To T
with all my gratitude
because he ran the
10,000 mile marathon
for me!

Sincerely,
M.T.G.

Nights in Heaven

a novel by
María-Teresa Guzmán

American Literary Press, Inc.
Five Star Special Edition
Baltimore, Maryland

Nights in Heaven

Copyright © 2003 María-Teresa Guzmán

Library of Congress
Cataloging-in-Publication Data
ISBN 1-56167-775-2

Library of Congress Card Catalog Number:
2002094233

Cover Art:
The Huntress (*La cazadora*), a gouache by Perl Estrada
Photo by Javier Sámano

Published by

American Literary Press, Inc.
Five Star Special Edition
8019 Belair Road, Suite 10
Baltimore, Maryland 21236

Manufactured in the United States of America

FOR STEVEN

Acknowledgement

Without the generosity of Dr. Jan de Vos, one of the most important contemporary historians of Chiapas and Tabasco, and that of the renown author Pedro Vega, whose literary name is Pablo Montañés, this book would not have been possible. Their laboriously-obtained documents, maps and research notes were made readily available to me. More important however, is the fact that they afforded me an invaluable and genuine life-long friendship.

Monterías

The year of 1822 marks the beginning of the history of exploitation of precious woods in Chiapas and Tabasco. We find a documented permit to Cayetano Robles, a public official of the government of Chiapas, to begin exploration with the purpose of future exploitation of precious woods in the Lacandon Forest. The objective at that time was to provide the country with all its logging needs.

Nothing seems to have come out of the first enterprise and future concessions were granted to Tabasco-based companies in San Juan Bautista, now Villahermosa, which became the capital of the state of Tabasco in 1880. Three names still survive: Bulnes, Valenzuela and Jamet y Sastré; they initiated a period of structured operations and a way of life. Then in 1892 the Romano and Schindler enterprises began a similar type of exploitation. In 1899 Romano, Bulnes and Valenzuela, following the act of law called *Tierras Baldías* [Empty Lands], divide amongst themselves some of the territory of the Lacandon Forest. Later, in 1904, a personal friend of Porfirio Díaz, Policarpio Valnezuela, receives a concession for the exploitation of 150,000 hectares of the Lacandon Forest, half of which will be later sold to Agua Azul Mahogany Company.

In 1902 another stage of exploitation of the area is begun, this time according to the *Ley de deslinde* [Law of Boundaries] of 1894. The rain forest can now be measured, separated, and divided; it other words, it can be bought.

In December 1925 the government of General Calles revokes all concessions, including those given to Casa Romano and begins their dismantlement. Soon thereafter, two articles which were crucial to putting an end to both human and forest depredation, and which constitute a testimony of the sub-human conditions of life in the logging stations, were written by a young lawyer, Rodolfo Brito Foucher. The first one was an article published on January 7, 1926 in the newspaper *El Universal*, and the second one was a speech published in 1931 in the magazine *Universidad de México*

This novel deals with one of those logging stations established by the Romano enterprises. The Romano family finally disappears to Spain in 1930 after perpetrating a huge fraud against Banco Nacional de México.

I

The table was set. It was the usual heavily embroidered white linen tablecloth, impeccable napkins neatly folded on the soup plate, monogrammed wine glasses and the grandmother's silver. The meal would begin. Her father would sit at the head of the table to initiate the austere ritual, which never varied. Nobody would speak unless addressed directly. They could answer and maybe add a few words that they knew would please the listener. The subject of conversation would be the one chosen by him, which almost invariably referred to strict moral observations. There was also the other topic, the one referring to him and his many virtues, which he voiced more for himself than for his family.

Clara was bored stiff, or perhaps more than that: she felt trapped and could think of no way out. Something about the whole refined setup disturbed her profoundly and she could neither find the reason, nor pinpoint it. She could not find a name for it; maybe it was just something similar to distress, like someone's death. She could find no meaning behind the silver and the glass. The smell of beeswax that permeated the whole house was glued to the feeling of utter loneliness and despair. Her mother's and hers. It was a reminder of their unwilling and unnamed passivity. Nothing was ever different. It seemed like they would always witness the same scenes till the end of time. Nothing was created; nobody thought up anything lively or or new. They would sit till doomsday to listen to the same words, sentences of rationalization and trite and tired jokes coming from the patriarch. He would paint the same picture, a good person with no vices, why he didn't even smoke! Nor drink! He was a loving father and a faithful husband. Always the same, whether in the privacy of their home or when company was present. He charmed the ladies then, by humbly kissing their gloved hand and almost clicking his heels just barely to remind them of his importance. The women swooned; the men nodded their approval. As a guest he would use his silence to draw attention to his importance and speak only when spoken to, and his conversation would invariably end by showing him in a glowing light to an audience at awe with the chief of the armed forces of the country. At times Clara would imagine him clearly ascending to the sky, like an image of a saint she had seen at catechism school one Saturday afternoon. Maybe her father would become a saint, he was so constant…and then again, weren't saints supposed to make one happy? Other times he would speak about books, especially history books and sometimes people ended by unconsciously identifying him with Napoleon Bonaparte. After all, France was close to Mexico, wasn't it? From 1864 to 1867 they had had an Austrian empire, which everyone linked to the French Intervention and nobody seemed to mind. Everyone spoke French because well, royalty was royalty; well not really anyone, but everyone who was anyone. Her father thrived on the opinion of others. They would nod, the guests, all the way through the conversation, which was more like the delivery of a lesson in morality, self-virtue and self-importance colored by world history. Yes, she realized that today as she sat down.

Her father arrived. His solemn face was neatly shaved, as always. He was austere in ways of money, time and affection. He had never made an effort of getting close to her, his only daughter and barely out of the convent. That meant…—Clara shivered—that she was on the marriage market! Sadly, she reflected, he had permeated even that area of her life and infected with his gravity most of her soul, like a cold and unforgiving wind. It was a wind that swept away any thought you might have had on your own, anybody you cared for, any idea that came to you…

The soup tureen was near her left elbow. She obediently took the ladle and put some cream of pumpkin flowers on her plate. Then she helped herself to some of the croutons. She sighed, wondering how she could have felt homesick. She had thought of home as something warm, and gentle. Instead, she felt to be an outcast; her blood froze and she did not know how to cope with it. Maybe the feeling would go away by itself like a gust of wind that passed moaning through barren fields?

Who could understand the world? Now she felt homesick for the convent, for the nuns, for her French teacher, a Carmelite whose honey-colored eyes matched her frock. She could feel those eyes staring into hers and the word courage whispered into her ear. She closed her eyes and could still visualize the small, neat hands of fine fingers with short nails pointing to her lips, showing her where the v sound originated. She smiled at her teacher for she had been kind and caring. Her fingers had touched the books as if they had been soft, velvety spiders. Maybe she could be kind and sweet like her teacher, maybe one day she could speak French and acquire her cultural refinement…maybe…The maybes whirled like dead leaves and dust in the deserted and cold land of nowhere and everywhere.

"Clara is to be married next month. General Heredia and his wife will come this evening to present a formal petition. Young Francisco is a very good candidate and nobody can say I have not done right by my family. Her future will be secure." Her father spoke to no one in particular. He was speaking to a captive audience and his eyes were looking into space. One could tell he was in a self-congratulatory mood.

Upon hearing her name, Clara's hand trembled and the heavy silver spoon fell onto the soup plate splattering her white, heavily-starched blouse.

"Sorry," she said looking nervously at her father, then at her mother and lastly, at her brother. And then it dawned on her that no one seemed surprised at her father's words and that no one would reach out to help her. She was doomed.

"She will go to her room without lunch. She needs to learn proper manners now that she will be the mistress of a house and the wife of an important man," her father sentenced with a controlled rage.Her father was that stranger who had distinguished lines on his face, a fine woolen suit with a vest which held in its pockets a gold chain and a huge watch which he consulted from time to time.

He never addressed her directly. Maybe he was just shy and she was not being fair to him. Ah, but she was forgetting, she was the aggrieved party! Or maybe just an ungrateful child? Who knows? What her common sense told her was that he was afraid of women and that it might be the reason for his feelings of repulsion towards her mother and towards her, an even weaker link in the chain. She had just returned home from the convent, she was barely sixteen, spoke a smattering of French, knew how to embroider in thin cotton and silk materials, could play some music in the black, austere piano which stood in the main living room covered by a yellow Manila shawl embroidered with red and purple flowers.

"It was just the surprise...could she, just this once...be forgiven?" It was her mother's halting, fearful voice that spoke out. A rare happening.

Her father ignored her totally, as if the words had never been uttered. Her brother, eleven months her senior, burst out angrily: "Go ahead! Defend her! Then they will return her as they did with the Limón woman, once the honeymoon was over! We will be the laughing stock of the city! Of the country! Our father is a general! Go on! That shows how much you have spoiled her! The money that was spent on her education will be wasted, with no refinement to be seen! So much for the best school!" He was their father's echo and this seemed to gratify the general, for he sat arrogantly at the head of the table.

Clara heard it all as if in a dream. Nobody looked at her; nobody spoke to her. She was being spoken about. Only Diógenes, the faithful servant, was waiting for a sign to help her with the chair. He too, was unable to understand the ways of the rich. Clara knew that she would be ostracized and that silence had already settled around her. She would be better off to leave.

She headed towards her room and sat in a comfortable chair with a fine blue bouquet of flowers and ribbons embroidered in petit point. Her window overlooked a garden which was enormous and filled with fruit trees and beautiful flowers. She was a prisoner, an object of barter in exchange for something she could not grasp. It was her own life, and yet she could not utter a word of opinion about it, or protest and say that she was waiting for the man she could fall in love with.

And what about love, a huge concept that should encompass all her life, everyone's life? Nothing. Not a word! On second thought, her father and mother seemed so ill-suited that she could not, for the life of her, understand how her brother and she had come to be born. They rarely spoke to one another, and when they did, it was on the war path. The usual one with the power, eliminating dissent with one cold stare. That was enough. She shook her head. She refused to live a life like theirs. She would rather die! She felt she had a right to happiness and maybe the only thing she could aspire to would be the silence of a convent and its apparent peace, because she knew very well that under the white, embroidered sheets, youthful, palpitating hearts were impatiently waiting for love and life to happen. Those girls had the goal of happiness, hope and joy before them. She was one of them and nobody could force her to the contrary. And now her father seemed to crush all that with a single master blow.

The more she thought about the whole affair, the less she seemed to understand the reasons. She thought that she had lived up to her part in the bargain. Her grades were excellent. She had been a good and gentle student. Her teachers commended her on her good disposition and her joy of learning. Now she felt betrayed; they had ganged-up against her.

She retraced her memories to her first view of the huge chandeliers of Austrian glass, and the Abousson tapestries, the oriental rugs, the Christophle silver and the embroidered linen. Oh, the world promised to be a beautiful place! After the austerity of the convent, this house had seemed paradise. What had gone wrong? Some time later, she did not even know how much, her mother came into the room and sat on the edge of the bed facing her.

"You are indeed fortunate. Your father has done very well in his choice of a husband. You will lack nothing in your life." She spoke in a longing voice.

"But I have not even seen the young man..." she started to protest.

"There will be enough time for that," her mother added. "You are very fortunate that your father will allow you to go shopping with me for your trousseau. We have ordered your wedding gown from Paris. You have no idea how expensive the whole wedding will be! It goes to show you how concerned your father is for your happiness." And she tried to smile.

"But I don't want to get married!" she repeated.

"This is a useless conversation. We have an appointment tomorrow morning with the designer for your wardrobe. Now get up and choose a gown for tonight."

Her mother had walked out with those words. She seemed afraid that Clara might make a scene and she could do nothing about it. She sat on the English chair that had belonged to her maternal grandmother, trying to observe the trees and the birds, but her mind was blank. She felt stunned by the constant 'peah' 'peah' of the blackbirds coming to their night refuge. Even they were better off than she!

Night fell and she hardly noticed it until her old nanny Justine walked in and turned the nightstand lamp on. "Mother of God, the holy Saint Mary, blessed Virgin! The guests are almost here! You are not dressed!" She crossed herself and begged, "Child, get going! I'm here to help you with your hair! Your mother urges…" the good woman stopped in the middle of the sentence and she approached the young girl to pat her hair.

Clara did not move; she simply uttered, "Nanny, tell Father I want to talk to him," she said determinedly.

"Child, don't create havoc. There is a commitment. You are getting married and that is that. You will own a beautiful house and carriages. You will ride your own carriage drawn by white horses, like the ones your grandmother had. You will be dressed in white and you will be holding a parasol. That is how she looks in the picture. I served her; I laid out her clothes and did her hair; I was present at her wedding. Now I am old and want to see you married. What other destiny is there for a woman of your status? You are lucky! You can convince your husband to buy a house nearby and you can visit your mother quite often. It will be a good life and you will blossom and be happy." She waited. No answer.

Finally old Justine heard the dreaded words: "I will not accept! Call my father."

Alarmed and defeated, the woman who had been an unwanted village orphan raised by her great-grandmother's family, walked out slowly. She was old and dragged her feet in silent, gray flannel slippers. She rarely left the house except for Sunday mass. The third generation nanny would be gone one day soon and she would feel lonelier than ever. Justine knew no other response but obedience to the master and she would be limited to being fearful for the capricious child. Clara could not blame her; she had known nothing else but the spirit of grateful servitude towards her family.

The general finally walked in. Pearls of sweat lay on his forehead. Clara knew what that meant. All the furies of his soul were surfacing and she would be the one to stir the beast. He appeared grand in full uniform, medals and all. How could she resist the authority that helped govern the country? In her mind she saw the grand table and signed Lalique vases with flowers all through the house. She saw the chandeliers and smelled the food cooking in the kitchen. His sole presence defeated her. She quietly stood up and began to get dressed. By then her father had walked out without having uttered a word.

II

Rigoberto López had left his house smiling as usual that morning. He had taken a gray felt hat from the coat and hat rack at the entrance; he had kissed his wife on her forehead while whispering, "I love you."

It seemed a day like any other. Neither of them had the slightest inkling that Rigoberto would be assigned the most unusual and dangerous task of his life. He had driven to his office in one of the few cars that circulated elegantly through the quiet streets of a city that would change drastically with time. He then walked into his pleasant office next to the House of Blue Tiles. He was always on time, and he was rarely faced with visitors. However, that morning he was greeted by major in the army who was standing across his secretary's desk. The clock on the wall was striking nine.

"Sir, Major Ramírez would like a few minutes of your time," his secretary said, rising from his chair.

"Please, Major…" he said as he opened the door to his office while nodding to his secretary.

The man must have been around thirty years old and had vivid eyes, which Rigoberto recognized as a sign of a quick intelligence.

"Have a seat, Major," he said as he himself sat down.

"Sir, I have a letter for you," he said as he handed him a white envelope with no return address.

He immediately recognized the stationery used by the President of the Republic. He opened it and found it to be a mere introduction to General Heredia. The message was absolutely clear.

"Well, Major, what else can I do for you?" he asked looking directly into the major's eyes. This usually made his listeners nervous. However the smile in his lips completed the message. He won friends quickly.

"General Heredia wonders if you could stop by his house around noon, Sir.

"With pleasure. I will be there," he answered quickly.

"Very well, Sir, you are expected."

Rigoberto was used to all sorts of interviews, but this one intrigued him because he had been summoned.

The morning continued as any other. He looked through some papers and signed others. Then he was ready to leave. Being indoors made him nervous, and he felt like a grounded child. Perhaps that was due to the fact that he was twenty-seven and in excellent health. He liked his city, enjoyed a morning walk in the sun, observed the colonial buildings with care and awe and arrived to the bustle of the coffee shop around eleven.

He dictated a last letter to his tall and thin secretary and considered him once more. He was so efficient that he seemed to be hardly human. He thought he could detect the usual smell of mint in his breath and he felt relieved. Rogelio Magaña was human after all! He was full of surprises because under the surface of distraction and indifference, was a quick and intuitive mind. He was so precise in his organization that Rigoberto had an efficient and smooth office which freed him up to pursue affairs that were entrusted to him. He suspected his secretary was a bachelor with no close family and he appreciated his good qualities. But that was as close as they had ever come. They were not friends because Rigoberto knew that the secret to a lasting work relationship lay in that precise distance. He was good to him, and gave him a yearly raise and periodic monetary incentives. They were an ideal team and he was sure that the powers to be had chosen this man for him with great care.

"Rogelio, I don't think I will be able to make it home for lunch today," he said taking his hat.

"Yes Sir, I could pass by there and let Mrs. López know," he replied without hesitation.

One of the things that Rogelio liked most about his superior was the fact that he was utterly devoted to his wife, a young woman with very light skin, jet black hair and hazelnut eyes. One could not say she was extraordinarily beautiful, but was charming and sweet and he felt accepted by her. And for this she had his undying gratitude.

That day she smiled pleasantly as she received a tea-cake he had bought for her, and thanked him sweetly for the message her husband sent. As she was closing the door, a malicious thought crossed her mind. This was the perfect gift for today, January 6, the day of the Three Kings. Then she sat down to have lunch by herself, in a strange and pensive mood. All the time she was imagining her husband's delight at the surprise of her own present. Still in that mood, she walked out into the garden where she sat on the bench built under the shade of a Jacaranda tree.

Meanwhile, Rigoberto López reached General Heredia's house located in the Ciudadela which was actually quite near his office and where many respectable families lived. It was five minutes of twelve when he knocked with the bronze head of a lion hanging in the middle of the front door. An older butler led him into a small chamber full of stained glass windows, tall stands with big flower pots which had abundant and overflowing leaves. He liked the room because the stained glass gave it a magic feel.

"The General will see you in the library," said the butler returning shortly.

He ushered him into a large room lined with bookcases and there, behind the desk, stood the general himself.

"So, you're the famous Rigoberto López," he said looking him over without reserve. He seemed to like what he saw, however, he considered the man before him was too young to be capable of the task before him. He felt this man could not possibly carry out what was asked of him. He was intrigued as to what his friend, the President of the Republic was thinking when he cataloged him was his best man for the job.

"Don Porfirio thinks that you are the precise person to deal with a minor but distressing issue…"

Rigoberto remained silent. He had apparently not yet received the approval. He did not like the man. Maybe it was a conflict of personalities. For him life was a continuous feast and the twinkle in his eyes betrayed the fact and he was fully aware of that if one were to study other people's eyes, one could clearly recognize the most zealously guarded areas of a personality. This conscientious study had helped him in his dealings with hardened criminals and other difficult members of the human race. He himself could not personally feel the evil, so he just read of it, as one might read the description of a toothache. Recognizing problems was enough for him to rapidly solve the puzzle that the person in front of him presented. One could not vouch for established methods, but he got them solved in the most surprising ways, mainly guided by his heart. He knew he could touch every single person in front of him, with mere kindness. Today, however, he recognized a different breed of evil, a more subtle and less detectable poison.

"Well, General, I am here to see if I can help," he said conventionally. The person the eyes betrayed was small, to the point of almost being unrecognizable. He therefore would let that small being who was dictatorial and rigid, do his thing.

"I hope you will not be offended, although God knows why you should be. I have had you investigated. I don't like your methods. Just yesterday…well, anyway, you are too soft with the most rabid criminals."

Noticing Rigoberto's silence, he continued, "Yesterday you visited the mother of one of them and gave her a substantial amount of money. You are free to do as you please with your own money, but that is not a way to deal with them!"

The general was doused with rage, an anger that did not belong to him. If to anyone, it should have belonged to the Church. The journalist in question had seriously criticized the Church. Nobody should meddle with established order—or so thought those eyes in front of him.

Rigoberto remained silent, trying not to let his calibration show. Nor did he want the general to know it bothered him to be investigated. He had nothing to hide, but there was no reason for this.

"How do you feel about that?" the general spat at him.

"I would have probably done the same," he answered non-committantly.

The general was pacing back and forth in the room, his hands intertwined behind his back. Rigoberto could see that one of the windows had a view of the garden. The top branches of a magnolia tree could be appreciated. There would be no magnolias at this time of the year. He had to keep his mind on something. The general's rudeness was supposed to sink down as a lesson in authority. When would he see it fit to reveal the purpose of this visit?

"I don't trust your youth. I can't imagine what my daughter's godfather, the President of the Republic, was thinking of when he entrusted you with such a high position," he continued looking down at him.

By now the picture in his mind was complete. A military man. That was all, not one to be reckoned with. The general was totally predictable: he would label human beings and file them away. Then he would think of them as the cogs of that huge machinery called army. His mistakes would be buried in the dust of time and in the chain of command. Yet how difficult it was for him to voice a need, a favor from someone who did not belong to the army structure. Now he understood why he had been summoned. An ordinary citizen would have gone to his office during working hours. He had been brought to this man's territory, probably the only place where he did not feel threatened in an affair that did not involve the army.

Rigoberto considered the arrogant figure the man wanted to convey. But he had finished his own considerations and wanted to leave the house of doubtful taste and elegance which was suffocating him. He decided to talk.

"You are absolutely right, General. You are the only one who knows what this is about and therefore you are the best judge regarding the most capable person for this problem."

They both remained silent for a moment. Then the general answered, "I know. I know. I asked my friend for his most capable man…Maybe you could work with someone I trust?"

"I am awfully sorry, General. I always work alone," he answered without rancor.

"See that! See that arrogance! That is because you are young!"

The general was visibly shaken. He walked to the window and pretended to inspect the tree.

"They have kidnapped my daughter!" he said finally. "My only daughter on the eve of her wedding day," he added with a coarse voice.

"Have you been contacted in any way?" Rigoberto asked. He now understood the nature of the plight.

"I will not be. It was a single, stupid kidnapper, and God knows to what ends!" he said vehemently.

"Do you have any idea as to who…?" he started to ask.

"The worse part is that I know who it was!" he interrupted.

Now the puzzle seemed scrambled and unusual. "You know?" he asked quietly.

"Yes! It was the gardener's helper! I will deal with him later! He has left me in a ridiculous situation; I will be the laughing-stock of the army! Of my family!" he complained feeling genuinely betrayed and abused.

Rigoberto waited looking quite attentive. In his mind, however, he was smiling. So, that was it! His daughter's fate did not really matter here. What was at stake was his role in society. Was it a love story? Was the girl running away from something? If it was on the eve of her wedding, did she love the man she was to marry? If so, why leave? He was sure she could not have been abducted. She had *fled.* As to the general's plans for the boy, those were clear. He would be shot in the back, claiming it had been an intent of escape— that is provided he could get his hands on him. Which he probably would. And his daughter's fate? Also very logical, she would be sent to a convent for the rest of her days. The family's life had been predictably planned by this man. But life affords surprises, General, he wanted to say. He was certain that the general would never lay hands on the boy. This revelation astonished him.

"There is nothing impossible for President Díaz, my friend! I hope for your sake you can accomplish the mission which is being entrusted to you!" the general said, finally looking directly at him.

He did not like being threatened either, but he understood that it was the only language the man in front of him had ever used.

"I, too, hope so," Rigoberto said in an unassuming manner. Then he continued, "Do you have any idea as to where they are headed for?" he asked calmly.

"You mean, where he has taken her?" he said in a correcting tone of voice.

"Exactly," answered Rigoberto.

"Then you should learn to express yourself correctly!" he retorted, trying to downsize him.

"You are right. Now, can you tell me when this happened?" he asked quietly.

"Last Friday. In the evening. Thieves need the darkness to perpetrate their evil deeds!" he added angrily.

"Do you know where the young man was from?" he asked again.

"From Cholula, in Puebla." The general answered a bit slower.

"I see…" Rigoberto said pensively.

"Don't waste your time trying to find them there. I have already sent the gardener, his uncle, to find him. He isn't there," he said shaking his head.

"Do you know the family?" he asked.

"Of course…wait! Catalina!" he called out in a loud voice.

Suddenly a middle-aged woman who was still beautiful stood next to him. She appeared very nervous and frightened.

"You have before you the person responsible for this tragedy," he said in a controlled voice.

The woman lowered her eyes and looked at her hands in which she toyed with a white lace handkerchief.

"Madam," Rigoberto said addressing her directly, "since when did the young man work here?" he said in a gentle voice.

"About a month ago. I did not ask the general for permission to hire him so…"

"Enough! You have said enough! Just answer what is being asked of you!" he spat angrily. It was obvious that he blamed her entirely and that she had taken the bait.

He observed her quickly. He now knew that she was unusually repressed for an adult woman and he tried to figure out the reason for choosing this husband. She had probably thought him to be dazzling and a good match. After all, he did have an unusually high standing in their community.

"What was she wearing? Was she wearing jewelry?" he continued softly.

"She was wearing a blue and white wollen dress and a matching coat. No, she wore no jewelry. I guess she still had on her school ring. Oh, yes, a hair locket that my mother gave her," she answered in a firmer voice.

"Did she take any additional clothes with her?" he continued.

"No, I don't think so. Nothing seems to be missing from her closet," the woman sounded a little more sure of herself.

Rigoberto raised his eyes and noticed her looking at her husband furtively. He was standing at the window with his back to them, as if absent from a scene that was not his.

"So your daughter was about to be married?"

"Yes. She was supposed to marry the following morning. She could not disobey her father even in that…" she said doubtfully.

She smiled timidly. Now she looked beautiful. She had white, even teeth and dimples in her cheeks.

"So your daughter was an obedient girl," he said vaguely.

"Well, not always… she said quietly as she eyed her husband again.

"Well, Madam, I will bother you no more. One last question. Was your daughter a good student?" he asked with a smile.

"She got first place in her class," the woman answered nervously.

Now he had the complete picture. His opponent was an intelligent young lady. Something told him she had to be beautiful. He knew that she had rejected the proposed marriage, even though her father had probably exercised his full authority in the matter. She had run off with the gardener's nephew. How very silly young people in love could be! They were full of life and eager to live it. It would be so easy to locate them. It was a simple explanation he had formulated because they would not let him see the workings of this family plainly. He also had to consider a third possibility: that due to the pressures of her family she had simply escaped. Something seemed awfully wrong. But he would worry about these imponderables later. There would be plenty of time while he traveled.

III

Clara Heredia cried by herself that evening in her room. The light had not been turned on and one could see a weak moonlight through the window. Gradually she began to feel better. The feeling of despair that had paralyzed her seemed to lift. Her brain started working. She had to find a way out.

She throught about the proposed groom. She had nothing against that young man called Francisco Monteros. Paco, his friends called him. He was not unpleasant and he knew how to behave in company. He seemed awfully boring, though, and she could not imagine spending a lifetime at his side, much less as his wife. Then she began to cry because she was so resentful that someone dared dictate her life. It would not happen. She would not allow it. How or when to avoid it, she did not know yet.

Last night the conversation centered around her proposed husband Paco, she remembered. He was young and yet he had a receding hairline. He wore thick glasses and yet his eyes shone intensely. He had long eyelashes but they didn't curl upward. He had tried in vain to hide his curiosity towards her but it turned out he could not refrain from staring at her. He was no paragon of romance. What to do? Was he maybe too passive? Who knew! Who cared! She, on the other hand, felt full of life, and why not? She was on the brink of it.

She cried because she was angry. She cried because she was disappointed in her mother, frustrated by her brother's caricature of her father and unhappy because she had been born into such a family. But she would not give in. At times she calmed down and prayed for guidance because she could not find the slightest clue to the mess she was in through no doing of her own. She had just grown up, like everybody else. In her whole world, the small world of her family, a small house and a huge garden with trees, she had only one true friend, the gardener's nephew. He was also the cook's second cousin. She would go out into the clear, sunny mornings to talk to him while her mother was busy talking to the cook about the day's menu. Other times, she found him to be her only company in an otherwise empty house when her parents had social engagements in which she was not included. He was an intelligent and happy boy who made her laugh. He expressed his belief that one was the architect of one's life. Life had to be lived fully and he seemed to find joy in the small tasks assigned to him. This was her only friend, and the garden was her only solace.

She returned time and again to her dilemma. What was she going to do against imposed events of her life? Why would her father dispose of her as cattle-raisers disposed of cows for mating purposes? That was an act of violence against her and for which she was supposed to be grateful. Well, she was not. They had turned marriage into something dark and sordid, instead of the light and happy relationships she might have had with other young people her age. She was shocked by the discovery that she would rather die, and that she was ready to do it.

For any event to turn in her favor she must take decisive steps. First she would pretend to go along with their plans, her enemy's plans, just to buy time. She had to make good use of that only chance. With that comforting revelation, she fell into a deep sleep when the dawn was beginning to light the sky.

The nanny entered the room with a cup of coffee and milk. "Wake up, child, your mother says you are going to the seamstress this morning," the old woman said nervously.

She woke up at her nanny's coaxing. Justine had lost most of her teeth, and her parents despaired when they tried to get her to visit the dentist's office. She would rather speak her broken sounds, because she said, nature knew what should be happening with time. Not that she didn't dye her hair. Well, she did so with the seed of a tropical fruit, which she burned on the cook top when she knew no one was a home. With the charcoaled seed she would touch up the roots of her white hair and her graying eyebrows. She had seen the black, shiny half-burned seed in her belongings once. She had also seen another one of her secrets, a small leather pouch with the old teeth, because, Justine rationalized, when she finally met with the Good Lord, he would plant them back. She kept her secret because she loved her nanny dearly, although she was not sure the woman really loved her in return; she would, however, go to the end of the world for her brother.

"Yes, yes. I'm on my way," she said as she tried to smile to Justine. The woman seemed relieved because she had expected some kind of negative reaction. She knew her child.

Clara drank the coffee in small gulps, she had a perfumed bath that Justine had drawn up and she dressed mechanically. She had to appear normal which shouldn't really be too difficult since nobody seemed to consider her.

They finally left in her mother's carriage, which was drawn by two horses. When they arrived to the seamstress' house, her mother carried in some material and a few fashion magazines. Clara quietly submitted to the measure-taking process. Then they proceeded to discuss the models that would be duplicated from the French magazines. She accepted everything without a word of dissent. She could not bear to look at her mother because she felt a strange thing called compassion which was mixed with her previous anger, and that feeling had to be tamed. She realized that her mother's life was no way of living.

The two women were discussing her. Her mother was giving the seamstress a full account of the previous night's dinner and the way things had evolved when Paco's father had asked for her hand and when her own father so full of himself and his medals had accepted and asked her, Clara, to go play the piano, Clara obliged by playing *Estrellita* by Manuel M. Ponce, a famous musician of their time. While she played she could feel tears welling up in her eyes. Nobody seemed to notice, and if anybody did, they would probably think she was so moved by the petition of her hand that she was a romantic fool! She could hear the two women congratulate themselves saying they had chosen "a good match" and a "nice, decent husband" for her. She had heard those words a millions times, in similar circumstances. Women around her seemed to have no other topic. This symbolized the reign of men. Clara hated them, the women, for submitting to it. She would have liked to go shake them and beat them until they woke up from their state of semi-sleep, or what they thought was a happy, fortunate life.

When they finally left, they returned home. They hardly spoke to each other. Her mother seemed relieved that she showed no further signs of rebellion. She interpreted her silence as fear of the married state. Clara thought: she should only know! She did not know her own daughter and her determination of finding a way out.

One sad realization came into her mind. She had no one to really love her. Her paternal grandmother would be delighted with the news, her aunts would commend her father, especially her spinster aunt Agnes. Nobody would help her in her quest for freedom. Nor in the search of her own path in life. They would cut her out to fit their established pattern. She would rather die and because she had been spiritually trained in a convent, she knew that physical life was a small price to pay.

Death. Well, if she had to die, so be it. She would die as the Good Lord had intended, a free spirit! Did they not read the *Bible* that spoke of self-love? Maybe things would not reach that point. But so what if they did? She was ready.

When they entered the house, her mother went to the kitchen to oversee lunch and she ran out to the garden to see her friend. She walked on the blocks of stone that constituted the pathway between the trees. Gerardo was there working and humming softly to the sun, to the flowers to the wind. He sang to joy! Pure, simple and genuine. This in spite of the fact that the gardner had used natural fertilizer to help his garden grow strong and beautiful. She herself did not mind the smell, but her family complained constantly.

He looked up at her smilingly until he noticed tears in her eyes. No harm had been done yet. He told her they would think of something. He asked for a one or two days in which to think how they could solve the issue of an unwanted marriage. He asked her not to worry and she knew it was no use, but at least she had the comfort of a friend. Maybe he could work a miracle. Was there a single way to solve her situation?

Sad and defeated she returned to her room. She sat on her grandmother's petit-point chair to look out the window as if to say goodbye to her beloved trees and plants. She could return to the convent. Or maybe she would run away.

IV

As soon as he opened the front door to his house, Rigoberto called
out his wife's name. There was no answer. He was aware that she
had already eaten and that they would spend the afternoon together.
Maybe she would like to go for a walk in the Alameda, then go have
tea.

He walked out to the garden. She was sitting alone on the stone
bench that surrounded a tree and seemed pensive, radiant. She
seemed to have acquired a new look of peace about her. He observed
her for a few moments, not wishing to disturb the intimate moment.
She was so beautiful! He had been blessed by life, by all the deities
around them. Rosa was happy; they were both happy and he knew
they had achieved it together. It seemed that they had known each
other forever, and then walked hand in hand through life, confident,
as if nothing could ever alter their fate. They would have children,
then grandchildren. Time would only strengthen their feelings; life
would grant them all the gifts that together would become the unity
it had always been. Did they know what it meant that harmony
prevailed in their lives? Did they know how fortunate that their
parents accepted them both as their own children? Rosa's family
felt grateful to him for their only daughter's happiness; his own
family loved Rosa as if she had been theirs.

"Why are you smiling by yourself?" he asked quietly as he
approached her and bent down to kiss her.

"Because it is the Day of the Three Kings," she answered
touching his hair with her small hand.

He kissed her hair. She smelled of sandalwood and jasmine, aromas of the orient. He could have never imagined life differently, nor even think of another woman in her place and he knew there had never been a question in her mind. He sat down next to her and could see the swallows fly around the trees. They remained silent for a few minutes, letting the warm sun of winter caress them. A small dry leaf fell on her hair and he picked it up.

"So…The Three Kings, is it? We will spend the afternoon together. Maybe you would like to take a walk and then go have tea and the *rosca* on the way back?" he asked softly.

"Speaking of which, Mr. Magaña came to deliver your message and brought us a cake that El Molino makes so specially for today. It seems like a good idea to have it here with hot chocolate, by ourselves," she said with a smile he had not seen before.

"Yes, that would be lovely. Are you telling me no one from the family will join us?"

"Not precisely, but…I would like to be alone with you," she answered furtively.

"Yes, yes, yes. We will drink our hot chocolate with the Three King's *rosca*! Would you like to go for a walk? The sculptures are waiting for us," he said teasing her a little. She loved to stop and admire the neo-classic white marble sculptures of naked women, excellent copies of French ones. They lay frozen in extravagant postures, a hidden treasure among the green, tall trees and the azalea plants. The *Alameda* itself was a magnificent and stately park in the middle of the city. Their parents and their families had spent many afternoons strolling there, meeting friends and going off with them to the coffee shops.

She had not answered the question for the second time, and yet, he knew her so well and could not understand why. Did she have some small surprise? Was she feeling all right? She was glowing, so it could not be that. They held no thought back and certainly had not secrets from each other. So he willingly accepted what he could not understand.

He said casually."The general is sending me on a short trip. Two days, maybe three," "Do you think you would like to go to your parents' in Coyoacán? It would certainly make me feel better because you would have their company," he proposed.

"No. This is our home. I will wait for you here," she said. She quickly added, "Unless of course you think it would afford you peace of mind."

He smiled. They seemed to think in unison. They certainly respected each other's concerns and feelings. "Stay here, Darling, but if my trip is longer…" he broke off. He could not bear it. Instead, he continued, "It is about a young girl who was surrounded by hostile people. Her father wanted her to marry someone that she didn't care for. He is rigid and terrifying. I can only imagine what she felt like! In any case, she has vanished."

She was listening to him attentively, with a worried look on her face. He then took her hand and started kissing every single finger. "Not everybody is as lucky as we are," he continued thoughtfully.

The housekeeper's presence interrupted the moment of intimacy. She seemed a little embarrassed. He looked up, questioningly.

"Sir, there is a young man who asks to see you," she said, handing him a card.

"Francisco Monteros," he read. "I don't know anyone by that name, but please stay here if you wish. I don't think I will be long," he said thinking how beautiful she was, how fresh and sweet. He kissed the top of her head once more, and thought of sandalwood. Something wonderful emanated from her, and he could not put a name to it. It was generous like the ocean and strong like Mother Earth.

He left her reluctantly, thinking how the gods had favored him. He walked into the living room furnished with his grandmother's antiques, and some of Rosita's mother's favorite pieces. There was a huge gilded mirror, quite ornamented, which they kept out of respect, since they felt it was a bit much for their house. One must keep a continuity, he thought as he fixed his tie with the help of the grandmother's French mirror.

Francisco Monteros turned out to be quite a nice young man. He did seem a bit boring and his visit intrigued him. He knew this to be the proposed fiancé for Clara. An ill match, he thought.

"Sir, I am General Montero's son. I was to be married to Clarita..." he said in lieu of explanation. The words choked him..

"Well, good, good. Let us sit down and have some cognac. I was about to have some, will you join me?" he asked to ease the moment while he proceeded to pour from the side table.

"Thank you, I think I need it. You see, I am terribly worried," the young man said earnestly.

"I would be too! Sad occasion, but cheers!" he said picking up one of his grandmother's monogrammed glasses.

They were sitting face to face on who small sofas next to the fireplace.

"Please consider me your friend and this to be your house," he said trying to ease the strain of the moment.

"You will probably ask why I am here. There doesn't seem to be much I can do, is there? I just wanted to tell you what I think. General Heredia is a very rigid and controlling man. I think he scared Clarita away. I would have liked to court her in my own manner, and then maybe she would have liked me. But he was definite, the wedding had to take place immediately. I frankly think she ran away!" he concluded taking a sip of cognac.

They sat there peacefully as two old friends, listening to the silence and the soft bells of the grandfther clock.. There were a few oil portraits and a French clock that kept time on the mantel.

"She is only a child," he continued. "She is beautiful, but too active and young to settle immediately and become a housewife," the young man concluded.

"It certainly is difficult to be so young and submissive. Those are two concepts that seem mutually exclusive. One day we will all remember this day and laugh together about it," Rigoberto said, trying to let the young man understand that he felt the same way. He was sure that Francisco had more to say, but did not know where to begin.

"I hope so. That is what I wanted to talk to you about. You should not have much trouble finding her. Please tell her that no matter what has happened, I am waiting for her as if she had never left home. We can still have a happy life together. My parents are quite different from hers, and we are all very religious. We know how to forgive, although I am sure there is nothing to forgive, so let's say forget. We must have all seemed quite intimidating to her. You see…she had just left the convent. What seems worse is that her father doesn't even seem to be aware of what he has caused!" he said drinking the last of his cognac and setting down the glass on the wine table.

"Amazing! We had the same type of intuition, therefore we must be right. I think Miss Heredia will be very happy with you in the future." By now Rigoberto had finished his drink and said, "I will begin my plans to leave immediately. Tomorrow morning I will leave quite early for Puebla. Maybe soon we can toast to your engagement. My wife and I would like to be invited to your wedding," Rigoberto said smiling confidently.

"That is the second thing I came to tell you. I am prepared to travel with you. My father and I are ready to assist you in anything that seems necessary," the young man said earnestly. Rigoberto could see the intensity in the eyes behind the thick glasses.

"I always work alone. Always, as I told General Heredia. Thank you for your kind offer and you will be the first to know if I need anything," he said smiling faintly.

"Can we help in any way?" he insisted.

"Certainly, we could always use a prayer next time you are in church," Rigoberto added smiling. He tried to further alleviate the young man's pain.

"Clarita is very beautiful, and she looks terribly intelligent" he said observing a photograph of the young lady that Rigoberto had received from General Heredia a few hours before.

"May I?" asked the eager young man.

"Certainly," Rigoberto replied handing over the photograph to the young man who thought he had fallen in love with a girl he hardly knew. He had fallen in love with her youth and charm and her strong personality. For him it was a trial to win his lady. He would rescue her from the clutches of doubt and paternal imposition.

Francisco Montero returned the photograph and made his way to the door feeling better. His eyes no longer spoke of defeat, now they spoke of hope. So the young man left in better spirits and he remained behind a changed and worried man. It was like packing up everyone's concerns and carrying them on his back.

"Please reassure Clarita that I love her and that nothing will ever change between us," were his parting words.

"I will, and I will convince her to return. Better still, I will send you a wire from Puebla, if I need your help. But as long as you have no news you will know I have none either. I hope this takes no longer than a week," he said closing the front door.

He walked out into the garden to join Rosa. He observed her. The more he looked at her, the more he was convinced that something was happening that he was not aware of. Maybe it was just a side of feminine inner mystique he had never seen before.

"Oh," she said as if coming out of a reverie, "shall we have some chocolate and bread? Maybe we should have invited the young man, but I wanted to be alone with you today," she said with innocent complicity.

They went into the house, hand in hand, smiling. Each one had his secret, a gift for the other. The table had been set for two in the breakfast nook. The cook entered with a pot of hot chocolate. It was foamy and aromatic. Rosita poured the steaming liquid into their cups. How many times in the future he would remember that last detail! She then pushed the platter with the coffee cake towards him and handed him the knife.

"You cut first," she said seriously.

"Ladies first, I was taught," he said laughingly.

"No, not today. Come on, do it to please me!" she retorted laughing with him.

"Your wish," said Rigoberto as he started to insert the knife slowly into the bread. He stopped when he felt an object inside the bread. He looked at his wife, his friend, his girlfriend, his lover, his everything, and laughed loudly. "I cannot say it was a trick, but look!" he said pulling out the small figure of a baby which symbolized the Newborn Jesus. "How did you know?" he asked her.

"Because the doctor confirmed it today!" she said filled with happiness.

Rigoberto looked overwhelmed when he saw her eyes fill with tears. He was confused. Suddenly he said joyfully, "A child! Our child! I am happy! I am the luckiest man alive!" He then jumped up and stood next to her. When he managed to calm down he approached her and kissed her hand. "What a present! You are full of surprises! Wait! Wait! Don't move!" he yelled as he entered the pantry and took out a bottle of champagne.

The maid entered the room with a bucket of ice. A few minutes later as he opened the bottle, the cork flew into the air breaking one of his grandmother's crystal bells. They both laughed. "It's a girl! It broke a bell, a feminine object. It's a girl!" he called out again.

"I toast for you, my dear husband, because you are the best!" Rosa said seriously.

"And I toast for you! You are the best of the world, the earth, the heavens and the universe! Cheers!" he said drinking the first glass quickly.

They were about to start on their chocolate and the cake of the Three Kings when Rosa picked up her napkin and found a small, square package under it. "Good Lord, Rigoberto, what is this?" she asked pleasantly surprised.

"When we became engaged I gave you my grandmother's diamond. She insisted on it, remember? Well, I wanted to give you my ring. Something made especially for you," he said watching her anxiously.

Rosita took the ring out of its case and studied it carefully, then she exclaimed, "The color is extraordinary. It is beautiful," she said quite pleased.

"It is a star sapphire, a pink sapphire, which can only mean one thing: our child his a girl!" he concluded happily. "She will be somebody like you, but quite small," he said teasingly.

It was then that Rigoberto realized that he had never thought his happiness could be greater. And this new dimension of life surprised him enormously.

V

"Ready? We have to leave today," Clara Heredia told Gerardo Zacarías. The young man continued trimming the blue and pink hydrangeas without the slightest change in his demeanor. She was visibly worried, and yet calm, so he himself, would have to convey a feeling of self-assurance.

"Good," was all he could answer. The least said, the better for there should be no margin of error. It would throw her off. He had promised help and he was going to keep his word.

The girl was standing next to him. The sun rays were falling directly on her face and her golden hair shone in such a manner that it was the outstanding feature. Her somber look of the last days had disappeared and now only her eyes seemed sad. Gerardo turned to look at her for an instant and then continued with his task.

"My parents will leave at eight for a service at La Profesa…" she said wistfully wondering if she would ever see her favorite church again.

"Very well. I will be waiting for you at eight at the corner in a carriage," he concluded as a matter-of-fact.

"Are you sure there will be no further problems?" she asked, wanting some further reassurance.

"Only the ones you take with you in your heart, which I hope won't be many. That way it will light and happy, like traveling without luggage, which we will," he added with definite conviction.

He continued to turn the ground near the root of the plants. "I have to hurry. I need to leave all these plants trimmed. They will be beautiful big, round purple spheres when May arrives. Did I tell you the lady next door made me pull out all the hydrangeas? What a pity! People are absurd!" he continued.

"Now, why would they want to do that?" she asked greatly surprised, and suddenly she realized she was thankful for a momentary respite from her present problem.

"Superstition. Pure and simple nonsense. Even the Church prohibits thinking like that. They think it brings bad luck…" he said shrugging.

"Bad luck! How?" she asked alarmed.

"Because according to them it means that the young ladies of the house will remain spinsters, saint-dressers," he explained impatiently while shaking his head firmly. It irritated him to see what plain human ignorance did to those beautiful and innocent plants.

"Well, I can no longer tell which is worse, to be a spinster or to be ill-matched," she reflected to herself. She quickly added, "That no longer matters!"

"You are very courageous, Miss Clara, yes, indeed very courageous! I think highly of you," he said earnestly, continuing his labor.

"So eight it is," she said quietly and turned around to go back into the house.

Clara did not know whether to laugh or cry. It seemed so easy! All one had to do was open the door and take the first step. What if they were caught? Her father would probably kill her, at worse, or send to her to convent for the rest of her days, at best. She knew him and feared him. She knew she did not want to spend the rest of her life locked up in a cell, for that is what the nuns called their tiny sleeping-quarters. These were usually cold and very austere. But then, would she be afforded the choice? Of course not! Who was? Who really had control over their destiny? She was not doing this as a mere tantrum, but as an act of survival. Nobody would ever be able to understand that, except maybe the young man who was helping her, and that was probably due to the fact that they belonged to the same generation. They were so utterly young. More than fear for herself, she realized she feared for him. What if he were to fall into her father's clutches? She shivered and prayed, "Grandmother dear, from Heaven you can help us!"

Clara's proposed wedding was to take place the following day. She realized she had waited until the last moment hoping for a miracle to occur. What did she think was possible? Absolutely nothing. Nothing but the usual preparations for the wedding: visits to the dressmaker, to the beauty parlor, tea sessions with ladies such as Rivas Mercado, Escandón, Lascurain, Limantour, Noriega and Carrera Stampa, the aristocrats of her time. On previous occasions, when visiting them, she was forced to sit quietly and acquiesce to the small talk of children and their illnesses, problems with domestic help and in general very immature reasoning behind everything. She felt guilty of not belonging to the "good families" in the first place. In the second place, she felt immense fear of becoming one of them. They were empty shells of people who smelled well, ate well and behaved well. Perfect people who slept between linen sheets and had their tablecloths and linens brought from Brussels. Most of them claimed to speak French and boasted a personal friendship with Don Porfirio.

There must be something wrong with her; she felt like an outsider who in no manner could identify with them and what she considered a childlike life. She had tried, talking like them, using the same vocabulary and holding conversations with the same themes. They approved of her then. But she wasn't really that, was she? To put it plainly, who or what was she? She didn't know. All she knew is that she had to leave tonight. Her future would not lie in the niceties of life like being beautifully dressed and carrying a parasol, nor in going in a carriage of white horses to Alameda Central park. That was her grandmother and her time. She had had little schooling and high aspirations. 'All right! Get over it, Grandmother, I am not like you! But do help me!' She prayed silently. Things in Heaven should be easier, because God knew everybody's heart, didn't He? The truth was always said and seen, wasn't it?

Wouldn't it have been beautiful for her father to have said, "Clara, you have to go away and find your path. That I cannot do for you, nobody can. Go, child, you have my blessing. Come back when you are ready"? No, it was not going to be that easy. She would have to stumble through life, by herself.

She had to focus on this day only, for one lived one day at a time. Each instant was precious and unique. What was on the agenda for today? To leave. What did she need for that? She realized there was nothing to prepare. She did not have a single penny. She could truly say she was indigent, and tried to focus on these facts while she was embroidering, pretending this was a normal day, just in case 'they' looked in on her. Her father insisted that all doors remain open at all times in order to exert better control over everyone's lives. They approved of the quiet, non-thinking activity. 'I shall sit here and embroider until we have lunch and dream of a wide, generous and beautiful world out there from which I am supposed to be barred, not shielded, barred. I will jump those bars and go, free and innocent to find out for myself what it is like to travel and laugh and run in the fields! Even maybe get to know the sea…'

Lunch hour finally came. They ate as usual in the big dining room where the pink marble table served its purpose. She had to look at everything carefully, concentrate on things, lest her nervousness be spotted. She had really nothing to fear, her father was busy thinking about his many virtues, her mother was listening carefully, as in ecstasy, and her brother was eating with an austere frown on his face.

Her father looked at her once or twice with what she interpreted was a feeling of disgust. He was furious for an extravagant expenditure. She smiled to herself thinking how much angrier he would be the next day! The whole wedding arrangement had been a useless waste of his money and he would feel cheated and betrayed. She had to see them clearly for the last time, because it was necessarily the last. She dared not return. If they had not accepted her before, much less afterward.

Her brother was eating silently. Her father began an utterly unjustified and furious tirade against her mother for the useless expenditure of a heavily embroidered Chinese handkerchief with which she was supposed to wipe the last virginal tears. And then? Done! She would be married! Honorably disposed of!

"It was an unnecessary extravagance. Who is going to notice a handkerchief?" her father was asking fiercely.

"It is a custom, that the bride have a handkerchief handy…" her mother answered in an apologetic tone.

"Quite an expensive one at that! Well, what a blessed tradition!" he said putting and end to the issue.

Well, she thought, at least everything continued on the normal track. She was used to this silly bickering about money. He was so extraordinarily careful about it that he even had one of the soldiers shop for groceries. The soldier, of course, was paid for by the Ministry of Defense. She had given up on trying to understand her father's stance on money. He was a miser, she concluded, for there was no other word to describe his attachment to money.

"The girl liked it; what could I do?" her mother continued. She could not leave well alone. She looked at her as if asking for her help. Clara would not give in this time to the undetectable game of motherly blackmail. Let her stew in her own juice! She and all the other women were absurd! She had never thought of crying at her own wedding or anyone else's. Why would she need a handkerchief? Thank God it was the last day of those major worries! She had better things to look forward to!

"I don't give a hoot what the child wants or not! She can want whatever she wants with her husband's money, not with mine! And as for you, when this is over, we have to think of a very different arrangement between us!" he threatened.

Her mother's look of anguish no longer moved her. She stood firmly grounded on her uninvolvement. Her thoughts went to money, what would they use for their adventure?

She spent the afternoon as best she could, reading and looking out of her beautiful window.

It was late in the afternoon when her parents got ready to leave. Her mother had come in to announce it, and claimed she was very sad because of her attitude. Clara remained inflexible in her feelings, and finally she looked into her mother's eyes. How many times had she needed her warmth! How many times she had longed for a loving and understanding mother! Nothing. Nothing but cold rejection and blame. She felt sorry for her and the condition she was in, always threatened and despised.

Eight O'clock. The clock on the staircase was sounding its first bell. She waited until the third stroke and started to go down the stairs trying not to make noise. She looked under the crochet carpet of the entrance table. The key to the front door was there in its usual place. She listened to see if she could detect sounds coming from the kitchen. Nothing. She softly opened the door, left into the night and closed the door to her wedding and her family for the last time. She ran to the corner where she saw the door to a black carriage opening. She climbed into it. Gerardo Zacarías held her hand trying to calm her down. Her heart was beating like never before.

"Freedom is but the first step," he whispered softly.

Clara felt like one of the characters of a novel, maybe the toy of Greek gods? Or was she the sinner of the Catholic world? However, this was the only way out and her instinct told her she had done the right thing.

She tried to calm down, but the excitement would not let up. She was afraid her parents would find her missing that same evening and then all hell would break loose.

All she asked was that they wait till morning to find out. Was twelve hours much to ask? Gerardo was informing her that early the following morning they would be taking the coach to Puebla In the meantime, they would spend the night at a friend of his. Which they did and where Clara had to share a clean but uncomfortable bed with one of the sisters, a happy and surprised teenager who welcomed the excitement of such a distinguished guest.

VI

Early one morning, Rigoberto López kissed his wife goodbye. He stood at the door and said, "Take care of my daughter and her mother. They are my most precious treasures," and he embraced her again not wanting to let go. Why? What seemed so different this time from the others? Rogelio Magaña stood at a distance, waiting for his superior and trying to give him some privacy.

Then together they got into his car and went through the city in the morning sun of the valley of Mexico City. The air was clear, the day was new but now he felt strange in his usual surroundings.

"Magaña, I think I will be gone for two, no more than three days. If my trip should take longer, I would like you to come next Sunday when my in-laws are here, you know, to check on things and to tell my father-in-law that I would rather Rosita go with them while I am away. Especially now." Why did he feel so uneasy? Why?

"Don't worry, I can stop by here everyday in case she needs something," he answered immediately.

"I have left several blank checks that are signed but, should she need more, please go to see Mr. Músqiz the bank manager. He will know what to do." He said this not because his wife was incompetent, but because he wanted to spare her any possible worry with the everyday chores.

"Sir, yesterday at closing time, President' Díaz's secretary dropped by the office to tell me that if you were to need anything while you are away, I should go directly to him," he added aware of the importance of the mission.

"Let us hope that won't be necessary. In any case we will keep an open channel of communication by telegraph. Nobody is to know any of this; it is highly confidential. The good name of a family is at stake," which was the most he dared to reveal to his secretary.

"If anyone one asks about you, I guess I could say you are on vacation…" he prompted.

"Sounds like a good idea. But I don't think anyone will ask. In any case, Lucio Velázquez will take care of anything that comes up for us at the police station. He knows I will be gone on a mission. You can send anything that comes up to him. After all, I will be back before you know it. Two or three days at the most…"

The last sentence he repeated to appease his own doubts. He had a nagging feeling that all was not well.

He was now concentrating on his trip. It took ten hours to get to Río Frío. They had changed horses once and by the evening he was resting with his driver in a guesthouse called *Los Volcanes*. It was the smaller of two inns and he had expressly chosen it for that reason. It seemed a relatively slow trip but he had to remember that it was a steep road and that the horses were limited by the slippery road.

Rigoberto proceeded to wash with some warm water they had provided for him. He felt better. His room was small and a bit cramped, but it would have to do for one night. He had to guess why his subjects would stay there, but it seemed logical; they had little or no money. He, on the other hand, stuck out like a sore thumb. The owner of the inn made no comment, but he knew she was intrigued.

Feeling rested he went into the dining-room where the good woman had immediately put a cup of steaming coffee and milk, and a delicious sandwich with crisp, freshly-baked, round bread with sesame seeds on top. He could still detect the aroma of baked bread. like Clara must have done, and like many others before and after him. They were the recurring travelers.

The coffee was good and sweet. As he sipped the last of it, he asked the good woman if he had seen Clara. She took the photograph carefully between her hands and looked at it. She answered that two nights before she had rented the very same room to the young couple. Everything seemed to fit so beautifully that he could not believe his luck. He would try to send a telegram immediately asking that the search be limited to the state of Puebla. That should spare the police from useless work and allow the secret service to carry on with their usual activities. He had welcomed her answer and after thanking her, bade her goodnight.

Next day, quite early, they had a good, solid breakfast. They drank coffee with milk, eggs ranch style with a well-spiced hot tomato sauce and Danish bread. He could not imagine anyone being that hungry so early, but they ate most of it. They were again on the road while it was barely light. The place of Río Frío had a history of highway robberies. In previous years armed bandits would appear from nowhere and hold up the passengers, stealing whatever money, jewels and good clothes they could.

Further back, in the early XVI century, in 1519 the Spanish conqueror Hernán Cortés, on his way to Mexico City, had traveled between the two volcanoes in what was later known as "Paso de Cortés" unaware that he was going to interweave two cultures, two religions and two peoples, thus giving birth to a descendant continent which would be known as *Nueva España* and which would present the eternal conflict of the vanquished and the vanquor, and an ambivalence that went on to torture its descendants and the class structures long after the Mexican people had taken the reign of their country and destiny into their own hands. The two volcanoes appeared covered by sempiternal snows; the Popocatépetl and the Iztaccíhuatl, shone in the morning light in all its immaculate splendor. One was a the figure of a legendary lying woman, known by all as the "Sleeping Woman" and her kneeling lover, who filled with pain at her demise, had not noticed the heavy snow falling on him and had remained by her side as a reminder of the birth of a new race, born out of love between a Spanish lady and an Indian man.

One more journey and they would arrive in Puebla. Should he continue that evening to Cholula? He could have done it, but the public carriages would never have traveled like that. His instinct told him he had to travel in the same manner Clara had done.

They arrived in the city of Puebla de los Angeles where Rigoberto decided it would be best to stay with his driver at a very famous inn called *Mesón de Santa Clara* which was quite well-known. His decision had been prompted because he was aware that the city was too big to go investigating every small hotel and guest house. He washed up and went to the central park for a walk, a main square surrounded by the usual colonial palaces with arches and stone sculpted figures and hand-painted tiles of Arab transplant. Puebla surprised him pleasantly every time he stopped there. It was one of the most conservative states of the Republic. The capital itself, also named Puebla, was a very clean city where people remembered the place they held in history and were unquestioningly loyal to their country. They were known for their struggle to keep up with their traditions and religion. He smiled, pleased at what he saw. He very definitely liked the place.

From his wallet he took out a card with a name and an address and started out to look for it. He had to stop twice to ask for directions in small stores that were about to close. Suddenly he arrived to a building with a very impressive, huge, wrought iron gate.

A few moments later, he was with the local chief of police who did not seem at all surprised, and who was very eager to receive him.

"Whatever you need, Sir, I am certainly ready to help you in anything," the good man said.

Rigoberto explained the affair as carefully as he could and showed him the girl's picture.

"We will find them if they are here. It shouldn't be too difficult. However, we must keep in mind that they have the lead, don't we?" the man asked quickly.

"That is true. True…" Rigoberto replied.

"However, a girl like that is not often seen around here, is she? Somebody might have seen them! I am afraid it is too late and everyone is asleep. But tomorrow at dawn we will search in all private homes where travelers sometimes stay. I don't think they would go to an inn or a guest house. That would be too obvious for them…" the chief of police continued.

"There is a slight possibility that they have gone to Cholula which is where the boy comes from. I will leave at dawn, but I would need a carriage and a driver. I would like to give the day off to my present driver. He needs a rest."

"We can send you a very good driver at five in the morning tomorrow. *Mesón de Santa Clara*, correct? Anything else we can do for you? Would you like to have dinner with us?" the asked affably.

Declining the offer, Rigoberto left the stately house after admiring the plants on the corridor. The chief had smiled proudly, "My wife likes her plants…" he said.

"Yes, so does Rosita, my wife…" and he stopped because he suddenly felt so lonely that it was painful. "Well, I'm off to sleep for a few hours because we'll be off early in the morning and then I will be back in the evening," he said tilting his hat. There was a strong wind that could be felt in the cold nights of Puebla.

Rigoberto slept quite well in a comfortable room and did not wake up until there was a discreet knock at his door. He felt ready to go.

The cook in charge had prepared a hot cup of coffee and milk and some freshly baked rolls that the nuns delivered to the inn every morning. He was imagining how different this trip would have been if Rosita were with him! But today he did not want to think of her. He had too much to do, so he quickly left the hotel crossing the surrounding garden.

It was bitterly cold and he mentally thanked his father-in-law for the heavy winter coat. Coffee had been great for him; it made him feel full of vigor and optimism. Maybe by tonight he would be back with Clara and they could start for Mexico. It was vital that he find her.

The road to Cholula was a short one. Three hours later they arrived in the tiny city that boasted three hundred and sixty five churches. Cholula had that refreshing smell that country places usually had. There were few wild flowers along the road that should be opening soon, when the first rays of light touched them. He had never been there before and was very curious about it. One could see churches everywhere, some tall and others tiny, and he was able to immediately recognize a yellow cloister. He would have liked to visit Santa María de Tonanzintla, the nearby church that was later declared as one of the wonders of the world. He knew it to be profusely ornamented with polychrome faces of indigenous angels, flowers, fruits, and plants that had graciously afforded their colors for that house of the Lord that was to accomplish the mission of visually educating the local people in the ways of the Church of Rome.

Puebla too, was part of it. There he had visited many temples like San Francisco and the Cathedral. They were ornamented in very different styles. Some were totally white, others totally silver and yet others totally gilded. They were fastidiously kept up by the officials in turn who also looked after the saint's clothes and the church treasure and their festivities in their one-year appointments. He would have liked to visit them too. Maybe he would do so that evening upon returning, because he was firmly convinced of the wisdom attributed to Napoleon Bonaparte 'When in a hurry, tread slowly' and slowly he would go.

The carriage stopped in the central park much to the surprise of its inhabitants. Cholula was a small dusty town then, not the world-renown city it was to become later. There was no royal highway, as the main roads had been called. To the left stood the small hill of Remedios with its cathedral on top. It represented the conflict between archaeologists and Church because they were sure that under it lay a pre-Columbian pyramid.

He walked briskly in the chill of the morning until he arrived at a house of three patios with thick walls.

"The Zacarías family?" he asked, sticking his head in the entrance door which was ajar.

"Who is calling?" a pleasant, smiling woman asked emerging from one of the rooms of the house. She had obviously been working because she was wiping her wet hands on her apron.

"I am looking for a young man called Gerardo," he answered quietly.

"And who is looking for him? she replied visibly alarmed.

"Are you his boss?" she continued while observing his attire carefully.

"No, I am his friend…" he said smiling.

"He works in Mexico with his uncle. Would you please come in?" the woman said politely.

"Thank you," he said accepting.

He could see several women peeping out from various doors surrounding the patio. They were curious about the foreigner. Children also came out to run around him. They studied his clothes in their child-like wonder.

"My name is Remedios Zacarías," she said shyly. "I am Gerardo's mother," she said, not daring to look directly into his eyes. Her hands toyed nervously with the edge of the white apron.

"Don't be alarmed, please…I want to help him," he said trying to appear reassuring.

"I will bring you a glass of cider. I work for them. I make the wires for *Copa de Oro* and they give me two bottles at Christmas and Three Kings," she said as she went into one of the rooms.

He looked around him. The children had been recalled by the adults, so he was alone. One of the doors led to the kitchen. He could see a tile stove and counter. It was clear the stove was a charcoal burning one. On the walls above it hung pots of clay of all sizes. The smallest one was the size of a thumbnail. The biggest one rested on a wooden stool and Rigoberto could see that it easily held fifty quarts of *mole* sauce. It was probably the one for important occasions like weddings and baptisms.

A young boy who seemed about ten quickly came out of one of the rooms with a chair for the visitor, then he returned to a room where one could see a loom. Mrs. Zacarías hurried out from a third door carrying a bottle and a glass.

"Please sit down," she said frowning. She was visibly worried. She poured from an open green bottle and handed him a full glass.

"It's cool enough. Last night was unusually cold," she said approving of his coat.

"And where is this factory located?" he said making small talk so she would feel at ease.

"Well...let's see. It is quite far, in Huejotzingo. That is apple country. But I don't really have to travel there. They come to bring us the wires so that we can make the mesh which holds down the corks. Then they come to pick them up periodically. I prefer that work to weaving on the hand loom. My aunt does that work and she sells the fabric to the store on the main square. They don't pay her too much and that is why I prefer to do my wires. Gerardo sends me money sometimes. I cannot complain about him. He is working in Mexico City with his aunt and uncle. You say you know him?" she asked curiously.

Rigoberto did not dare to look directly into her eyes. She was a mother who was hopeful for her son. He could not tell her the truth either. Upon reflection, he realized that sometimes he wondered about his job. He would rather be a good person than a good investigator.

"Well, I know him very little. How long has it been since you last saw him?" he asked casually. Then he added quickly, "The cider is delicious."

"Yes, it is the best of the local ciders. Well, let me see. I haven't seen Gerardo since he left. It was my brother who came to visit yesterday. I have a bad feeling about that. I had begged him not to leave. He could have stayed here and asked for his father's job at the foundry. His father passed away a couple of years ago.

"Yes, yes, I see. Well, maybe he is too intelligent for that and wanted to see the big city," Rigoberto answered sipping from his glass.

"Well, he did start to go to school and he was a good student. The teachers liked him, but...well, he wanted more out of life. You seem to have understood that. My son is not a bad boy. I don't know what led him to do certain things, but I know that he did them in good faith. I assure you. I know him. I can see my children's faults, and he is not evil. He is the best one of my five boys.

She tried to give him a second glass of cider.

"Thank you. I think that was enough. I should be going to have some lunch." He had said that without thinking that the result might be an invitation.

"Did you travel from Puebla?" she asked eagerly.

"Yes, I started out quite early. But never mind," he said studying her dark, handsome face.

"Please wait. Drink this cider," she said pouring more golden liquid into the glass. I am going to give you some *mole*. Yesterday was my niece's wedding. It was my brother Pedro's daughter. Pedro is the owner of the bakery store," she explained.

"I don't think I should impose. And I really should be going back," he said politely.

"Well, you do have to eat and you will find nothing in this town. And it will take you another three hours to get back to Puebla. Or are you just going through?" she asked.

"Well, I do have to return to Puebla. I came to bring some papers for the governor," he said. She was looking into the distance, to the hill with the church.

"Wait," she said determinedly as she walked into the kitchen.

He would accept the meal which had been offered to him with such good will. He needed to know more about the family. The escapees were almost two days ahead of him. It was also true that he was suddenly hungry and wanted to taste the home-made *mole* with delicious, fresh, white *tortillas*... So he drank the second and third glasses. Meanwhile Mrs. Zacarías had brought out a small table and a spotless, white starched tablecloth.

She set before him a copious plate of turkey in *mole* sauce. He could taste the delicate flavor of the roasted chili pods, the touch of chocolate and almonds. Next to it she placed another dish with red rice, an embroidered round cloth container with the whitest corn *tortillas* he had seen in a long time. He ate silently as the good woman walked to and from the kitchen complementing whatever he might need to have a perfect meal. Lastly she offered him a sweet-potato elongated dessert with ornamental sugar flowers.

It was then Rigoberto became aware of the fact he loved women in general. They were hard working, industrious beings who loved their families and homes. His thoughts went back to his wife and the other women of his family. He could picture the goings and comings of his mother's kitchen during the holidays. Each one of the female members had a specialty that they would practice to outshine the previous year's tastes. He especially remembered his grandmother's sister who miraculously on a white cloth on her knee, stretched out big, round, paper-thin *buñuelos* that she fried and and later served with a syrup she prepared with rich, dark sugar and all kinds of fruit of the season.

After lunch he bade his goodbyes to Mrs. Zacarías, Mellitos, as she was known. He embraced her trying to express his gratitude and to calm her fears.

"If Gerardo shows up here, tell him to go directly to the chief of police in Puebla. He should refuse to talk or deal with anyone else. He will then be directed to me. I am going to help him, because I am his friend. Do you believe me?" he asked looking into her eyes earnestly, handing her a card with chief Blanca's name and address.

The good woman suddenly seemed to have remembered her pain. He would have liked to spare her, but at this point it was impossible. So they accused him of unorthodox behavior, so? What harm was there on being sensitive to other people's problems? And those who had had any kind of dealings with him were forever grateful.

He left the three-patio house where small and big tragedies brewed and came to fruition. His fears were true. The trip had been almost useless. Gerardo Zacarías would have been too intelligent to return to Cholula, or even to remain in Puebla.

He had no further clue as to their whereabouts. General Heredia's arrogance and pride had delayed the investigation for precious hours. He felt at a loss, probably for the first time in his life.

VII

Clara liked to think that the trip she had taken had been the most uncomfortable of her life, when if one were to examine the truth, she had rarely been out of her city, except for the few times when her parents had gone to visit relatives who lived in Cuernavaca. Anyway, she was too young to have traveled. It was only after marriage when a proper young lady could feel she was ready to face the whole world. Then one could think of a luxury cruise to France. And that was the reason that all the young girls should have French survival skills. It would not do to leave the hotel without being able to say a plain *bon jour* or *merci*, would it? She had been to a school that knew how to prepare its pupils for the life they would be fortunate enough to lead.

As she sat on the coach, Clara Heredia could see herself as she had done many times in her mind, waving goodbye with a gloved hand to friends and family. She would be wearing a wide white hat with a red flower in the middle. Then she would smile to begin her new life with whomever destiny had assigned to her. Her mother, happy and tearful at the same time, would have waved back with the same apprehension, or maybe even a little jealousy?

Instead of that, she was surrounded by strangers and traveling to God knows where! Gerardo said Puebla…while she was too stunned by her daring action.

A few times, when they stopped to go walk for a bit or to eat, she would feel free like the wind in spring. Maybe that was happiness. She certainly felt like all the characters she had read about in the novels, those characters who fought against all the odds to achieve their goals. She clung to that fantasy because she did not want to face the future. She needed to live only the present. She did not even want to think of a group of men, police or soldiers, surrounding the coach and taking her and Gerardo prisoners and looking like common criminals to the rest of the passengers. Gerardo would surely die at her father's hands.

Gerardo was behaving splendidly. He put up a brave front and she did not want her lingering fear to take over. They would get lost, lost forever without a trace, even if that meant going to the end of the world. Anything rather than going back to the paternal house!

Many times in the future Clara would think back on those first days, her first big trip and the surprises she had along the way. Here she was just another person. That was a big relief. Anonymity was more than welcome. Some of the passengers viewed her curiously in the beginning and that had made her fearful. Once they arrived, this would no longer be important. The whole experience caused her fear and happiness and then happiness and fear. Nobody wanted her, nor loved her. Why must she feel guilty? They seemed to want to get rid of her by marrying her, so she would help them. She was not afraid of God either, because he was Perfect and being perfect, was All-Understanding. It was this love that allowed her to feel at peace and happy. Just as well, didn't Gerardo have enough on his hands to have a emotional creature to deal with? And what good would repentance do? She had taken the definitive step!

By nightfall they had arrived in Puebla where Clara was surprised to see a colonial city with its huge buildings and big churches. They sat on an iron bench in the main square. Some tall trees surrounded the cathedral. Blackbirds were coming back to their evening retreat, squeaking their raspy 'peah, peah.' Then they saw the police arriving at the coach station. The driver had already unhooked the horses and turned to talk to them. Without a word they started to run down the street towards the outskirts of town. Once there, they hid behind some bushes where they would be less visible for they were sure the police search would continue. It was bitterly cold and windy and there would surely be frost at dawn.

"It might be a good idea to buy a blanket," he said after it was dark.

"No!" she said without thinking. She was terrified at being left alone.

"You need new clothes. We will be wearing the same thing for several days," he observed.

"I know and I don't care," she replied.

"You will be fine alone for a while. I will hurry because the stores are sure to close soon. Nobody knows me. Maybe I will even go to the big market. It is so impressive. Too bad, I think you would like it, but you would certainly be recognized because they are looking for us," he said nervously.

Gerardo started on his way and she was to remain hidden there until he returned. The hours seemed long and tedious and it would probably be some time before Gerardo returned. Two peasants from Cholula appeared on the road carrying their fresh vegetables for the next day's market. They were so engrossed in their conversation and so eager to get out of the cold, that they would not notice her. She, in turn, hid as well as she could from them. Finally Gerardo showed up smiling. He had a long woolen skirt and a big shawl for her. Hurriedly Clara put on the new clothes on top of the old ones and tried to find a comfortable spot in which to spend the night.

Gerardo then explained to her that he had initially thought of going to Cholula, but then realized it would be a terrible mistake. The police or even army people would be lying in wait for them. His uncle would be forced to tell them where his mother lived. Then he felt very sad, because he thought of his mother and what he would be putting her through. Clara, on her side was thinking of Nanny Justine who walked incessantly from the kitchen to her room and back with trays and flowers and her ironed clothes. She needed clean clothes and warm food.

So they had the lead, how was it possible that they had caught up with them? Had they used the new invention, perhaps, the telegraph? How about the rest of the state of Puebla? Would they be on the lookout for them? He had not dared to find a place to spend the night, because in Puebla people were ultra-conservative and they would never allow them to have a room. They had a saying, "Clear things and heavy chocolate" and he would have never been able to explain Clara's situation to anyone. The good women who let rooms would never let a young couple, whose legal situation was not clear, spend a night under their roof. There was also the financial aspect to be considered. They were almost out of money. They needed what little they had to buy food.

"I brought some round sandwiches called *cemitas* with head-ham and cheese and avocado. You will love them for dinner! Sorry we don't have a cup of hot coffee and that we have to eat out in the cold and dusty road."

"I will love it. I have never seen such a beautiful sky and have never slept out in the open. Please be patient with me, I have so much to learn! Maybe someday I can do something good for you," she said sobbing.

He held her by the shoulders trying to comfort her, but she was having a crisis of some sort. She was tired, hungry, sleepy and cold and all kinds of black thoughts passed through her mind. She tried to get rid of them but did not know how.

Soon she had calmed down. They ate and she finally fell asleep on Gerardo's shoulder. She woke up shivering; the cold wind continued moaning for a long time. "Don't be afraid. It is only the wind. There are no animals, it is too cold for them," he said trying to get her to go back to sleep. But she couldn't. And that is how they had spent the longest and most uncomfortable night of their lives. They rationally knew they would get over it and rest up somewhere. After a while they decided to get up and go back to Puebla. They were exhausted and hungry.

They spotted a small café that was about to open. It was too early. They sat down and ordered coffee and ate everything they had to offer. They ate so fast that the cook could not believe her eyes. The young woman who had served them said very quietly, "The owner will be here any minute. He has to do his duty and report you…The police are looking for you. I believe in love and wish you both much happiness," and with this she gave them small change for the pocket of her apron.

"Thank you," they said as they started to run down the street. They needed to go in the opposite direction. Now the police search was a certainty. When they finally reached the road, they saw a black coach coming their way. Gerardo made a sign for it to stop. The young man who was the driver, obliged them, while the other passengers were merely curious because Clara was dressed in such an extravagant manner.

They got in barely saying good morning to the other passengers, but they did not say a word to each other.

"You were lucky I had two empty seats," the driver had said to them. "You barely made it!"

"I'm sleepy," Clara said and proceeded to close her eyes in order to avoid further conversation.

"Are you from Veracruz?" a tall, lanky man dressed in black and wearing gold-rimmed glasses asked.

"Yes," Gerardo replied.

"Well, coaches are very much on time, you were nearly left behind," he said kindly.

"We were saying goodbye to our friends," Gerardo said as naturally as he was able to.

"And your luggage?" the man asked.

"We don't have any. We are going to visit family; we will be all right," Gerardo lied.

"But still…" he said shaking his head doubtfully.

The rest of the people looked on with interest.

"Well, we will arrive soon enough and change our clothes," Gerardo continued.

"Your sister looks tired; we should let her sleep," the man continued.

"I'm very tired also," Gerardo said laughing and closed his eyes. He thought it funny that people might think Clara could be his sister. Even better, they would not suspect. And he closed his eyes, if only to escape more comments. It would have probably aroused more suspicion. He thought of Clara and could not make out her thoughts. But she was really sleeping in spite of the wind that seeped into the coach.

They were traveling so slowly! However, the weather was becoming milder. The sun was shining and Gerardo was eager to reach their destination, maybe it was Veracruz, and try to get lost among the people, the sailors and the taverns and maybe see the ocean. People knew Veracruz was a port. Neither of them had ever been to the ocean, and they had never seen so many varieties of fruit and products of the sea. This would be a treat for them, they thought as they went from one surprise to the other.

Lunchtime had arrived and the man dressed in black had insisted on sharing his basket with them. Neither could resist. Clara was used to her meals on time and Gerardo declared to not be hungry because Clara was avidly eating most of the fried chicken. Mr. Barrios, as the man claimed to be named, insisted Gerardo eat the rest. Something, he suspected, something was fishy. He would not be the one to ask. He merely observed the beautiful and refined girl sitting opposite him. He had rarely seen her type of beauty. She had huge green eyes and hair that shone like gold. Her teeth were perfect and her hands were soft.

"The good woman who cooks for me has sent far too much fruit and dessert. Be so kind as to eat it or it will go to waste," he said as he handed over a bottle of a sweet beverage made of the Jamaica bloom. He was amused to see her drink so quickly and smile at him. The spontaneity and innocence in her eyes spoke to him of the creatures of the Lord: "He who loves me will love my children." And he felt the Lord had touched him and for this he was grateful.

Mr. Barrios did not seem in the least surprised when after lunch they both wanted to sleep. He knew they did not want any questions asked.

Clara felt contented. She let the horses' even pace mark the rhythm of her breathing. In her mind she decided to do a recount of what her life had been up to then. She tried to think of her first memories and of her mother and a cold house. She grew up with her mother's little deceptions, harmless things, like holding a cigarette with a hair pin so that her husband could not detect the odor of tobacco on her fingers. Many times he had ostracized her for days and would let no one speak to her for what Clara considered minimal details. She had to obey his strict decrees which seemed to have no logic at all. Her mother seemed to go through it all silently and walk around the house like a ghost.

Finally, in the early evening they had arrived in Tehuacán. Clara woke up to the beauty of the place as if emerging from a nightmare. The name of the spa and its thermal waters and of the city were familiar to her and it was enough to make her smile.

VIII

The sun was shining with full force. It was warm now. He had
walked around a small canal that bordered the house of the Zacarías
family and proceeded to the *zócalo* or main square, where his carriage
was waiting. The horses seemed to have had water and his driver
was polishing the leather seats. He was a good policeman and he
had his orders. He did not dare ask anything; he merely waited for
instructions. The older man smiled when he saw his passenger who
smiled jovially at him.

"Sorry not to have been able to give you time for lunch, but
now we are in a hurry, Taurino," he said as he boarded the carriage.

"No problem, Sir. My wife gave me some nice sandwiches and
I brought coffee. So you see, I had eggs and sausage," he replied as
he closed the door for Rigoberto.

"Cold…" laughed Rigoberto shaking his head. "Well, there
seemed to be no alternative. I, on the other hand, have just had the
most delicious of *moles*. Sorry, I owe you one," he said laughing
good-heartedly.

Maybe he had laughed because he felt at a loss. Where were
they? Where to begin? Maybe the plump, good man whose hair
was thinning, the Puebla chief of police, would have some kind of
answer. Maybe Clara Heredia and Gerardo were already at his place.
His mind wandered along the dusty road. He felt, somehow that
they were within his reach, very near him. The trees seemed tall and
bare and sad. It was the arid winter scenery which upset him.
However, he was sure he would soon return to the warmth of his
own home. The affair at hand could not take all that much time.

Before he had left he had sent people to Cuernavaca, Coyoacán and Taxco. Those places were not far from the capital. Now he must go back on his orders. Another pleasant discovery was that his instinct had not failed him.

It was around four thirty when they reached Puebla again. He asked Taurino, his driver, to drop him off at the chief of police's house. Blanca and his wife were sitting in the comfort of a big dining room. It had twelve-foot ceilings and was still cold. It would have been perfect in summer, but now it was chilly.

They welcomed him warmly and invited him to join in the meal. Blanca had just had dessert and was asking the housekeeper for coffee. He was pouring two glasses and smiling. "I have news. Yesterday around six they had breakfast in a tiny restaurant called *don Chema*, not far from the main square. Chema came to report his guests too late, around ten O'clock. You see, I got a telegram yesterday and we made the rounds of all inns, guesthouses and restaurants, leaving word that they should report them. This morning we made the rounds again; we even had to wake up a few people. I realize we have an urgent matter, don't we?" he asked casually.

"Yes, you are right," Rigoberto answered, trying not to let his impatience show. He needed the gist of it, directly, not in a roundabout way. Now the explanations were not needed. They had lost them. Patience, patience. He had to go at chief Blanca's pace. He smiled and drank a delicious aromatic coffee. Puebla was a coffee-growing state, maybe this was Cuetzalan coffee. So, to divert his mind he concentrated on the big, hand-carved furniture, on the family oil portraits, which were hung too high for his taste, on the cabinets where the finest glasses and china were kept. He recognized the well-known fact that the people of Puebla were conservative and zealous guardians of their cultural inheritance.

Chief Trinidad Blanca was an extremely cordial host, as were all the heads of families in Puebla. He was nice by instinct, not by duty. He watched him pour cognac into the two carmine-colored monogrammed glasses. They must be antiques. He slowly savored the cognac and realized that it helped take out the chill of his body.

He relaxed and watched a very concerned and discreet Mrs. Blanca. She too, was drinking coffee. Where was Clara?

"Well, Chema in person came too late. I really didn't except anyone to report them so quickly. They had a huge breakfast. Coffee with milk, *chilaquiles* and fried eggs, tortillas, rolls...Well, it goes without saying that young people are always hungry, regardless the fix they are in!" said Blanca as if speaking to himself.

Rigoberto drank his coffee. The moment of despair had passed. He would go at the chief's pace, and chief Blanca was stalling, because he considered to have failed in his mission. He now understood. They had been there!

"So our birds took to flight leaving behind no clue! Well, we'll just have to take it from there," he said as he emptied his glass. He was impatient to leave.

"Do you want to talk to Chema yourself?" he inquired eagerly.

"I don't think that will be necessary. What did the carriages have to say?" he asked quickly.

"One leaves for Veracruz at six and the second one for Córdoba at six-thirty. The employees there forcibly see everyone that gets on the coaches. No one matching their description got on. They seem to have disappeared into thin air!" Chief Blanca showed his frustration this time.

Mrs. Blanca came into the dining room with a plate of cookies made by the nuns and the typical sweet-potato bars.

"By the way, chief Blanca, I would like to ask you a favor. If Mrs. Zacarías, Remedios Zacarías, comes to see you, please receive her personally because she might be the bearer of news. You will under no circumstances arrest her or her son Gerardo. Just question them naturally. As to the boy, send him directly to my house in the company of a good officer. In any case, I will keep in touch with you by telegraph. I will sign Rogelio, my secretary's name, just to stay undercover," he said to the embarrassed chief.

The man was quite attentive and his wife, an attractive woman over forty listened carefully, trying to be unobtrusive. She was disconcerted with this case. They had not been able to have children, but they had adopted a little girl named Leticia to be their very own and beloved daughter. She was a young lady by now.

"I'll be leaving now and maybe I will return. Madam, my respects. This is the state of the Republic where the best food is prepared. I will return soon with my wife Rosita, under different circumstances."

As he walked through the central square he thought of his Rosita and the small being which was growing safe and loved in her interior. Women on the streets crossed quickly, covered with woolen shawls; the men were wearing wool jackets. The temperature was descending quickly. He finally reached the arches that formed the main square and stopped before a colonial palace which served as the coach station. He was directly across the Cathedral. It seemed deserted at the time. He went into the house that had a big patio which seemed to serve as stable. He tried to see everything through Clara's eyes. Had she felt repelled? She was not a young lady who was used to traveling. Was she curious, uncomfortable? Maybe she was just tired and maybe just curious. Did young people ever feel tired? And then she was forced to continue traveling, but where to? The street sweeper!

It had been difficult to locate him, but the man stood before him half an hour later. He looked quite clean for his trade, only his dark, calloused hands betrayed his occupation. He seemed like a sincere man. He eyed Rigoberto's gold coin suspiciously.

"Why for me?" he asked looking at the young man again.

"Just tell me what coach the young couple got on this morning…"

"The ones who almost lost the coach? And that is all you need to know?" he asked still suspicious of the man who wanted to give him a gold coin.

"Yes, those," he said quickly.

"Why do you want to know? Are you family? Don't worry, they left at six-thirty to Veracruz. The young lady was very pretty. She had on a big, wide, blue coat. They barely made it. They were running so fast! Young people oversleep, while we, the old people, are afraid of falling asleep; we will have enough time to do that six feet under," he said smiling widely showing his lack of teeth.

"Those drivers sometimes 'forget' to report the last minute passengers. Ernesto would never do that. So when he comes back, he will probably report them. He does not like to be late, so that must be the reason he just took off," he said quite happy with the gold coin between his fingers.

"So the young lady had on a long, woolen coat?" asked Rigoberto once more.

"Yes. I have never seen anything so elegant before, and I doubt I ever will again. It was very wise to wear it. It can get quite cold around here at this time of the year," he said toying with the two-peso coin.

It was already evening. There was nothing more he could do but drink coffee. First he would stop by the telegraph office. He missed his family and would have liked to be on the way to Mexico City. He must stop trying to dream.

Rigoberto smiled to himself as he wrote his telegrams. The longer one was for the chief of police of Veracruz, the second one was to his wife. The man in charge read them both trying to hide his surprise. He proceeded to transmit them as quickly and precisely as possible. The man standing in his very own office must be extremely important! He had made his day! How could a man of such importance be so young and happy? He hesitated for an instant and the man smiled at him, as if to ask, 'well'?

"I'm done. It's just that it is very strange…strange," he said in spite of his usual indifference.

"Love can be strange, but stranger even is lack of love," he replied non-committantly. He then paid and left.

He was now certain. The girl had fled because she felt no love. He admired her strength of character and now he was really curious to meet her personally. It was going to be very sad to be the one responsible for returning the captive girl to her jailers. He now understood her perfectly and could find no way to solve the dilemma they were all involved in. Well, he had plenty of time for that! Now he had to concentrate on the thought process that was directing her. He had to remind himself that he must continue with this search because that was the task assigned by the President himself. First he would do what was asked of him, and then he would try to find a solution to save the girl and later the boy.

He tried to convince himself that as long as Clara was traveling in the coach she would be safe. It would be when she got off that the matter changed. The police would hold them until he arrived. He would get there, and return with his charge to the city. He would be free to go back home.

When he arrived to the main street he spotted a restaurant which had a side-walk café. He sat down. He was alone. Everyone had gone inside because of the chilly wind. But he had wanted to sit outside to observe the Cathedral with its splendid wrought-iron gate crowned by angels in bronze. Puebla de los Ángeles with its tall palaces with stone-carved figures and hand-painted tile. Puebla had been distinguished with the honor of inheriting the trade of hand-painted ceramic tiles and earthenware and it was there where kilns had been installed with the purpose of producing *Talavera de la Reyna,* the Spanish Queen's favorite ceramics. They had originally produced the classic blue and white, and with time the New World had enriched them with an infinity of colors. He enjoyed sitting there and savoring the history of its traditions where patriotic holidays were respected and foods were created to celebrate them; others were created with the colors of the national flag, as was the case of stuffed peppers bathed by fresh walnut sauce adorned with green parsley leaves and red grains of pomegranate. His mind went back to the meal he had just had and the delight he experienced in seeing a true Puebla kitchen at Mrs. Zacarias'.

Maybe he was just hungry and that is why he was thinking of food. He would probably go inside and order something. At that precise moment chief Blanca spotted him there.

"My wife insists that you have dinner with us. I promised to come out to look for you and am a bit embarrassed. This initiative should have come from me. We should also offer you hospitality in our home," he said sincerely.

"No, no, no. Thank you very much. I will, however, come have a light supper with you, but I will remain at the hotel because I will leave very early for Veracruz since our friends are headed that way," he said as casually as possible.

When he lifted his eyes, he saw chief Blanca quite upset and he thought he possibly might be cold. This was not a good time to be out there. "Would you think it is a good idea to go inside and have a Carlos III brandy?" he asked the man.

"That would be fine," Blanca answered but Rigoberto could see he was still quite perplexed. The young man from the big city had given him a lesson in efficiency. How was that possible that he had found their whereabouts in such a short time? He had assigned twenty of his best officers...

They went into the café, property of a man from Galicia who greeted chief Blanca in a very friendly manner. Everyone turned to look at the foreigner while he observed them with a twinkle in his eye. They had interrupted a game of domino.

"Welcome to our table," a couple of them said, hoping the young man might want to play.

"Next time maybe…" Blanca said leaving the cue to Rigoberto. When the young man did not answer, chief Blanca continued, "My wife is expecting us for supper."

It was a pleasant place, full of cigarette smoke and clearly the meeting place of the older generation.

They sat at a small table with marble top; the Austrian chairs had woven reed seats.

"Do you play domino?" Chief Blanca asked him.

"I seldom play it, yes. But I would rather do other things," he replied pleasantly.

"I used to play frequently. But we adopted Lety and I like to spend time with her because one day she is going to get married and we will be alone again," he said longingly.

Rigoberto thought of his own parents and Rosita's, and in the cycle of life.

"Then you will have a son, and grandchildren. Chief Blanca, fate is a strange being. If you observe the Heredia family, they have a sweet child and they have decided to destroy her. They are her enemies. She has a strong spirit. A woman ahead of her time. I am to be a father soon, and for that reason only, I think I side with her. I am beginning to understand a lot with her flight," he said in a confiding manner.

Blanca had listened to him attentively. "Well, maybe the parents acted thinking in the best interests of the girl," he said.

"Would you force your daughter into an unwanted marriage?" he asked Blanca who remained silent. Noise of the chips hitting the marble and glasses being set down could be heard. Cries of joy from the winners were clear.

Rigoberto continued, "I hadn't thought of it that way. The truth is that this case alerts us as parents not to make the same mistakes. Maybe that is why nothing like this has crossed your mind. My mission is to return her to Mexico City. Obviously the wedding will not take place. But what about the consequences? The irony of the case is that the candidate chosen by the father is quite a nice boy. Maybe if the father had let events develop by themselves, we would not be sitting here today. But just now, it is very urgent that I find her. Maybe later I can try to talk to the general. My orders come from the top...the very top," he said sighing.

The man before him had changed. That was what was so surprisingly wonderful about youth. Foreign to them, Clara Heredia had changed them both, forcing them to examine fundamental issues.

"I wouldn't worry if I were you because you will never have that problem," he said trying to reassure the man seated before him. Blanca was balding; he probably was very much aware that he was getting older and thought he could not understand the values of young people. Those values were so different from what seemed important things to his generation. He was disconcerted and now he knew he had never noticed that with his own father and mother. It was as if a generation gap had not existed then.

Chief Blanca sighed, as if waking from a dream. He looked around him and then said softly, "Thank you, sir. Now I know why in spite of being so young you have this important assignment. *Sagesse du Coeur*, as my grandmother would say. She was a very chic Parisian who lived in a God forsaken town called Lait Charbon. She had fallen in love with a peasant whom, curiously enough, I ressemble. It was a terrible scandal in one the castles. Here we are. Their descendants. Surprisingly enough, they were very happy. They had ten children," he said smiling.

"I appreciate your sharing that with me," the young man answered. Do you think we will have time for another glass of cognac?" he asked, noticing Blanca's empty glass.

"Well…the chocolate will be ready…" he said kindly.

"Let us go try that famous chocolate prepared by the nuns…" he said thinking of the scented aroma of cinnamon.

"And their miniature pastry," added Blanca proud of their traditions.

Blanca bade farewell to all the other patrons. They had probably known each other most of their lives.

The ice-cold wind returned them to a different reality. There was a full moon and the stars shone brighter because the sky was so clear.

"The coach will pick you up whenever you wish. I see you have been to the telegraph…They will be waiting for you in Veracruz," chief Blanca said casually.

"Five O'clock will be a good time," he answered thinking that he was finally seeing an efficient and intelligent man at work. The more he thought about it the more he realized the appearances can be misleading.

"It might be too early. Our roads have been quite safe for some time. However, I would suggest six O'clock might be better because of daylight. I have already made some arrangements, I hope you will forgive me, but I was aware of the content of your telegrams. Forgive this seemingly intrusive act, I guess it is part of the trade," he said finally.

Then they walked in the silence of the night for a short way until they reached the chief's house. Only their quick breathing of the cold air seemed to hurry their footsteps on the square stones that paved the deserted street.

IX

Rigoberto López had traveled from Puebla to Tehuacán. He felt at peace with himself. At that time it was the only way to arrive in Veracruz. Clara would have been forced to follow the route. He was hoping to put together a picture of the girl by trying to see the world through her eyes, the eyes of a young, protected girl. How had she been able to cope with the rigors of such trip? And what would the conditions be for them in the future? For surely the situation would go from bad to worse, if even for the sole reason of having no money. They would be surrounded and captured by tonight; he had carefully planned it that way and he tried to remember that each time a pessimistic thought crossed his mind. It was a relatively easy project now.

For Clara it would mean the beginning of the end, for she would have to go again under her father's protection. Something in the whole setup told him there would be no wedding with Francisco Monteros. Why? Well, maybe because she had committed the worse sin of all, not to go on the track society had designed for girls like her. That, they would never forgive. This meant she would be entering into the closed circle of the rejects. She obviously had not considered things carefully and had acted on an impulse, which showed very little common sense. But that was not the case, was it? Maybe there had been no alternative to her situation. And deep, very deep within his heart he was hoping she could evade him and go to another world, another time, another existence because he felt her fate was not necessarily one of raising a healthy brood and putting up with a dull husband.

Once in Tehuacán it had not been difficult to trace the house in which they had spent the night. The woman in charge gave them the details. Sure, she had been surprised to see a young lady there, traveling among salesmen. At least there was a priest with them. The girl seemed so tired that she could not get a word out of her. She remembered that she had gone out for a stroll with her young man. The woman could not tell if they were going on to Veracruz city itself, but she supposed they were because they were traveling in the coach headed there.

Rigoberto left the house in a good mood because at least he had not lost her. The weather here was milder than that of Puebla. He then proceeded with his driver to a hotel called *Los Manantiales*, the springs, much favored by the Porfirian society. The spa boasted General Porfirio Díaz's patronage and from then on, the big living room displayed a life-size oil portrait of the president in full military regalia surrounded by dusty pink velvet drapes and French furniture. It was an elegant place and its patrons belonged to the upper echelons of society. They had comfortable rooms with embroidered linen; the china used in their dining room came from a special factory and it was called "pigeon's blood" because its transparency lent a reddish tint to the bone china. The hand embroidered tablecloths and napkins came from Aguascalientes. Rigoberto asked himself if Miss Heredia had not felt regrets when remembering all that. He liked the young lady; he respected her because she had not given in without a fight. She had not compromised her integrity.

They left early the next day for Orizaba. They had to cross Cumbres de Acultzingo which were a dangerous series of descending cliffs that had amazing green and blue colors. They seemed an unending experience of zigzagging twists and turns. The scenery however, made it worthwhile. One mistake was all it took to have a fatal accident. The coach drivers were the best in the country. They had to travel very slowly and hope the horses did not want to take an initiative of their own. Rigoberto smiled. He was a fortunate man. They had assigned the best driver of the police force to him. The man was quick and resourceful and knew all the secrets of the area. He thanked his lucky stars to have said no to chief Blanca when he had insisted on sending Taurino with him.

Upon their arrival to Orizaba, after he had recuperated from the slight feeling of vertigo, he went out to continue his search. The passengers of the coach had all stayed at a place called *Las Cumbres* and the young couple seemed to have continued on to Córdoba with the rest of them. It was not a long trip, but they were ahead of him. They must have enjoyed the rich and varied vegetation of the generous land. In Fortin de las Flores, the flower vendors offered hearts of palm carved out to hold fragrant blue and white gardenias. Surely Clara had never seen such profusion of flowers nor swam in a pool perfumed by floating gardenias. By now maybe she had gotten used to traveling among strangers through fascinating lands. She probably had never been so close to nature and she might be absorbing it all as the greatest adventure of her life.

He was intrigued. Where did all that money for travel come from? He asked the owner of the boarding house. Had she noticed a medallion his sister was wearing? She good woman said yes, naturally she had admired it and could not help wondering how a young lady from a good position came to be traveling with such a young man who did not seem to be her relative. The girl did not appear frightened although she was quiet and shy. She didn't give it much thought later because she was used to all kinds of travelers.

He went out to a sidewalk bar and sat down to drink a couple of beers in hopes of seeing the medallion pass by in some woman's neck. No such luck. What was Clara doing for clothes? Surely this was a warmer climate and she would stick out like a sore thumb. His mind went back to the medallion. It had been elaborated with eighteen carat gold in Florence; it had the hand-painted profile of a beautiful girl wearing a red cloak on her head and it was on a thick chain of red, yellow and white intertwined strings of gold. They should have been able to get enough money for both things to continue on their way, which was, where?

Still pondering on his facts, Rigoberto went to bed and slept peacefully and happy thinking that it would be so pleasant to travel here with his wife and walk with her through the scented fields of flowers. The peace of the province. Yes, she would have liked that. He was in a hurry to get back to her and tell her about all the wonders of a world she had never seen. He also wanted to tell her that he now understood the reason for Clara to have run away with the gardener's nephew. He felt a keen pain of separation because now he had two women and one was his daughter. He could picture Rosita holding the little one in her arms and signing a lullaby. And then he became sad. By now, he realized, Rosita would have probably moved to her parents' house and their home would be left empty and lonely. Houses had souls too, that he knew. He had to come to terms with the conditions of his profession. A man's work was an important part of a man's life and he loved it because it was a challenge to his intelligence and creativity. To him it was like a game of chess, a puzzle. Up until now he had always turned out to be the winner because it had always been so easy for him. Now he had met his match and he understood that and was ready to continue the chase.

His mind went back to the first time that General Díaz had called him. He now realized that the general had been taken aback by his youth. He had hesitated briefly before confiding a state secret to a twenty-three year old. It had to do with the disappearance of official documents that were concessions of mines in Santa Rosalía, where there was a church designed by Eiffel, in the state of Sonora, where land was arid and most of the state was a desert. The documents represented a great and solid source of wealth, just recuperated from a French company. The whole file had disappeared without a trace. Overwhelmed and intrigued that something of that magnitude would happen in his offices, Díaz had sent for him. Surprised by the young man in front of him, Díaz seemed to doubt for an instant. The young man's eyes spoke of his intelligence and Díaz finished by confiding in him, hoping that at the very least it would teach the young man a lesson in humility.

"So?" he asked him once he had finished his exposition.

"Well, sir, with all due respect, I do not want to speculate before a proper investigation, but it should not be too difficult to locate those documents," he had replied smiling.

Maybe Díaz had felt provoked by his attitude, on the one hand, but on the other, he realized the words were spoken with no malice. It was part of his personality, for Rigoberto always proved to have a sixth sense to solve what seemed impossible. His theory was that the most obvious answer was the correct one. The key to finding solutions was not an easy one, precisely because it was there, in the open.

His mind went back to the first time he had walked into the National Palace. He knew Díaz to be the son of modest middle class parents who had entered the military after a few years of attending law school, probably because he knew that Santa Ana was a dictator turned traitor and a strong man was needed to overthrow him. He had also been one of the leaders who had defeated the French in Puebla on May 5th 1862. Incarcerated, the escapee had become a hero of the liberals. When Emperor Maximilian's power collapsed, Díaz originally from that state, commanded a formidable army in Oaxaca and his was the first liberal army to enter Mexico City as the conservative forces withdrew. Rigoberto was also aware that Díaz later had privately deserted liberalism in favor of his own political interests. The army of Oaxaca had remained loyal to him, especially after his Plan of Tuxtepc. It had given him the opportunity to capture the government. Rigoberto was puzzled by the descendant of Mixtec and Spanish blood. He had become a living legend, the prototype of a new Mexico, with all its virtues and vices. The President had become by now a man of refined tastes, quite ambitious socially and was married to a woman from one of the most distinguished families.

On that first occasion when he had entrusted Rigoberto with a puzzle, Díaz was surprised to be holding the retrieved documents between his hands only twelve hours later. Overwhelmed and speechless he studied the young man carefully. After a few seconds he asked him, "And the person responsible?" he asked fearing the answer.

Rigoberto, who knew that would be the case, answered casually, "Haste, Sir."

Díaz was extremely surprised as to how he had worded his answer. He looked into his smiling green eyes.

"And just how did this happen?" he asked, knowing he did not really want to hear what the young man was going to reply.

"They were mislaid. The only question was to find out where," he said reassuringly.

Díaz had remained thoughtful for a moment. He had ordered coffee, he said, with sugar. It had become a habit. Not that Rigoberto disliked it, but he was before a dictator and he knew it. He tolerated it and somehow had a soft spot for the man who ruled the nation and would continue to do so for a long time. That day it had been a subterfuge of Díaz's to stall for time while they drank the coffee. He had sat down with the young man in the more informal gilded chairs next to a coffee table where a discreet officer had placed the two cups and had left the room closing the door softly after him.

And then came the question which seemed far more difficult than any of the battles he had fought. "What would you do in my place?" he asked quietly addressing the man he was beginning not only to respect, but also to like. It was then he realized he had grown old and insensitive to people. That is what power did to you. His soul felt old and corrupted and the man in front of him was a breath of fresh air. How lonely he had been and had not even realized it! Somehow he was encased from others by the walls of power. This young man did not even seem to notice them. He seemed to float in freely from the outside world to provide a ray of sunshine.

"Well...I would probably send my private secretary as ambassador to Timbuctu," he replied half in jest.

Díaz was not offended. One could not be offended by the young man's spontaneity. What he would learn about Rigoberto later was that his answers had been very carefully contemplated beforehand. He would never be caught unprepared for any possibilities.

"I fail to understand your sense of humor," he said pretending to be very formal. The truth is that he could let his guard down. He had never been faced with such a man before. He had forgotten that people lived in a different manner outside the army and the police forces.

"I do. It is unbelievable but possible. Timbuctu is so far away that important papers would not be lost and even if they were, it would not be as important. They would have never arrived to this city in the first place," he said very simply.

It was at that very moment that Díaz knew he had a friend. The man sitting next to him wanted or needed nothing from him. He had arrived to where he wanted to be and Díaz needed him there and no place else.

General Díaz observed him carefully and tried to place his family. He liked what he saw, but could only remember his father was an outstanding lawyer and notary public. He accepted the fact that he needed this young man very close to him. The most important factor was that he spoke his mind very clearly. The second fact was that he did not fear him and his respect was probably the respect he afforded an ordinary citizen. That was a precious feeling for a president! And thirdly, and possibly equally important, was the fact that he had shown a great amount of good judgment when evaluating the situation. He had proved to be very objective. Did he know he had saved him the embarrassment of a military trail to a member of his own family? Pretending not to notice, Rigoberto knew that Díaz knew that he knew! Anything else was best left unsaid.

The following morning Díaz's private secretary was quite surprised when he received the assignment of ambassador to Spain. From then on the post was likely to be used in the same manner. The sensitive, diplomatic solution did not pass unnoticed by the interested party. That Christmas Rigoberto received a case of the best brandy Spain produced.

Díaz's respect for Rigoberto could only grow. They seemed to be linked somehow and their minds seemed to work on the same track. He would never dare to try to contradict or change his methods. He had thought of promoting him to a ministerial position but knew that Rigoberto would not like that type of promotion. The loyal and disinterested friendship was more valuable than power or money, and Díaz had learned the painful lesson. He also learned from Rigoberto that discretion was part of their relationship.

"Heights are lonely places," the young man had told him one day and Díaz was forced to accept his fate. Curious, he thought, how this young man can tell me anything and it will never offend me. He is my own conscience, young and strong, which returns me to reality and brings me down to earth. Nobody but a president could understand that.

Rigoberto was extremely surprised when the day before his wedding he received the news that General Porfirio Díaz would be more than happy to accept signing as a witness to his marriage certificate. Rigoberto was pleased because he had not suspected the depth of appreciation the strongest man in the nation conferred upon him. Even his own parents could not understand it and Rigoberto guarded the precious knowledge to himself. They had become accomplices of sorts. It was in that spirit that when the general needed something, Rigberto complied willingly. He also understood it was part of the service he owed his country. As to the rest, they rarely met socially, and when they did, they were courteous and distant.

That was the friendship that bound him to Díaz, who knew very well that a man with so much power could never be sure of his loyalties. However, with Rigoberto it was different. He was not a 'climber' he was a winner! And Díaz admired that type of people. He doted on him like a father and the young man paid him back in the same currency. From time to time he would receive a card stating that the general would receive him as requested and Rigoberto understood that he was expected at five O'clock sharply at the office. Two cups of coffee were already set next to them and he would willingly sit down to listen to the older man. Díaz was getting on in years and he was feeling it. Rigoberto, in an inexplicable manner, left him feeling revitalized. It was a strange and fortunate relationship and that was the reason that he understood that General Díaz was entrusting him with something important, his goddaughter, Clara.

The affair with Miss Heredia had become quite complicated. How could he help the young girl undo the mess and lay out her future? Maybe he could talk to his friend, a new friend called Francisco Monteros and together they could prevent the terror that her father had prepared for her. They would improvise as they went along. At the moment it was imperative to solve the issue of their disappearance.

X

A sticky breeze, curly hair and a fresh scent of fish seemed to announce their arrival at the sea. It was evening and the lights shone at the port. She knew that there was plenty of life down there. The sailors would be drinking, dancing and having their way with life.

Clara was not exactly tired, but she was stiff and bored, which was something she could not understand. They had said goodbye to the traveling companions with the same reservation with which they had traveled. Then they had found a guest house with the curious name of *Balcony to the Sea*. She loved the name and the green color of the building. Clara had been forced to give her medallion to the woman in charge. The woman whose eyes lit up when she received it, prayed to all gods that the young couple would not have enough money to pay for the room and that she could keep it. In exchange she would offer them two camp cots.

Once having settled in, Clara and Gerardo, free from all cares, ran down to the port in search of something to eat. They got to the main square where they could see the Cathedral, and next to it, stood a restaurant called *Café de la Parroquia* which was extremely famous for its coffee with milk, *café con leche*. After drinking their coffee with sweet rolls, they went down to the port where two boats lay in wait. One could clearly hear the bustle of life and laughter of bars and nightclubs. When she saw the beauty of a sea, which encased jewels of light, the women dressed in skimpy dresses of attractive colors, Clara realized that her experience of life was extremely limited. The world was beginning to yield its secrets to her, be it by accident or will. Vendors roamed all around trying to sell their wares from all the corners of the world. She inspected the coral necklaces, ashtrays and ornaments made of seashells; she saw the red spheres of Edam cheeses and Havana cigars being peddled. On the improvised store windows she could admire the Chinese and Philippine tablecloths and shawls. From China came also soap and powders. Clara had never seen such a variety of things, nor had she seen the women who peddled their night trade even during the day.

Gerardo too, in his own way, was absorbed in this new world. He had a smile on his face, unaware that the police of the area was frantically looking for them. They were looking for a girl with a long, blue woolen coat. Nobody had seen any such girl. The coach station knew nothing. Maybe they had been left elsewhere? In one of the small towns on the way? They were waiting for the next coach. The driver was finally located and he described the couple and told them that they had asked to be left at a short distance from the terminal. He was almost sure they had gone to visit relatives. The police questioned him as to the whereabouts of the other passengers but they had disappeared into the night. Each one had gone his way and they could not add anything else. Their young people were being quite discreet.

The police was all over in their search while the culprits were happily walking by the docks without a care in the world. They had stopped at an ice-cream store with the name of *Nevería Jiménez* located in the Alhóndiga Street where two young ladies standing on the street called out: *güer, güer, güero güera*…much in the style of the middle east, to attract cutomers. There they bought ices made from *marañón, guanábana* and tamarind fruit. New flavors, new scents and scenery. Everything was new to them. They were delighted.

The police had finally located a guest house called *Balcony to the Sea* where a surprised matron swore that no one of that description had stopped there. She had seen and recognized the opportunity to keep the medallion. It would be enough to tell them that she had helped them with the police and the jewel would be hers, no questions asked.

The unsuspecting couple slept that night in the quiet of the province, away from the activity of downtown Veracruz. The cots were made out of white, thick cloth and were extraordinarily clean. The owner herself had belonged to a family of money and when her husband had been killed with a *machete* by an offended husband, her world had crumbled. She had lost everything, except the four walls of her house. She had then been forced to sell her jewels to prepare some rooms for boarders. She was a good-looking matronly woman with long, black, wavy hair and jet-black eyes and a white and delicate skin. She had never had any dealings with the police, and so she planned to continue. The young couple would be the beginning of her good fortune and her jewelry. Her business too, was going well. Her house on *Damas* street had not been too far from the theatre on *Nava* street and she had a good many guests.

Clara woke up early to the vendors cries. They offered all kinds of wares such as fresh fish and coconuts. Their landlady had prepared a hearty breakfast for them. She served them fruit, coffee, and fried fish which she offered on a clean and beautifully laid-out table. Clara was happy. Life was smiling down on her. She had initiated a conversation with them assuring them she was their friend, and confided that she too had eloped with her husband. She would help them. First she would give Clara some clothes and dispose of the ones she had on. Clara agreed that she would have been immediately noticed and that the weather would become unbearably hot. The woman gave her some used clothes that were well starched and ironed, some old sandals and a palm hat. Clara's heart overflowed with gratitude and a sense of well-being. She had rested and was not aware of the police search. She was certain they had slipped undetected. However, they were never far from her mind.

"Oh, you can walk freely around, but I will instruct you how to dress and walk," the woman told them. "They won't know who you are. And make sure you don't walk together, especially downtown," the woman said sensibly.

She looked at Gerardo insistently, trying to understand the ways of love. She also knew that it was none of her business. Her business lay elsewhere. Anyway, love was love, especially when one was so young. This must be a little rich girl's whim and nothing else. Not that it really mattered as long as they went on their way.

A short while later they went into the city. The good woman had handed them two pesos and a few coins, and it seemed the world smiled at them. Clara felt very comfortable in her new attire. The cotton clothes were cheap and faded, but that should work in her favor. Her feet felt free and light and she felt as if a bolting of light had passed through her body. This she interpreted as a sign that had past had disappeared, that a new one was about to begin. When she saw the boats she wondered which of her friends were in the process of embroidering or going to a ball, or maybe even walking down the aisle. Most would be happy and because from their confidences at the convent, she knew they were loved and welcomed in their families. She also realized that her fate had nothing to do with theirs. Each one had her own. Her life had irreversibly changed. She was wearing working-class clothes and shoes. Was that the price of her freedom? It was minimal, insignificant! Hadn't her father always claimed that everything had a price and could be bought? Well, she was buying hers. But of course she had no way of knowing if further payments would be required! So, what if she had to be a working-class woman and scrub floors for the rest of her life?

Gerardo was worried. What seemed terribly urgent was that they disappear. They walked to the second street of *San Agustín*, turned on to Main street and again to the *Pescadería* which was the fishmongers street. They observed the many varieties of fish and then went towards *Puerta del mar*, then to the dock where they found the buildings of customs and the water fountain, *la Aguada,* where young girls filled their jugs and dreamt with their lovers while the water ran, incessantly and inexhaustibly. There one also found the *Puerta del mar* where one could see the silver shivers run down a blue infinite mirror of water. Then they walked to the Fifth Beach where sun-toasted children with yellow hair played happily.

Clara breathed deeply; she filled her lungs with levity, sun and salt, with life itself. She seemed to be in a curious state of mind where her body met with the magic of the place and responded with every pore of her skin that tingled at nature's whim and call. She was too young to understand her sensuality and the fact that her body was opening to nature as a budding flower. She felt her thighs and breasts tingling and attributed it to the sun...

The care-free girl noticed Gerardo by her side. He was observing the horizon where sea and sky became one and the confusion of everything began. Clara's presence returned him to the real world. It was imperative that he find a job, any kind of work would do. He would like to earn enough to pay their bill at the guest house and retrieve Clara's medallion. The near future worried him also. At the same time they had to flee. But, where to go? He looked at the boats thoughtfully. Some were quite big and there was a smaller one that was unloading wooden crates filled with bananas, big jute sacks of cacao and coffee beans, Mexico's gift to the world. He sighed and continued to dream. He thanked Clara for her initiative and for their future. Otherwise he might have never experienced the vastness of the sea with its seagulls, nor the majesty of the boats.

In different circumstances he might have just returned to the family home, to his ethnic group to run and play with his brothers and cousins in the patios. He would continue to celebrate religious holidays and take part in the pilgrimages organized each year to the hill of Remedios, the patroness Saint of Cholula and after whom his mother was named. He would return to savour the women's cooking, the *moles, pipianes* of the area and set up the altars for the dead with flowers and their preferred foods and objects. Each year, they set up one for a small child his mother had lost. He was in charge of getting the acid, yellow flowers called *zempazútchitl,* and the purple velvety *garra de león* or lion's paw, of taking down the photograph from its place on the wall. His mother would light the candles and set up the child's favorite food, pumpkin in dark heavy syrup, amaranth *alegrías*, and tamales with the cacao flavored corn gruel. His younger brother Miguel was in charge of the toys and serpentines. He had exchanged all that for...the world! He was not sorry; he felt very optimistic. One always tended to look inside, now was a good time to look outside!

Clara was walking up and down. She had a remarkable idea, maybe Gerardo could find a job on a boat? If he left her there maybe she could help the woman who kept the boarding house. She did not mind menial work. She would learn to wash those beds, sweep the floors and set out the sheets to dry in the sun. She knew the police was on their heels. She had reached the realization that she had to disappear, because by now her father's ire would know no limits.

Gerardo walked towards the smaller boat. She followed him.

"Does that say 'Grijalva'?" he asked unsure of his ability to read.

"Yes, it does," she answered thinking she had not really paid much attention to her protector. She realized that she had been privileged to attend a good school. He had only had dust and work in Cholula, and later the plants of her garden. They could not separate, for they complemented each other.

The Grijalva turned out to be a passenger boat and Gerardo climbed the plank to see if there was some work to be had, enough to pay for his sister's way. The sailors laughed at him and said they saw no sister. Clara had hidden where she could not be seen. At that precise moment, Gerardo saw a strong, tall man walk towards them.

"Speak with el Tiburón, the Shark," the sailor closest to him advised as he spit on cover and wiped the sweat off his forehead with the bandana that had been tied around his neck.

Gerardo understood it was now or never and approached the man called Tiburón. He was a rough sailor, a feisty drunkard.

"Sir?" Gerardo started to say timidly. The man walked quickly without paying attention to him. He was very upset because he had ruined the only chance they had had of leaving and becoming untraceable.

He joined Clara and together they walked silently until they reached the main buildings, the Corn Exchange or *Alhóndiga*, the Palace and the *Escribanía* or Judge's Office and onto the *Plaza de Armas*. It must have been close to noon when they reached the palace in front of the arches where restaurants placed tables and chairs on the sidewalks and which was a place patronized by sailors, musicians, tourists and women of ill-repute. Sitting alone at a table they discovered Tiburón. Gerardo instructed Clara to wait inside the Cathedral. They should separate and then start back to their guest house.

He went straight to the Tiburón's table and gathering up all his courage approached him. He stood in front of him. Tiburón spoke first: "I don't miss a thing. Did you kidnap her?" he asked while he emptied his glass.

He was utterly surprised. Tiburón's black, thick beard shone with the liquid which he wiped off with the back of his hand. He was wearing a sleeveless T-shirt and a tattoo of intertwined hearts showed in the middle of his hairy chest.

Gerardo waited, at a loss.

"Okay, I'll take you. But your sister must pay for her fare," he said burping.

"Thank you, oh thank you, sir. How much is her fare?" he asked glowing.

"Two pesos and fifty cents. Is that all right?" he answered mockingly.

But Gerardo was too happy to notice. He gratefully answered, "Of course!" and watched the man eagerly down the fourth glass of white rum.

"When those lazy bastards finish loading we will leave. They still have to load shoes, cloth and hardware stuff. Sit down, have one on me. I am a terrible man, and maybe you will be sorry to have met me. Maybe not, because you might really want to work. I will put you in charge of the storage room. Not a nail must be missing. Honesty has no price and I don't trust any of the ones on board. If I find you stealing, you will not forget my teeth. Now you know why they call me 'Shark!' Do you know where the thieves end up?" he asked laughing quite loudly. "With the sharks!" he reported gleefully.

Tiburón's look was beginning to become glazed. Gerardo knew quite well. There were a couple of drunkards in his town. Tiburón ordered two more drinks. The earring loop moved incessantly.

"Come on, man, be happy! You have your girl, and if you are honest you have nothing to fear," he said burping in his face.

"I will try, Sir, I really will!" Gerardo answered earnestly.

"Drink up!" he said when the waiter brought the two glasses. "I was young once, too, you know. See these two hearts? Do you know where Carmela is? She was the owner of this one," he said looking down at his chest and pointing to one of the hearts. Then he turned to look at him steadily, earnestly, as only a drunkard can look. "Well, you seem to know nothing of life, so I will tell you... Well, better not, but I will tell you the third party is part of the history of the sea! Yes sir! Cheers! And here is to the sharks!" he said raising his glass.

Gerardo had understood very little, except that his heart was happy because they would disappear the same day.

"Thank you for the drink, Capitan," he said as he stood up. "I will go get her," but the man no longer seemed to listen. He had retreated into his private world and had his eyes fixed on the empty glass.

Gerardo walked fast to the guest house. Suddenly he stood cold on his tracks. He had not even asked where the boat was headed for! Then he started on his climb again. Did it really matter? They were like two leaves in the wind, towards an unknown fate. He should thank his lucky stars and Tiburón for the opportunity. Maybe Tiburón was being generous because he was drunk, and would he remember when they set out to sea?

XI

As soon as Rigoberto stepped into the police headquarters he knew something had gone awfully wrong. There was nobody waiting for him and the only policeman on duty appeared very nervous and worried and claimed to have no knowledge of anything. Rigoberto crossed the street and sat down at one of the restaurants in the main square and ordered a cup of coffee. He drank it heavily sweetened trying to concentrate on something totally alien to the problem of the moment. He did not want to think what that absence of policemen at the station meant. Where was everyone? Where was Clara? He did not even want to think about it. He sat trying to integrate into his own, the rhythms of the music from the percussion instruments made of wood, the marimba and the rattles. For a few coins the musicians perpetuated Caribbean songs. They sang to their fruit, their women and everything they loved.

He observed them carefully. They were wearing strictly white trousers and bright-colored shirts. Their heads were covered with palm hats in spite of the hour and they seemed immersed in their black rhythms. He looked around him and saw extravagantly-dressed sailors in different stages of intoxication, older vendors offering their wares from every corner of the world. The whole atmosphere was one of rancid food and alcohol. The prostitutes walked by freely offering their services with a smile. What else could be expected of a port? The whole scene could have been a nightmare, a strange and attractive dream. It was life in chaos, but rather it was life in a different order. Here night was day and day was night. Intensity was the keynote with which to follow in the dream.

He sat facing the Cathedral, known as *la Parroquia* which had been originally built of wood in 1622 and the only traveling cathedral—or so the locals liked to think— because it had been a guest of The Brothers of Mercy in 1650 when it was on the verge of collapse. Later it had been rebuilt in its original site. The *Parroquia* was closed at this hour and he could not visit its interior. He did not know if he would be able to at all, because tomorrow morning, quite early, he had to go running after a crazy dreamer. He was uneasy, as if he had been presented with a new puzzle to solve. The only difference was that now he realized he had a next to impossible task.

Clara had somehow evaded them. Where was she headed to? If he had been in her place he would have returned to the big city to try to get lost in the relative anonymity it could afford. Maybe he would have headed to one of the small surrounding cities like Coyoacán or Xochimilco with its tall skimpy trees and floating gardens. Instead, she was going further away into the wide world. He was certain that Clara and her friend did not have a plan, which meant that they improvised as they went along, and that would make things much more difficult. He was sure they were no longer at the port. He somehow felt that he had missed them by a few hours.

He refused to think about the possibilities so he had to try to concentrate in the world around him. The military band was beginning its Friday concert. It was seven O'clock and they stood at the square surrounded by chestnut and orange trees and date palms. The round fountain was the attraction of the gray pigeons that stopped to drink from its fresh water. The vendors roamed with all kinds of things like Cuban cigars and locally grown tobaccos from los Tuxtlas and pistachios from far away lands. A young boy was selling small flasks with soapy water and demonstrating how to create magic, multicolored, and ephemeral bubbles. The ice-cream carts rolled in the square, together with the vendors and their fruits, Dutch Edam cheeses, black and red coral necklaces and jewelry of amber produced in Simojovel, filigree necklaces and earrings and

Puebla's embroided dresses and shirts. It was a mixture of cultures in very creative order-disorder.

Waves of fresh air impregnated with salt toyed in and out of buildings, caressed branches and trees and touched the water in the fountain raising small shivers on its surface. Rigoberto sat there as one of the many travelers of centuries. A cigar from Tuxtlas was set on his table; he accepted it and paid for it. Then he proceeded to light it, maybe in despair.

Suddenly a tall and overwhelemed man stood before him and he knew that if someone were to look for him, he would stand out like a sore thumb in that crowd.

"Good evening, Sir. Well…not so good," the man said with bitter irony.

Rigoberto looked at him and quickly surmised he was a military man.

"Sit down and let us have a drink," he said looking around him. There was life and movement of the people, poor and rich alike.

"You have to sit down anyway to tell me where you think Miss Heredia and the boy have taken off to," he prompted slowly, realizing he had already accepted the fact, while the man seemed paralyzed by his fear.

"I don't know. I can't understand it!" said the man who was obviously overwhelmed. He finally sat on the opposite chair relieved that Rigoberto had voiced what he dared not.

"Well, I would like to think that the first thing we need to do is have a drink. Then and only then can we sit down put our heads together about this matter; then we should eat dinner and then we should get a good night's sleep. Miss Heredia is no longer in Veracruz, I am sure. Now I know what you are going to say: no one here has seen her. Yes, she arrived in a carriage. You and I know that," he said observing the smoke from his cigar.

"But that is not possible!" the man insisted.

Rigoberto realized that he did not even know his name. "Well, two desperate adolescents with no experience do desperate things. Tell me, do you think they got into town or did they stay in the surrounding villages?" he asked while instructing the waiter to bring two bottles of beer.

The city itself was not too big. It was protected by a wall dating back to the 16ᵗʰ century when the Spaniards had felt the need to protect themselves from the pirate attacks and pillage. By 1880 a great part of the wall had disappeared since such protection was no longer deemed necessary. Eight of the nine bastions had been demolished. They had been origianally named with religious names such as Santiago, St. Joseph where the military quarters were, Saint Barbara, Saint Gertrude, Saint Xavier, Saint Matthew and Saint John near the Door to Mexico and the bastion of the Holy Conception near the Door to the Sea. There were four other buildings that were the warehouses of Californias, which, as its name indicated, were stored all the goods entering or leaving the New World since the discovery of America.

Rigoberto drank the beer slowly. The breeze was warm in spite of its being winter. "Well?" he asked the man in front of him who seemed intent on the foam of his glass. He looked as puzzled as a stargazer.

"Well, the young lady and her companion disappeared in the outskirts of the city. The driver thought he was doing him a favor by leaving them close to their relatives'. Now we know they were purposely trying to evade us. Do you think they know we are looking for them?" continued the worried man.

"Of course! Although I do not think they realize how important they have become to us. Our orders come from the top, my friend, Efraín Sosa, correct? Well, the best hunter can loose his prey. Don't worry. I suppose you looked in every inn and guest house. You have performed a valuable service and this escape was unavoidable. The driver had no possible reason why not to help his passengers and allow them to get off near relatives. No one could foresee that! Now, with regard to the future, because you see Efraín, the past is no longer here, it is only the future that lies before us with endless possibilities…" he said sighing for the first time since his adventure had begun.

The man facing him was an extremely nervous person and Rigoberto could almost tell him he had an ulcer or would be having one very soon. He wanted to reassure him because recriminations had never helped any situation.

"I will be fired," the man said as if talking to himself.

"That is nonsense! You see, I need you and you precisely, to be my liason, because now the case has turned really difficult. So I am naming you a temporary assistant to the Metropolitan Police for as long as my mission lasts. After that I will see you get the proper compensation in the local police force. So, now with everything clearly set up, do me the honor of dining with me here to see if we can begin to plan our future actions," he said absent-mindedly.

"Of course! I will do anything necessary to help. I do not understand how this came to happen. We have been searching for them since last night and at dawn today," he continued perplexed.

"Plain good luck of those who want to run. That is all. I assure you they slept in a quiet, clean bed last night. The question is which? And that we may never know. Now if you don't mind, I will register at this hotel mainly because it seems close to everything and that makes it comfortable. I think I should have enough time to take a shower before they finish preparing our meal," he said standing up.

They were in the bar of an inn called Palacios, which with time would be known as Hotel Colonial.

"Of course, sir, of course. What about your luggage?" he asked quickly.

"Never mind, I will be down in ten minutes. Please ask for a Red Snapper filet in Veracruz-style sauce, and a bottle of white, dry wine. You order whatever you would like. And now, forgive me, I cannot be without a shower for a minute longer," he said as he opened the door to the lobby.

Efraín Sosa was suddenly a distant past as he got into a luke-warm shower and lathered with perfumed soap. The affair at hand was lying on the restaurant table. Here he was alone with his shower. He had trained himself to function that way. With the feeling of cleanliness came also the feeling of having washed away the unpleasant situation at the front desk when they had demanded money in advance because he had no visible luggage.

He had regained his composure and he felt light and hungry. At that moment his mind was set on fish and wine dinner. He did not want to think about Clara because the thought was too obscure. It was better to remain calm in order to be able to dissect matters in the best possible manner.

"Sir, they could not have left. The coaches had strict orders not to pick up anybody outside their route," Sosa exclaimed when he saw Rigoberto return.

"What kind of boats were docked?" he asked happily as he sat down. The waiter was arriving with bread, butter and a bucket full of ice. A bottle of Valdepeñas was opened and he tasted it. Good. He liked the vibrant life of the port, the music and mainly he liked to see the musicians enjoying their work.

"Do you think…? No. They are still here, a Russian boat and an English transatlantic. They could not have been accepted there. The captains have their instructions. So, how? Did they have money?" Sosa asked. But Rigoberto was busy looking at an elderly lady who was scandalizing. She was heavily made-up and wore a light and very flashy dress that did not conceal her sagging flesh. She went from table to table asking the sailors for a drink. He was not really observing her, he was lost in the possibilities of his escapees.

"All right, we will go talk to the coastguards. This morning another boat could have sailed. But right now, let us taste this delicious fish they are setting before us," he said happily enjoying the aroma of good cuisine. He loved the olives and capers, and the tomato sauce with spices that was added.

Rigoberto could see Sosa was a very shy, insecure person. He had ordered the exact same dinner. They ate in relative silence, listening to the music playing at their side. Then another four musicians appeared with their *marimba* and started playing the port's favorites. Before his eyes lay an unexpected international mix of traditions and temperaments.

When they finished dinner, both felt better. They walked towards the Customs building. The officers in charge knew their trade well. They immediately confirmed that towards noon that very day, the *Grijalva* headed for San Juan Bautista in Tabasco, had set sail. No, they had not seen any such couple. The police had already been there. They would conduct a second round of questions in the morning, just in case somebody had forgotten something.

"No, it would be useless. The couple we are looking for are on that ship, What kind of ship was it?" Rigoberto asked urgently.

"Well, it is not a passenger ship. It is commercial ship that buys and sells products. The captain is Eleazín Rodríguez, who is better known as 'Shark' by his friends, is a huge man who looks more like a pirate than a sailor. He disposes of people caught stealing by feeding them to the sharks. Let's say rather, that he takes justice into his own hands," the officer explained laughing while shaking his head.

The people of the port were happy people Rigoberto reflected, because they were friends of the sun and the water and all the creatures born therein, and with that thought in mind, he thanked him and they returned to the main square. They left behind them the wharf, the lighthouse at the island of *Sacrificios* and the Castle of San Juan de Ulúa. The castle was the first fortress of the New World in the second half of the XVI century and had been the headquarters of multiple needs, and it had served as a protection to the city of *Culúa* where Juan de Grijalava, a subject to his Royal Majesty, the king of Spain, had arrived one day in 1518 when the patron saint was honored. It had been a castle to the governor, or maybe several in the XVI century; it had been a prison during the XVIII century where narrow, damp cells called *tinajas* had seen many a prisoner languish. San Juan de Ulúa was present history, with a glorious past which would extend many centuries into the future.

"Tomorrow I need a boat to take me to San Juan Bautista. Can you arrange that?" he asked Sosa.

"Certainly. That can be arranged. It will probably not be a big ship but it will take you safely. Now, in all truthfulness, let me tell you, you will not get there before the *Grijalva*. They have the advantage of some twenty hours. I can go with you and we could take a few additional elements if you judge it necessary," he answered feeling more optimistic.

"Thank you Sosa, that will not be necessary. You see, it is only a young girl I need to bring back, and possibly a boy. That is why it is imperative to stress the need for the utmost discretion. Let me put it this way: it is almost a state secret," he said smiling. He knew he had conveyed the seriousness of the situation to the chief of police.

Rigoberto looked at Clara's picture and sighed. Then he showed it to Sosa. "Believe me my friend, I have never run after a girl so much in my life!" he said laughing as he took the picture back.

Efraín Sosa waited. The band of the Marine had finished its concert and the musicians were putting their instruments in their cases. The people gathered in the square were beginning to leave.

"Come inside for a few minutes so I can write two telegrams that you will send tomorrow," he said opening the door for Sosa.

The deserted lobby was astonishingly silent. The laughter, music and sounds of the vibrant night did not reach it. The man at the front desk was staring at him, ready to oblige. Rigoberto asked for pen and paper which he handed to him with a smile.

"They have brought your luggage and I have sent it up to your room," he said a bit embarrassed.

"Yes, thank you," he said automatically. He was thinking of the wording of his telegrams. His happiness disappeared. What would he tell Rosa? When could he promise to be back? What could he tell his in-laws? He understood that words would carry no meaning.

"Have you ever been to San Juan Bautista, Efraín?" he asked Sosa as he sat down next to the coffee table.

"No, sir, I have not. It is wild country. It is tropic. The heat is unbearable," the man volunteered.

"I know," Rigoberto answered. "Until what time are the big shops open?" he asked suddenly.

"Until nine O'clock. Let's see, it's eight," his assistant answered.

"We will leave the telegrams for later. I need to buy some clothes. Would you mind going with me? I am not familiar with the city," he said.

"You will need linen and cotton clothes. We have some excellent English clothes," he said as they left the hotel.

They walked for a few blocks until they reached *Almacenes de Francia* where Rigoberto purchased three pairs of white linen slacks and three long-sleeve shirts called *guayaberas* which had the characteristic of having tiny pleats all along the front. Not too bad. He would travel the world, visit the tropics and see for himself that things were as everyone described them. He felt at the beginning of a new adventure. He smiled happily and paid quickly. Then he realized he might not have enough money.

"Sosa, I need a favor. I seem to have little cash. I can give you a check or sign a voucher at the station…" he started to explain.

"Don't worry. How much do you think you will need? I will be right back with it," he answered.

"Maybe two hundred pesos. I suppose I could always go to the chief of police at San Juan Bautista, if I need more further on," he said.

"Of course. We will send word for him to expect you and of course to check on the passengers of the *Grijalva*," he answered quickly.

"Good, that's settled then. I will write the telegrams and meanwhile you tell the front desk to wake me up forty five minutes before departure so I can have some coffee," he said as he sat down to write.

"Yes, yes, of course," Sosa answered quickly.

"Come on, Sosa. Don't worry so much. I will be back in three or four days, with my charge…"

"Certainly, Sir, certainly…" he said walking towards the front desk.

Rigoberto wrote his telegrams quickly. He needed them to be cryptic and yet clear enough to allow Rosita to understand something of the situation. Rosita…hum, soon, soon… Rigoberto marveled at how things had become so complicated and difficult, so then he drowned any thought of returning in the waves of the sea, with its hidden azure and its fish. It was a silent wail that he sent into the sweet breeze of the night.

XII

Clara Heredia could not understand how she could have imagined for an instant that she would be traveling with the other passengers. It had not dawned on her that she was not really a passenger, but rather an exception that must be kept in the dark.

The rest of the workers had finished loading and the ship took off. From where she stood she could see the Castle of Ulúa and she could still picture the chapel of the *Santo Cristo del Buen Viaje* where she and Gerardo had worshipped that morning. It was a chapel where travelers from all over the world had gone to thank the Good Lord for a safe arrival or to ask for His blessing when embarking on their next trip. It was a small chapel built on the outside of the city's wall with square stones from the sea which had ingrained fossils of fish, that which showed how close sea and eternity were. What Clara had prayed to the Good Lord for, was that her father might never find her. She would always remember that morning at the banks of the Tenoya river and little did she imagine that years later it would meet the city towards Boca del Río. While standing there she concentrated on the city which had been so lively and electrifying. She thanked Lord Christ for the rebirth she had felt there and asked Him to remain forever to greet and help other lost souls like herself, find a new way.

She loved the sea and could not seem to get enough of it; she would spend most of the afternoons just watching how it stretched ahead in waves until it became an enormous and graceful silver serpent which was by now a river. She admired the different shades of green which she had never been able to distinguish before. She had to give it a name, and she called it city daltonism. Here was nature, abundant and never ending. She liked to watch the workers tending to their copra coconut palms on the banks and watch their happy family lives in the huts along the river. She saw the fishermen for the first time in their mahogany kayaks, moving about in a sea that was their home. She learned of river routes where men and women came and went selling and buying their goods from another part of the same state or another one close by. She enjoyed watching Gerardo take his work very seriously on the bowels of the ship. She could not go down to visit him because it was a man's space where no women were allowed. She waited for him on the lower deck.

It was there, among the workers of the ship, that Clara Heredia, pupil of the Carmelites, had begun to learn about life. She had been assigned a hammock with the cook who taught her the names of fruits and plants and new ways to cook, who also taught her about men and women. She would come into the room some nights with different men and Clara tried to shut out the laughter and moans of ecstasy and pleasure.

Other times she would simply enjoy the free skies like the sea gulls that followed their boat, drawing white check marks on the azure infinity, as if to express their pleasure in the creation of the world. She enjoyed the feel of the sun on her skin and the changes in her complexion. She would sit in a small stool on deck to eat her meager rations of fried bananas and beans with tortillas. The cook must have begun to like her because sometimes she found a piece of pork meat in the beans and she would insist Clara drink light cups of coffee instead of the water on board, which she argued, was not fresh.

The past would creep like an unexpected guest and she chased it out realizing she neither had the time nor desire to serve it. The monstrous figure of her father seemed to have vanished definitely. She felt safe here, as if in a magic circle where nothing else seemed to exist. Long gone were the embroidery classes of the nuns, and forgotten were the rosary prayers, the French classes and the visits to the hairdresser and seamstress.

Here only one thing remained constant. Beauty. A beauty so total that it managed to obliterate everything. A freedom so total that she floated along with the river, soft and natural. She had observed miracles of a moon plating the river with liquid silver and pleased herself with her image which was reflected on the crystaline surface. She also knew of colors of moons so red that dripped their vermilion to set the river on fire; she saw fire dancing on the cool waters of the night; she saw images that never before had anyone seen. She had been allowed to peek, a humble observer of the Truth!

From time to time she could hear laughter and voices from women in formal dinner clothes. In the daytime she had seen women in linen dresses and elegant hats protecting their white complexion from the sun and elegant men dressed in white linen with immaculate white shoes. But downstairs the story was quite different. There was sweat and work, coal and fire.

They never stopped for long in the riverside towns. The boat floated majestically like an enormous bird of the sea. Clara had fallen in love with it for no known reason, except for the sheer delight she experienced. She enjoyed a feeling of liberation until she heard the human voices from upstairs, which took her back to a past that was no longer hers. She had chosen well: freedom versus the constraint of perfumes and silks and jewels, including the medallion that had served its purpose. And tears of gratitude welled up in her eyes when she remembered the wise grandmother on her deathbed who had insisted on handing the jewel directly into her hands.

The winter of the city had evaporated, so had Puebla and its traditions and Veracruz with is jumbled-up gaiety. She could not even try to imagine that there were people elsewhere feeling cold or hungry, because here the land was prosperous and warm, life came easily, and all beings seemed to live, like herself, in the innocence of Paradise.

In the sunset when the translucent fish jumped in and out from the liquid crystal of the water, Clara raised a thought to the Creator of All for the mystery of her life and the adventure and she thanked

Him for guiding her way into very secret and mysterious paths. She in return would be happy, learn to feel total happiness because this was a world where no limits were set and therefore no fear was felt. Other times, Clara would discover a tear or two when the enemy of temerity crept behind her. She could not believe her boldness.

The hours passed, smooth and long, hours of delight on sweet waters. Hours with no time, just alive and palpitating. She did not want them to end. Had she been born a man, now Clara knew, she would have worked on a ship, she would be endowed with thick muscles in her arms and she would have learned to spit and curse and drink cheap alcohol and go with the women of the port. That was, she knew, just a show. For real life was the water. She loved the liquid that generated life, and was swayed by the moon's fickleness and the fish. Whenever they ate fish she felt as if it were an act of depredation. She, being part of the lesser-noble side of nature, would sit down to enjoy her meals.

She tried to imagine what San Juan Bautista in Tabasco was like. She could have bet that none of her friends would ever get to see it. Her parents had never spoken of the place, and yet it sounded so beautiful! If only they could see her so happy, smiling, free and pleased! Was there evil in that? That was where they differed. She had even spared them the expense of a wedding and a dowry. Maybe they should be grateful. But no, they would never forgive the public affront she had put them through. Wrong reasoning, she realized, it was they themselves who had created the whole situation. It was so tragic that it became a laughing matter. She thanked them from the bottom of her heart for sending her off into an adventure that would liberate her unconditionally.

Clara had never seen a sunrise on a ship. It was the most beautiful of beauties in the world. First one could see a lilac ribbon on the celestial vault, then, as if by magic appeared a second one, and a third one and then a pink ray created a contrast of incredible pastel colors in a totally white sky. She had seen *the beginning,* dawn and its freshness; she rejoiced to be living it! She could almost touch it with her hands, and it had certainly touched her heart, transforming her.

It was dawn when they arrived to a small town called Frontera. She was curious as to the women and children who came to the pier to sell fried plantains and coconut milk. Clara, who had never tasted the coconut milk, found it to be pure and pleasant-tasting. So she drank one, and then another and a third one, as if nothing could quench the thirst of an arrival to the land of bounty. She ate the *empanadas* stuffed with *pejelagarto*, those strange-looking fish, half-fish half-lizard or with shrimp and doused with an extremely spicy sauce. She realized she was privileged above all. Nobody would ever have such a delightful experience which filled her with vitality and joy. She would not have recognized herself. Her demeanor, her whole appearance, the color of her skin and her hair, everything had changed! She had been revitalized by the magic of the sun, the salt of the sea and the beauty of the river.

Soon thereafter, the workers had finished their work and the sailors returned on board. Clara knew that it was time to continue the trip. A few more hours until they reached San Juan Bautista. Nobody had ever talked to her about the place and she did not know what kind of life they would be forced to lead. It did not matter. Mexico was a huge country, a cornocupia of wealth. Her teachers had repeated and it was true; she knew it to be true, as she ate fruit of the land, plantain chips, *guineo*, they called it and she savoured the word and the floury texture of the fruit.

Tiburón would sometimes appear on the deck. Once he stopped to observe Clara for a long time. She, in turn, was lost to the river, lost in her reveries. He smiled, 'food for kings' he thought. He would help these lovers if he could, but nothing else. He did not trust himself with her. As to Clara, all she felt for him was a strange mixture of terror and gratitude, because she knew that he had made an exception with them.

They arrived in San Juan Bautista towards noon. It seemed like a true city, she told herself. They had traveled into the Grijalva river for some time now. Water was no longer salty. She realized she hardly ever spoke with anyone. She and the cook would exchange a few words because she knew the woman did not like white people. She did not trust them. She would show up shyly at the door and she was handed a plate. She would then sit on deck to eat while caressing the water lilies with her gaze.

"We will be arriving soon," Gerardo was saying to her. He had come up for a few minutes. He looked worried. Then he added, "I will speak to the captain and we will find something to do. Well, he might know people who need work done…I don't know. But don't worry; we will make due."

The captain was busy giving orders as to the wares they would be taking back with them to Veracruz. He could already savor the night he planned to spend with the local women. Maybe he was in luck and would meet Juan Beuloc, the captain of a small ship called the *Clara Ramos*. They would usually have a few drinks together and maybe play a game of cards or domino. It was quite an elegant ship. It belonged to the owners of a wood-exploitation enterprise and its passengers were the wives or children of the bosses.

Gerardo approached him and spoke to him briefly. "Well, I could send you to Tenosique. What would you do there? And will you like it?" he asked doubtfully.

"Anything, I am willing to do anything to continue on this trip," he told Tiburón, the good-natured sailor. He was afraid of the police, more for Clara's sake than for his own.

"All right. Leave separately and go to that boat. You stay there until I can have a word with Juan Beuloc, who aside from being a joyful person, is also generous. You are quite lucky, my boy. I was your age too, you know? I also plucked a beautiful flower," he exclaimed with nostalgia as he spat on the floor. "You have served me well, so don't wait till they finish unloading. Disappear!" he ordered, handing him a few coins.

Gerardo approached Clara and he told her they must head to the *Clara Ramos* that was docked next to them. That she should get off first and walk towards the ship and look for captain Beuloc, and if he were not there, she should wait. He would arrive shortly after.

Clara felt blessed. They could continue on their trip, moving further away from the capital and her family. She felt light on her feet, happy, in her cotton dress and her mesh of hair hidden under the tattered hat. No one would have recognized a girl from the convent who spoke French and had been groomed for high society.

She immediately went to a well-preserved boat which boasted its name in big, black letters and climbed the wooden ramp. The sailors looked at her with some suspicion. However, once upstairs, she asked to see the captain. They laughed goodheartedly and she felt tempted to turn around and run. At that same moment a tall, robust man of a brown and shiny face, impeccably clean, was ready to disembark. He observed Clara and asked her to explain her business.

Clara explained to the captain that she needed to get to Tenosique and on hearing the name of Tiburón, Juan Beuloc smiled. The rascal! But Tiburón had never asked for a favor. At that moment Gerardo came on board. He was visibly worried; the police was on their trail. They were talking to Tiburón who denied having seen a couple and he had not given a ride to anyone, as Gerardo told her later. Tiburón and Juan Beuloc were people of the sea, who had freedom and in their veins, and together they would make a love story possible.

That how it what happened that Clara and Gerardo never got to see San Juan Bautista. An important city, like any other, Clara said to herself as they set sail.

XIII

Rigoberto López took a deep breath of the sweltering air of San Juan Bautista. The atmosphere was sultry and it was extremely difficult to breathe, as if one had to swallow gasps of warm vapor. He was landing from a navy boat on the wharf of the Grijalva river and not too far from the city. The chief of police was waiting for him. By the look on his face, Rigoberto expected the worse. As soon as he was able to think, he knew Clara had not been located. The usual smile and pleasant disposition had disappeared suddenly. Frowning, with a bag in one hand and protected by a jipi hat of the finest palm, he walked slowly towards the man who was obviously the chief.

"Mr. López, I am captain Sarlat, welcome. I am afraid we don't have such good news for you..." he said waiting for the young man's reaction.

"Miss Heredia has disappeared..." the foreigner answered.

"Worse than that, we could never find a trace of her. She did not arrive here either by land or boat. Yesterday we interviewed the captain of the Grijalva which is a steamship and does not accept passengers. We were there when it arrived and we watched the few travelers get off. There was no young woman with that description. We have a list here and everyone is from the region and quite well known. Miss Heredia never left that boat. It was the last one yesterday and nothing else has arrived since," he ended his account at a loss and not daring to look at him directly.

Rigoberto hastened his pace. Clara had escaped from the net like a fish anxious to live. Bravo, Clara, bravo, he cheered mentally.

One of two things was possible: she was extremely shrewd or she was terribly lucky. Maybe he applauded her shrewdness because that was the reason she was able to slip by unnoticed. Where to this time? The clues had ended here. It was not possible. Nobody had seen her. They had combed time and again inns and guesthouses, bars, restaurants, nothing. What about Gerardo? Was it possible that no one had seen either of them? Nobody. Rigoberto, a child of fortune, could not believe what was happening now. What next? Should he return to the capital and tell General Heredia that his daughter was irretrievably lost? How could he justify the whole police force of the country?

"I need a beer," he told Sarlat, because he felt faint.

"Of course, sir, of course," Sarlat answered. He was a short man of dark complexion. "We can go downtown," he suggested.

"No, I want to go to the bars the sailors patronize…" was his answer.

"Yes, I see…Although I must warn you that it will be useless," he said defeated.

"We still have to try, Sarlat, we really must! By the way, is your name French?" he asked casually while trying to solve the puzzle in his head. This was a defense mechanism, small talk to be able to continue with his solving skills unmolested.

"Yes, my grandfather was a rich Frenchman. I am one of his grandsons. There are many of us living around here, including a doctor, which I hope you will never need in a professional capacity," said the man feeling more at ease.

They walked for a short distance to a *champa*; they sat under the palm roof which was held up by four posts of the chicozapote tree. The climate was such that this type of construction was the most practical and sensible.

"Two beers," Sarlat ordered.

Rigoberto looked around him. He felt uncomfortable in spite of its being winter and the locals claiming that the climate was mild. The place was deserted, but soon local men started walking one or two at a time. Some time later two attractive women sat down at a neighboring table eyeing the men.

The waiter returned, saying the cook sent word of having very fresh river crayfish with the name of *pigüas*. The chief of police seemed at a loss, and Rigoberto said yes. He wanted to know and experience all the possibilities of the place, because if there was a way to find Clara, he must follow her footsteps.

"General Heredia has sent a telegram for you. Would you like to read it?" he asked Rigoberto.

"No, I am not interested. Don't bother to answer it. Just ignore it." He explained to the man who looked puzzled, "What can I tell the man? That his fifteen year old girl has been more astute than the whole police force?" he asked sadly. Something was definitely very wrong and he knew it. He had to hurry. He had to catch up with her before she reached her final destiny. Which was where?

The visit to the outdoor restaurant yielded absolutely no results. The *pigüas* were well-seasoned crayfish, which he surprisingly ate with relish. The steamy atmosphere was really getting to him. Sarlat joined him happily. Life was after all so pleasant, so momentaneous, that the problems, he seemed to think, could wait. Where were they going anyway? A couple of hours could not make much difference.

The beer had become warm by now and Rigoberto motioned for another bottle. Sarlat looked at him trying to rationalize the waste it meant.

"Was there any other boat on the pier that day?" he asked Sarlat.

"Yes, the *Clara Ramos* a four hundred ton freighter. It belongs to Casa Valenzuela and it was headed for Tenosique," he said without much enthusiasm.

"Wait! What time did it leave?" he asked anxiously.

"We can check that out. But do let me tell you that your logic will not work. You see, we were present from the moment the *Grijalva* arrived until it departed. We would have spotted the young lady at any given moment, even if she had tried boarding the *Clara Ramos*," he assured him.

"Well, my very dear Sarlat, Now I will tell you what might have happened. You were not looking for a woman alone when you were watching the passengers board. You were looking for a couple. Am I right? Well, you were not prepared for the other possibility, that she looked like a working-class woman," he said smiling as he took a big gulp of the cold beer.

"You mean to say she wore a disguise?" the astonished man asked.

"Well, it would not be exactly a disguise. You see, she came from Mexico City where the temperature is awfully cold. It is winter which means we need to wear heavy coats and warm shoes and socks. She simply changed clothes to suit this climate. Maybe she bought them, and maybe someone gave them to her. I don't think they have much money left," he said as he drank more beer which afforded some solace to the heat.

The man in front of him was frankly astonished. He was not used to investigating the whims of a spoiled child, and he could not understand the subterfuges used by her. He understood crimes of passion and alcohol. He put men in jail all the time for those reasons. But spoiled daughters of generals running away from home? Never!

Finally he could no longer resist saying, "Can you tell me what is so terrible that a kid runs away with her boyfriend? It happens every day around here and everyone has learned to accept it as part of life. Are you here to marry them?" he asked again trying to find the reason for so much upheaval.

Rigoberto López never lost his temper. He smiled. The proposal seemed simple and logical, even childish. It was the first time he had seen the realities of life taken so naturally and later he would also realize that women in the tropics seemed to require less care than those in the city. How could he convey to this man in front of him that she was really better off without her family and that they were relieved with her disappearance? He had to accept a new way of looking at life in a different latitude.

"Sarlat, the only thing I know is that our orders come from very high up. And it is our duty to carry them out whether we understand them or not," he said slowly and smiling calmly, because he could not convince the man in front of him that it was imperative they find the young lady.

"Yes, yes, of course and we have spared no effort. This I swear to you. I simply do not understand why so much is at stake. We take those things with simple philosophy," he answered wiping perspiration off his forehead with a red and white bandana of the region. "Yes, yes, of course...we must continue the search," he muttered to himself.

Rigoberto asked for more beer. "Sarlat, where was the *Clara Ramos* headed for? I must follow it immediately. The further away this young lady travels, the less clues we will find. Am I right in thinking that Tenosique is already rain forest?" he asked. His green eyes had acquired a new gleam; he was on the right track!

"Yes, that is jungle. But, boy oh boy, is that complicated and far. The climate is terrible. I think I should go there myself and find her with the help of the local police. However, I do not think they traveled there. How could they? I would suggest you wait here and let me take over. I would probably be gone about a week. Please think about this, because that is terrible land, wild and dangerous. You might as well be in another planet," he said earnestly.

Rigoberto realized the man was sincere in his concern and he himself was beginning to feel alarmed. "Would you say a girl would be in a greater danger there?" he asked uselessly. He knew the answer.

"Well, it depends what you call danger. I don't think she would be killed. I don't think she would be robbed either. Is she carrying jewels or money?" Sarlat asked.

"Nothing. She has nothing," he answered impatiently. "When can we start out?" he asked with urgency.

"Well, we need to wait for the next ship that covers that route. But that could mean several days and then it would be too late. It would probably be a good idea for you go to the hotel to rest up and maybe take a shower..." he suggested.

"No, let us go to the headquarters to find out the earliest date possible," he said standing up and leaving some bills on the table.

Together they walked to the building near a big church called The Lord of Tabasco, with two belfries, so tall that it was visible from any part of the city. Next to it was the governor's palace and the police station. There was a central garden of big chestnut trees cut in the shape of umbrellas to protect the pedestrians from the unforgiving rays of sun. People walked calmly and happily. These were good natured people who wore bright colored clothes. They spoke with a different tone; their food and music were also different. Rigoberto wanted to absorb everything, as if from that picture he could find the answer to his plight. He searched in every face for Clara's because in his mind he could see her and almost touch her joy and hope.

The city had surprisingly narrow streets, a fact which served the purpose of protecting the people from the hot rays of the sun. Otherwise, the paving stones would hold the heat, turning the homes into a blazing hell. Everything was calm. Most people seemed to be eating, and he could see them through the windows that necessarily had to remain open to get some kind of cross-ventilation. Others would be sleeping the midday nap and he could see the hammocks swinging from the hooks. Soft music could be heard coming from other houses. In general the city was calm.

"Well, here we are," Sarlat said waiting at the door so he could walk in first. There were few furnishings. There were two desks behind the counter where two policemen were studying documents. Other two younger policemen were drowsily sitting on a wooden bench which seemed to be intended for the public.

Rigoberto studied the scene quickly. He saw no possible and efficient solution. Things seemed to have lost their importance here. Everything could wait. He knew immediately what he had to do, and that was what he hated most. He did not like to use his authority in order to get things done.

"The best thing would be to wait for the *Carmen* or the *Sánchez Mármol*. They should be arriving soon now," Sarlat was saying.

"Impossible, I must leave today. I don't know how my dear Sarlat, and that is a problem I am passing on to you, because I do not know how things are done here. But it is imperative that I follow immediately," he said with all the strength he could gather.

"Yes, I understand," Sarlat answered quite nervously. "We have no other alternative. One of the ships of the *monterías* is liable to come soon. Those are the ones who travel that way and the only ones who can reach Tenosique. We could send you on a smaller ship which makes frequent stops and that would be even slower! We did not realize you would be traveling that way, otherwise we could have asked don Polo Valenzuela to wait for you and he would have helped."

The policemen looked at each other. Rigoberto knew when the other party was right. He had no alternative and he was beginning to understand the area and why in central Mexico little or nothing was known about these distant lands. He realized that maps did not even exist of the region; the French called it 'Virgin Forest', inaccessible, impenetrable, unaccountable. That was what he was facing: nature with all its power, the same bounty that eroded the human soul. There was no way of getting there except on a ship that traveled to the *monterías.*

He would not despair; he would take things rationally. He would send his telegrams and he might even write a longer one to his wife. By now he had given up part of his optimism. He was facing the biggest challenge of his life. Besides, he could take off a few days to search in the city for the girl. He would not let the situation overwhelm him before it had even begun! He had his own rules for solving matters, and the first one consisted of adapting the mentality of others. Where in God's name was Clara? And he realized the question was beginning to obsess him because it popped up in the middle of any other thought and he realized he was beginning to fear for her personal safety. She was like one of those wonderful flowers of the tropics that disappeared in an instant when discovered by an army of ants.

Rigoberto checked into a hotel built with brick and where the roof was covered with French clay tiles brought by European ships that came from France with such wares; otherwise they would have had to travel in total emptiness on the way to Mexico to pick up huge logs of precious woods from the Lacandon forest. They looked for mahogany, *palo tinto,* or *ceiba*, the sacred tree of the Mayas, in one word, all the finest of the finest which came to be known as 'green gold'. The wealth of the rain forest was in the hands of a few concessionaires.

He took a shower to try to cool down. It was the first time in his life he had considered the hammock, an art of weaving that afforded a comfortable bed. He felt so good, and welcomed in the pleasing hammock which afforded ventilation through its thousands of threads when one balanced to and fro. If anyone had seen him! He laughed out loud and could not understand the reason. Was he desperate? Angry? Or extremely mad? He did not know. It seemed to be a mixture of everything, which made him realize that human beings do not know themselves. Where was the efficient, happy friend of the President? Reduced to an object swinging from a hammock and thanking the dark, swift hands of the weavers.

In the afternoons he would live the life of people like him. He would sit in the main square and order coffee. In the evenings he would sit at some restaurant to listen to news and happenings of the forest. Some were unbelievable and wonderful, others terrible. But he knew he had to change now. He had to become one with the rhythm of the place, he had to have some of those unheard of adventures, he needed to know about the life of the animals of the rain forest and to eat in a chaotic way, and savor innocent creatures without wondering why.

Intuition, my intuition which never fails, thought Rigoberto. I will spend some time running after a dream that a young beautiful child had one day. And I will love the wilderness, and the rain forest and its rivers and lakes and the work people do. Maybe he was rational and maybe he was only dreaming, because he found he could no longer distinguish wake from sleep.

XIV

The captain had told Gerardo he could substitute one of the stokers in the mast hole since the *Clara Ramos* ran on coal. He would be assigned to work with an older stoker during the night and a second team would substitute them in the morning. As to Clara, she would have to be the cook's helper and do the dishes. Knowing they had no money with which to pay for a fare, Clara accepted gracefully because she knew she could cope with it moderately well. She did not mind at all. The workers would rise early, around four in the morning to light the stoves, make coffee and begin with the breakfast preparations for the passengers and the crew.

Captain Beuloc invariably ate with the passengers with whom he seemed to have a personal friendship. The owners of the big lumber companies or some of their children would sometimes travel with him. It was usual for the young people to be sent off to study in Europe, usually London or Madrid or to some cities in the U.S. like New Orleans. There they led a life of luxury and leisure with the fortunes amassed in the rain forest. And then, after that carefree time of travel and study, they were forced to return to the austere and difficult towns and cities like Tenosique, San Cristóbal or Ocosingo, and some were to live for a few years in the *monterías*. In other cases, the owners would offer the outposts to less fortunate members of their own families back in their places of origin. They would then become the liason and negotiators to other members who lived in less rigorous cities. A few of them had made their homes in San Juan Bautista, because they realized it was necessary to be in closer contact with the European countries, consumers of the riches of the Lacandon forest.

Clara felt akin to the captain and in spite of that, she tried to keep to herself and become a willing apprentice to a middle-aged cook who seemed to resent Clara's lack of knowledge. Little by little, she too began to accept the girl to whom she delegated the chores she herself disliked. Clara was in charge of dicing the vegetables, of slicing the huge plantains that would be served over white rice or as a dessert topped with condensed milk from a can. She would wash and prepare the fruit that would be served in the dining room. Clara was adapting to a subterranean type of life.

She was happy to oblige with anything the cook asked of her because she knew that her situation would last only a few days until they arrived. The name itself, Tenosique seemed to encompass a world of exotism beyond words. Meanwhile she concentrated in the manual labor for that was something she knew she was capable of performing well. She learned the names of vegetables and fruit she had not even suspected existed. She tried the *posol* a drink elaborated with ground maize and dissolved in water. The sailors would add salt and spice to quench thirst and hunger. She understood the importance of corn and the inextricable mystical Mayan world of the men of corn. Clara observed their physical characteristics; people here were of short stature and their figures tended to be square; the bridge of their noses was high and their color was bronze.

Clara remained among these working people, distanced from what was going on in the upper deck where the evenings were full of music, dance, laughter. She could hear traditional guitar songs and sometimes even waltzes played on an upright piano, somewhat out of tune. She would walk in the moonlight and dream of other worlds that were now hers, the river and its tributaries, and recall the delicate tones of the water lilies. She could make out the shapes of trees along the river banks and see the mangrove swamps. She would bless the water, generator of all life. There, under the stars she had a stunning revelation. She realized that the chains that bound her, those chains of her inner psique were gone, gone for good and disappeared. The repetitive dream was no longer with her and she knew in her heart that it would never visit her again. It was not unpleasant, and for that, she could not consider it a nightmare. It consisted of a young girl, much like herself, standing barefoot, clothed in a transparent gown under perennial trees. The rays of the sun gilded her hair and suddenly there came a rush of gold flakes lavished on her from the sky. The girl never moved, she just stood there with both hands raised to receive the blessings with a feeling of joy. Yet Clara would wake up sweating, as if an urgent message was being sent to her somehow. Maybe it was her destiny. And now that she was fulfilling it, the dream had disappeared. Mysterious ways of a strange and wide world.

Clara would stroll in the sun at siesta time. She felt fulfilled by it and she roamed to and fro under a tattered straw hat the cook of the *Grijalva* had pushed into her hands the day she had left. The woman was somewhat hysterical at times, and angry others, but she had shed some tears when the young girl left, remembering a daughter who had just walked out one day and of whom she had had no further news.

Other times Clara would sit on the well-scrubbed wooden floor to think. She realized that it was one of the other luxuries of the sea. She would contemplate her new hands. Hands that spoke of labor and toil and she felt pride in them. Joy because she was she, alone and free.

She would avidly learn stories that the cook would tell her when the day's work had been done and she would be rocked to sleep by the gentle tiny waves of the river. She rarely saw Gerardo who seemed a graduate of stoking. His face was blackened and one could admire the white, strong teeth behind his smile. He was proud of his newly found trade, and the word 'stoker' came like honey to his lips. He too had come to love the sea and the river, the adventure and the vicissitudes of navigation. Clara found the simple joy of his friendship to be like the connecting thread of her life.

Sometimes the cook observed her handling with loving care the china that the upper deck used. It was certain that Clara could understand their meaning and the cook wanted to know no more.

With the same care she would wash their humble dishes and their blackened pots and pans. She would spy her walks on deck in the early hours of the evening when the breeze would scatter her hair, and she somehow thought Clara belonged there with the violets and lilacs of the sky or with the deep vermilion of a dying sun that drew a liquid work of art on the surface of the enormous and generous river. She saw the girl watch the heavens and could not guess that Clara was seeing carriages with gods of water, Chaac and his royal entrourage and with it the harmony of the universe.

The trip had been too brief; for Clara it could have well lasted all eternity. She could see herself spending the rest of her life from kitchen to deck to cabin. She was traveling to unsuspected places of the world. From San Juan Bautista they had navigated through the Grijalva river to Jonuta, where they had made an intermediate stop to buy supplies and fuit. They had picked up some aromatic *anonas* and big, green guavas; they had stopped briefly at Ciudad del Carmen near the astonishing forts of times of pirates, where Playa del Carmen boasted some of the finest shores of white fine powdery sands that with time would attract some of the richest of the rich. The city itself was very important. People spoke of mansions with French furniture and big gilded mirrors and curtains of Damascus silk. Clara dreamt of them, as if she had seen them. Her real world, her very own, was the boat where they continued to Balancán, area of cattle breeders, where the cowherds loaded some young bulls that seemed to resist going on board. Clara felt empathy towards the young black bodies, because not unlike her, they knew not where their final destination would be.

In Balancán, the cook told her, there was little to see. It was cattle country and they would only stop to buy a few things such as big cans of lard, meat jerky and animal skins that would be used for making furniture.

She, herself, felt very much at home in the *Clara Ramos* for she saw more than a coincidence in the name, and she felt a happiness that she could not explain when she scrubbed the blackened pots and pans and scrubbed the floor. She wanted everything to shine with pride. It was her home with many levels.

Some nights, protected by the darkness, she would surreptitiously climb to the upper deck to look through the window to watch the travelers singing and dancing. The big room was beautiful. The mahogany walls were finely varnished. The lights shone on tables and chairs that had been carved out of *palo tinto*, a wood as eternal as life. That type of wood had the peculiarity of polishing itself further with each use. The women sat quietly smiling, looking fulfilled, while their husbands always dressed in white, seemed to enjoy their travel. They would sing until the wee hours of the morning, aided by fine liquors from overseas. There were a few tables where the men could play cards, domino or roulette. She knew their world; she loved their music, but was happy in her new condition.

In the lower deck similar things happened. A sailor had a mandolin and two more played with reed flutes songs of nostalgic notes that seemed more permanent because they spoke the language of the rain forest. It evoked the solitude of forest and river and the freedom and peace achieved through her daring action.

All during the trip she had seen captain Beuloc twice, times when he was happy and gentlemanly with his passengers. He would give her a wink and go his merry way. Only once, when he saw her in the upper deck, had he briefly spoken to her about the need to remain in the anonymity of the lower deck. Clara knew that he was right. And from then on, until they reached Tenosique, she kept very much to herself in the lower deck.

She knew she needed a change of clothes and a good soaking. Maybe when they got to Tenosique she could please herself in the cool water of the river, like the children she had seen, growing free in the elements.

As to Gerardo, they would laugh at his appearance, delighted in their innocence. His health was strong and his skin now darkened even more by the sun, that which seemed to help him adapt to their new habitat.

When they finally reached Tenosique, they were met with the news that the city was still a respectable distance from the pier and that the romping in the water would have to be postponed. They bade their goodbyes to the captain separately and started out to where the city began. It lay there, quiet and hot, a steaming door to infinity where their escape would be definitive into the jungle.

It was only occasionally that she remembered her family and her city. It was as if a master stroke of this very nature she now contemplated, had banished it from the Painter's cloth. Overjoyed she knew herself to be one with it, as if by integrating she had disappeared. She marveled at the concept of Time and was overjoyed to understand it did not exist. It was like the river, a long fluid becoming, and unfolding before them. It was a big wheel that became the cycle of life and death. And she was there, a part of that, and happy to breathe its substance.

XV

Once in Tenosique Rigoberto López was sure to have lost the slightest clue to Clara's whereabouts. She and Gerardo had disappeared, swallowed by the enormous and magnificent beast of the Lacandon Forest. He was desperate; his good disposition seemed to erode away with each negative. Nobody had seen them. Logic told him that everything in the jungle ended up in change, change of essence, including the human beings whose personality could gradually or brutally be altered. He himself could vouch for that. He was beginning to experience unsuspected feelings and moods, and this made him lose his bearings. Now he understood that the purpose of the trip was to map new boundaries within himself, for now he was open to unknown facets of his personality. He reacted with anger to the frustration he felt when faced with a feeling of impotence. The reason being, he had invariably been able to foresee solutions to everything.

'Is this possible?' he asked himself as each door closed in front of him. And yet, there they were! Doors closed one by one without the slightest possibility of scrutiny. What to do? Where to begin? For once he realized that the lesson to be learned, was one of humility and the acceptance of his shortcomings. 'I do not know,' he muttered for the first time in his life. The retaliation was not to think of the 'other' world, of his family, of his wife. 'They do not exist, from now on I shall concentrate on each day, and thank life for this opportunity to grow.' He would come to appreciate the small favors and continue tracking Miss Heredia. 'Work will save me,' he concluded.

Other times he asked himself to what end. The possibility of never finding Clara finally emerged as a clear concept. He had swept the small town from top to bottom. He had challenged each store, including the home vendors with a few miserable articles. The big stores he had done first. Valenzuela sold denim overalls with orange color fringes that read *Orilla de Coral* on the labels and denim shirts of the brand *Traje Azul*. They also sold women's sandals, bright colored necklaces of hand-blown glass, artificial flowers for the graves, axes, picks, shovels, saddles and hats. In one word, everything needed in the *monterías,* including thick ropes and hooks of all types, yokes and chains. Nothing. Nothing. Nothing, he repeated time and again.

Disoriented, he walked back to his hotel. He lay on the hammock to perspire and despair. It was time for the noon meal, *comida*. It was usually siesta time also when the dampness of hot air vanquished good intentions. Out there, forgotten, lay the glorious Usumacinta with its cascade of steps leading to the pier and surrounded by fulminating orange flowers of the Indian Laurels, the intense blue sky and the fresh, undulating water of the river where everything wilted or slept until four or five in the afternoon.

He would wake up with a start. The thought of Clara and her companion would make him return to reality. By now he feared for them and with regards to him, well…he had more than surpassed the time he thought it would take. A mission. Yes, but would General Díaz understand the impossibility of the situation? Certainly not. Nobody could understand the magnitude of something endowed with so much danger and strangeness. He tried to stay within the limits of reason. He had to think clearly, now more than ever because as the hours passed, he knew the danger increased for them. What would Clara's parents think of the state of things? General Heredia would see it as a failure due to his youth. He had told him so directly. That part he didn't mind. What he did now see is that a mission that had begun with so much optimism should not have lasted so long and that he had been arrogant because things forcibly had to end the way he had intended them to. During the trip, in quite a decent ship called the *Sánchez Mármol*, which had been purchased in New Orleans, he had the nagging thought that the end could be different.

He racked his brain; he despaired, but that was only his gut feeling. He should not give in to it. He refused to give in to it. Maybe the unexpected would happen. And he contemplated the wharf again: all green with papaya and banana trees of many types, even some called *machos*, the plantains, or the tiny ones called *dominicos* and the *cochi* thus named because they were fed to the pigs. He could see the chaotic growth of the most splendid flowers that grew wild and spontaneous in backyards where hammocks swung to the rhythm of their happy and indifferent sleepers in the sensuous calm of midday. He himself felt lax and slow and recognized how easy and gradually a human being was lost in the immensity of an overwhelming nature.

He did not even realize that he had fallen into a restful lethargy and that he woke up bathed in perspiration when the afternoon provided a milder temperature. He got up, took a shower and proceeded to the downtown cafés. That was the custom to try to regain a few useful hours. Coffee, thick and sweet, too sweet for his taste. Or maybe it felt that way because his disposition did not agree with the pleasures of the flesh.

He sat on a small table near big pots of plants and flowers where he was greeted politely by other guests. The people of the town would look at him trying to understand who he was and why he found himself there. Speculation, nothing else. He knew he had better be careful with his anonymity.

Finally, the chief of police came to greet him. Rigoberto asked him to sit down and ordered another cup for him. "Hum…Aladino Acopa," he said. "I like your name because Aladdin made things appear…" while they waited for the coffee that was brought to them shortly after by an attractive woman clothed in the sensuality of red.

Aladino had set a graduation ring on the reed table without saying a word. Rigoberto looked at it without daring to touch it. He had hoped it wouldn't show up and that Clara Heredia would have gone to a less dangerous and equivocal place. It was the first time he trembled in his life. Both men had their eyes glued to the ring. Finally as Aladino stirred his coffee, he said, "This was taken in payment of two pairs of shoes from Comitán, an overall, two cotton dresses and a silk one, two white cotton shirts…"

Rigoberto López knew he had won the battle and probably lost the war. Now he had confirmation that he had not followed the wrong path, because now it was obvious they had been there. The man sitting next to him could not decipher his silence.

"The description could add up. Tens of men would fit it. But there was no woman," he said without looking at him.

Logical, Rigoberto thought, that she tried to keep as inconspicuous as possible. For surely, by now, they were aware that the police was on their heels. Someone had alerted them. The girl was more than intelligent; she was reckless. And yet, the very fact that she kept out of sight might mean that she did not feel threatened and that they wanted to continue their flight.

"If you were young and wanted to disappear for a while, Acopa, where would you go?" Rigoberto asked, picking up the ring and carefully reading the initials and the 18 karat gold seal.

"To the *monterías*," he answered without hesitation.

Rigoberto studied his features. He was endowed with bushy eyebrows and a square jaw, undoubtedly from Spanish ancestry.

"The *monterías*?" he echoed because he had not heard the word before.

"Yes, deep into the jungle, where God himself could not find you, I assure you don Rigoberto," he ended, like a happy pupil who knew the correct answer. "Yes. These are places in the jungle where workers are badly needed. They are so isolated and dangerous that few of them survive," he added.

He still could not understand. He had never heard of the said institutions or working camps or whatever they were. That very fact went on to show him how little he knew of his own country where there were many worlds and languages, so different in conception, so vast, that Mexico City now seemed like a town to him.

Acopa interpreted his silence as a requirement of further information. "They cut precious woods, especially mahogany, don Rigoberto, to be sent to Europe and the United States. But is it in the middle of nowhere! There are no exact locations in the jungle. Trees are cut, then the timber is floated down the river so that the Usumacinta floats them down to Frontera and Ciudad del Carmen. It is extremely difficult and hard work. Few survive," he said wiping his forehead again with the *paliacate*.

"Would you like to drink something else?" Rigoberto asked Acopa.

"No, thank you," he said while folding the bandana carefully and putting it into his pocket.

"Well, suppose you wanted to go work somewhere you would never be found. What would be the best place? Logically the *montería*, yes. What steps would you have to take to get hired?" he asked.

"None of the people here would do such a thing. It is like walking into hell never to come back. You can die of a snake bite and that is a horrible death because all the veins in your body explode, or you can contract dengue or malaria…No, no one here would do that sort of job. Well, of course these young people would have no way of understanding the perils that lie ahead. Oh, but the young girl…no, that would not be for her, definitely not!" he said very firmly.

"Are women not wanted where men are working?" Rigoberto was eager for the answer to a question which had not even occurred to him.

"On the contrary! Quite the opposite! But this young lady would be in a lot of danger because she is not used to the way of life in the jungle. She would probably have to help in the kitchen and then serve the team as their woman. Of course they welcome women; very few venture there. Then on the other hand, we constantly hear of crimes of passion. We learn of them long after they have happened when the culprit or culprits have disappeared. Those things are settled on the spot by whomever. We have known of some cases…never very exact or reliable information. Nothing can be done there."

Rigoberto's heart skipped a beat. A cold sweat invaded him from head to toe. A malaise took over and he felt powerless. It was extremely urgent that he find Clara, now more than ever. "All right, Acopa," he said weakened by the news. "Let's begin at the beginning. Where would you go to look for such a job if you were a young man from another state?"

He felt defeated and overwhelmed. These feelings were new, and more importantly he felt impotent. He possessed no elements from which to begin to unravel the puzzle set before him.

"Well, invariably it would be the *enganchador*, a representative of the real employer who would give you a cash 'advance' and with whom you had to sign up. These are contracts of one or two years, but rarely does anyone come back. It would not do to have survivors. See? They can tell tales which would go against the owners of the lumber companies. Now, as to the representative, you would have to go find him in the evenings and well into the night in *Heaven,* a cabaret in Pueblo Nuevo…a little ways from here," he said pointing in the opposite direction from where they were sitting.

"And what would be a convenient hour to get to *Heaven?*" he asked.

"After seven O'clock. The women should be sleeping or about to get up now," he said consulting his wristwatch.

"Good. We can wait. Would you like to take a stroll with me to the wharf? It is so pretty out there. Those flaming trees that are reflected on the water is one of the most beautiful things I have ever seen!" he said, asking for the bill.

"Oh, yes, we call them Indian Laurels. There are others which are very similar called *Llamarada*, Flame. When the sun is going down you should see the river! It seems to bleed. Come on, and if you like, I can take you around to see the store," he volunteered.

Rigoberto was happy to see that the people there had not lost the element of surprise. They still had time and sensitivity to admire that which nature had given them so abundantly.

"I have already been there. They will tell me nothing. I guess it is the biggest store; isn't it? I think it would be better to go to the river to see if together we can think of something," he said walking towards the door.

"They must have had to go somewhere to eat. Now, the question is where and how," he continued as if thinking out loud.

"Well, the owner of the house would have fed them to earn a little extra. They would not necessarily have had to go to a public place," he answered.

"You mean, the house where they would be staying? And where would that be?" he asked eagerly.

"It has been useless. Nobody seems to have seen them. Now that if they had two hammocks, well, nobody needs a house. All they had to do is find a couple of trees from which to hang them. They did not buy them in the store. They would have necessarily had to have them. Otherwise, how would they go into the jungle? Well, we could go find the two hammock-sellers. They are from Yucatán and they come and go selling them. They are not so cheap. Maybe they used the money of the 'advance' for that purpose, otherwise, why sell the ring?" he said puzzled.

"Good thinking, Acopa, good thinking! Let us go see the two Yucatecans," he said as they walked slowly to the wharf. By then the sun was beginning to go down. It was one more day, he thought, but in a strange way, it had been a fruitful day. But tomorrow? It was too early to think of tomorrow. That day would arrive uninvited and alone, without help. It was a technique he used to avoid anguish which would only hinder his thought-process.

They were in the downtown area. One could see the central park with its kiosk in the middle, and surrounding it were the usual buildings, the government palace, the police station and the justice department. Tenosique was a city of plenty of financial activity and prosperity. Its cobbled streets spoke of the indefatigable transit of the men and of luxuriant women in bright colors, seducing the world.

They sat under the umbrellas of tropical almond trees that had interesting leaves. On the one side they were green and on the other they were red. There they found two men speaking a Mayan language among themselves. They were wearing white cotton slacks and white typical shirts. Their heads were covered by *jipi* hats which were woven in damp caves by the very women who had woven the hammocks. On their feet they wore rough sandals and on their brown, smiling faces one could see signs of malnutrition.

"How much is your hammock?" Acopa asked them.

Extremely interested by the promise of a sale, they rushed over to them.

"Good price, cheap. This is good quality. Forty knots," said the taller of the two. "Silk, here touch," he said smiling.

"How about those?" Rigoberto said pointing to the other vendor's.

"Those are not for you, Boss. Too cheap. These are for the jungle workers, not for you. These silk ones are better," he said extending a pink hammock.

"Well, I like the ones for the jungle workers. A whim, if you like. I am following my brother; two days ago he bought two of these," Rigoberto said, not feeling the need to explain the situation in its entirety.

"Well, the bosses of the haciendas use the silk ones. But the workers themselves don't. Are you a boss? Did you just arrive from Spain?" asked the taller one who seemed less shy.

"I will let you in on a secret. I need to get lost for a couple of months," Rigoberto said in a confidential tone.

"Who doesn't?" answered the younger man who seemed quite intelligent.

"Come with me. Let us go get a beer and see if we can agree on the price," Rigoberto said walking to a open restaurant that seemed to sell small bottles of *Sol*.

"Well, if the boss says so, why not?" he answered shrugging.

They sat at the metal tables and Rigoberto asked for shell fish, *pigüas*, fried fish and acid cheese from Ocosingo. He sat facing the river watching the sun in its descent, and the flowers which seemed to float in the water of ever-changing tones. The two vendors ate avidly and drank the *Sol* beer toasting to his health. They enjoyed the evening and the relief the change in temperature afforded.

Aladino Acopa took life as it came. He was smiling and seemed to be enjoying himself too. He realized it was too early to reach

Heaven. He participated with good humor in the food. The two Yucatecans were hopeful of a sale. One never knew…clients could show up from anywhere.

Rigoberto could not deny that the beer seemed to produce a slight feeling of relaxation and that his mood was changing. He tried to eat a little because he realized he was becoming dehydrated. Later he learned that it was one of the reasons why pernicious anemia was rampant in the area. The inhabitants suffered from lack of potassium. And that in itself was a contradiction, because nature offered it generously. It was a manner of providing what it depleted them of.

"So, it happens you don't know many people here…" Rigoberto said wanting to start them talking. He needed to see what effect the beer could produce on his guests.

"Well, we don't know many people here. We are from Calkinik, in the Mayab region. We come and go selling our hammocks. My sister and sister-in-law weave them. The women have specially good hands for that," the taller one said.

"Yes, Boss, one can see you are a good person. You must be an accountant or something like that. Look at your hands; you are not just anybody. One can see you are an important person. You work behind a desk," the taller man continued.

The shorter one, who seemed very shy, finally said, "Hands that know how to write numbers." He was toying with a hammock between his hands.

"I think I will take the silk one," he said, "but I will come back later. Now my friend and I have something to do. How much is it?" he asked trying to look interested.

"Six pesos. Well, the boss has been good, so maybe five fifty?" he asked.

"That sounds fine. We will be back later," he said standing up.

It was beginning to get dark. Light was vanishing, almost as if one could touch it. They walked silently. They finally arrived at the newer red light district called *Pueblo Nuevo*. The place was poorly lit.

"That square building there, don Rigoberto. The owner is Camilo Mandujano. Would you like me to locate him?" he asked trying to be as useful as possible.

"Not for the time being. I need to act as Gerardo did, without any help," he said.

"Yes, yes. Whatever you think is best," he answered hurriedly.

XVI

Even though it had grown dark, one could still distinguish a big building in the corner of nowhere. And Rigoberto asked himself bitterly, how he would spend his first night in *Heaven*. It sounded poetic, mystical, happy. He could almost hear soft music, which was in total contradiction with what Pueblo Nuevo represented.

They approached the building and one could hear marimba music interspersed with laughter and loud talk. A spontaneous voice out of tune could be heard singing a romantic song from Yucatán. These were inebriated people living a dreamy nightmare, and this time it was a terrible and unknown nightmare because it was going to turn into reality. One could hear people yelling and when they approached the door, they saw a man and a woman arguing. The woman had slapped the man, and he, surprised, had abandoned the building while she had returned with a quick step into its interior. The drunk man stumbled upon Rigoberto, swore at him for getting in the way, and started to walk downhill.

"Go home, Acopa, I will see you tomorrow," he said in a low whisper. He could no longer distinguish the police chief's silhouette because there was no street lighting.

The man started to protest and Rigoberto stood firm. He did not have time to explain to him why it would defeat his purpose if it were known that the chief of police was helping him.

Acopa then said, "Yes, sure," and he disappeared into the night.

Rigoberto entered a poorly-lit galley. There were candles on each table. He counted eight open doors around the building. Three of them faced the street. The two rear doors opened to a banana field.

Heaven was a well-attended place because it was where the action took place. The patrons were young indigenous people, peasants in various stages of alcohol. A woman spotted him at the entrance and she rushed over to him. She was young; she had a white complexion and wonderful, smiling eyes with long curly lashes. She asked if he would like to sit with her.

"Of course," he said as he followed the young woman who was wearing a shiny deep-blue dress. She knew her trade well, he thought, her smile was provoking and she had a nice figure.

"Shall we order something to drink? It's hot…" she said looking for the waiter. She had not even studied her new customer.

A young man who must have been around thirty approached them, "*Fundador, Zorro, Comiteco*…" he recited without looking at them. He had to pay attention to his other tables.

"Look, the don here is a man of great importance. How dare you ask, Bas?" she said as she turned to smile at her customer. She knew the pleasing trade. She was good at it.

The waiter returned almost immediately carrying a bottle of *Fundador* brandy and two glasses while asking for the bill to be settled.

Rigoberto paid and gave him a good tip. It was very strange to him to be asked for advance payment. Never mind, he thought, the more I live, the more I learn.

"What is this name, 'Bas'?" he asked the young woman.

"Bas, yes, *Basura*, Trash, that is what we call him. We have known him a long time. Bas, only, Bas…" she replied pouring brandy in the two glasses.

Bas was a nervous and smiling man. He was blond and had a huge nose and a big smile. He was pleasant and did not mind being called that strange nickname.

"He has never had a fight with anyone. He has a good disposition and he helps us. Cheers, foreigner!" she said clicking her glass with his.

Suddenly the music had started again. He could distinguish a man playing the marimba. A few couples had gotten up to dance.

"Do you always have this music here?" he asked trying to distinguish the musicians in the shadows.

"Yes, it is the *marimba* of Querubín Bolón from Campeche, and Leandro who plays the saxophone is from Jonuta. They brighten out nights," she said drinking the last of her brandy and pouring more. She looked at his glass and complained, "You're not drinking anything! Would you rather have some beer? I know it's hot. In a couple of hours we can feel better temperature," she assured him.

"This is fine," he said toying with his glass.

He looked around him. On one corner stood the musicians and in the other, almost opposite to him, the owner stood behind a bar supervising his business. Next to him, on a table was a man who was talking to two peasants and instructing them where to sign. They seemed slow in understanding, or maybe only drunk. He had to repeat his instruction.

"The *enganchador*," he whispered in a low voice, looking at the young woman.

"Yes, Avelino Sánchez, but…no, that is a horrible place, an evil place that *montería*. Nobody gets out of there alive!" she said drinking from her glass.

"Don't tell me you want to go?" she said jokingly. When she realized he was silent, she added, "No. You don't even know what it is all about, do you? I don't know…" she said looking him over carefully for the first time. "Are you a relative of don Pedro Romano's family?" she asked trying to understand the situation.

He shook his head. He did not want to change the conversation because this one seemed vital.

"How long has Avelino Sánchez been here?" he asked her.

"He's been coming here about a week every night. I think they must be needing plenty of people this time of the year, because the dry season is almost here," she answered.

"Has a representative of any other *montería* been here?" he said looking at her eagerly for an answer.

"No, nobody else has hired people up here or in any other house that I know of. You see, sometimes they use somebody's house for that purpose," she explained, studying him more carefully.

"What is your name?" he asked the young woman who had turned out to be an unexpected source of reliable information. He stared at her and apparently this made her uncomfortable, for she started toying with her bead necklaces. They had attracted his attention because they were blown glass. He saw she was also fixing the fresh flower on her hair. Her long eyelashes flickered in excitement, "They call me *la Ballena*, the whale, but my real name is Nenúfar. I have never told anyone before. It is a pretty name; it is the name of a flower. I think maybe it is a water lily. Do you know? And what is your name? If I told you, you can tell me. Or is it a secret? Yes?" she asked in a flirting way which came naturally to her.

Rigoberto nodded slightly while he drank a sip of his brandy. "I trust you and you must trust me, but I cannot tell you; nobody here must know. Will you keep my secret?" he asked looking at her directly into her eyes.

"You are quite a ladies' man, aren't you? Yes sir, a ladies' man! There is only one way of keeping your secret. I'll let you know which, later. Shall we order something to eat?" she asked casually.

"Sure. You do the ordering because I do not know what they have here, Nenúfar," he said. He liked the name and the girl. He thought she looked smart and knew that under different circumstances she would have been more than a languishing figure of *Heaven,* 'serving those who left forever.'

This was a battle, he knew. He had to take it seriously. He needed to prepare a possible escape route. "Do you live around here?" he asked her.

"Yes, with two other girls. You know it is difficult to work here because there are no hotels we can use. So we share a house and we are all right. We try to help each other out.

The music had changed to a livelier rhythm. She brightened up and called to the waiter, "Hey, Basura!" and he rushed to them.

"Bring us two Mexican-style steaks and some cheese," she said firmly, looking for his reaction. But her client seemed intent on the men with Avelino Sánchez.

The waiter came back in a few minutes and he watched her eat avidly. While she ate he surreptitiously watched the men behind the counter. The scene indeed was very interesting.

He had little time to think about his companion. She was happy eating, perhaps her first meal of the day. Avelino Sánchez was distributing money and reviewing his list. For a moment his eyes fell on Rigoberto and then he hesitated, as if he were thinking of leaving.

Suddenly, Rigoberto had made up his mind, and without a word, he went up to Avelino Sánchez's table and waited next to the man who was following the man's instructions and signing with a cross...for sixty pesos, the man repeated, sixty pesos was a lot of money, he could go buy his wife plenty of clothes and drink until he could no longer walk, or dance all night. All in exchange for one year's labor. And in the jungle, Avelino continued, life was good. Nobody bothered you and you came back with some savings.

The man had taken the money and left. Avelino turned to him, "Yes, what can I do for you?" he asked Rigoberto.

"I need to work," he said without hesitation.

"Well, well...Who would say?" he said sighing. "Well, after all, to each his own. There are no questions asked here. But you are not a peasant, nor are you a *kichán*, an indian. You know how to read and write..." he was assessing him carefully.

The music continued with other melodies of the region. The songs were soulful, and the woods of their forest lent them material for the instruments and some were tropical rhythms, fast and happy. It was as if musicians and trees and forest had become one, and in their becoming had encompassed those present. It was a primeval feeling. The shadows and the tobacco smoke should have been a premonition of the hell he was about to enter. He did not even turn to see Nenúfar; he might lose his courage.

"I don't need to know anything else. But I warn you. If you are honest, you earn well and no one will find you. If you are found missing one cent, one number, nobody will find you either. And you are in luck, don Fernando needs a man for the store," he said turning the papers over to him and giving him a pen.

"I understand, yes, of course I understand," he said eagerly.

"I suppose you want some money…" he said tauntingly.

Rigoberto turned to look at Nenúfar and was worried.

"Of course! Who is going to pay for the *Fundador!* I should have known, *la Ballena*, as always! Well, the most I can give is you is two hundred pesos…" and he waited for the answer.

Rigoberto blushed and then smiled. It felt like an offense to him and he understood he needed to remember his purpose for being there.

"Sign here. It is my receipt and tomorrow you go to the wharf at five in the morning. Well, let's say in a while. You won't forget, will you? And now go join your young woman and enjoy your last night in *Heaven* for a long time," he said laughing sarcastically. He could afford that because he was the boss here. Rigoberto signed with his secretary's name. He needed to leave behind a clue, just in case… Then he took the bills and put them in his pocket and left the boss's table to go back to his own. He had taken a quick look at the names on the notebook. It was in vain. The name that interested him so much was not on it.

"You'll need a hammock and a hat!" Avelino called out to him.

Rigoberto returned to his table and without saying a word to Nenúfar, sat down and swallowed a big gulp of *Fundador*. The young woman poured more into his glass and asked, "Did you sign?" Her hand was visibly shaking and her eyes betrayed the fear she felt.

"Yes," he said watching her carefully. Here was a stranger he had met scarcely half and hour before and she was capable of worrying about his fate! He appreciated her gesture. He was not worried about himself, but could not deny he was afraid for Clara and the boy.

"You don't know what you have gotten into! One hears horrible things about that place. I get goose pimples every time they mention that name. Well, you have done it, so there is no use trying to change matters, is there? Maybe one day you can tell me what it's all about. You must really want or need to get lost, because you have just performed a desperate act. You don't look like a thief. Maybe you were set up. Someone set you up, didn't they?" Nenúfar asked earnestly because she felt she had already fallen in love with a very masculine face and his green eyes. She would have done anything for him, anything! One could see he would not allow it; he had the demeanor of an honest man.

"You could return the money...maybe they would accept. I can pay for dinner and drinks. Basura knows me and will give me credit for a couple of days. Don't go!" she urged again. With her eyes she pleaded. "I have a friend who can hide you in his ranch all the necessary time. Of course you would have to help him bathe his cattle...Now, if you had chosen another *montería*, there wouldn't be so much to fear," she continued visibly frightened.

"Don't worry woman, I am going to work as an accountant in the store. There is not much to fear. But I tell you what. We will make a pact. You are offering to help me and that is terribly important to me, and besides, I will need you someday. Now, with regards to leaving tomorrow, don't worry. I can take care of myself. If I get malaria or something like that, I will come back, because I don't think they are prepared for medical emergencies," he said voicing a concern he had not even considered before.

"They don't cure anything there!" she said quickly drinking the rest of the content of her glass. "They die! They get weak to the point where they just die off!" Tears were showing in her eyes. He guessed them, because it was difficult for him to watch her distress. He was moved by it.

They were silent for a moment. It was an intimate moment of communion. Two lost souls that could not speak the contents of their hearts. Two strangers that came from nowhere and that were headed for the unknown. It was a brief instant. It was a precious instant he would remember for the rest of his days. He suddenly experienced a flash of intuition, Nenúfar's gesture would be with him to comfort him on his deathbed someday, ah, but would he be there for her in her hour of need?

"Well, drink up! I wish you luck anyway," she said clicking her glass on his.

"Nenúfar, listen! Listen!" he said holding her by the wrist. "I will come back and I will take you with me! Do you believe me? This night will not be the last thing between us, I swear!" He was desperate. Was he trying to convince her? Or was it to himself he was talking to? In any case, he knew he would have liked to help her.

The woman facing him must have been in her early twenties. She was nodding and started wiping her tears away with a handkerchief she found in her cleavage. She had beautiful breasts, he noticed. She was quite attractive. She then motioned to him, "Come, come. Let us dance!" she said standing up. "They are playing 'Women to the Sky! I like that music. How about you?" she asked drawing her body close to his.

"I do too. All women should go to heaven..." he replied vaguely. He did not want to think of his wife. Not tonight, not here, on the verge of a precipice.

"Come! Loosen up! Dance with more rhythm! One can really tell you are not from the region!" she said laughing. "You must be from...well, let's see...Puebla? You must be a puritan, eh? But tonight you will forget all that. I will see to that!" Her soft movements had an impressive sway, the sway of the water in the river, or of flowers in the breeze.

"I have already forgotten everything," he said shortly after. "Come, let's go for a walk and then we should go to your place," he said taking her by the hand and pretending not to look at Avelino.

Nenúfar left him for a while and went towards the banana patch behind the building. She was smiling when she returned and started to look for the waiter. Don Owner, as she called Mandujano, was busy preparing bills and counting money. Avelino Sánchez, pretended to continue with his job of hiring and studying his notes, but he was watching Rigoberto's movements and that made him slightly nervous. He would rather be outside, walking and breathing the fresh, moist air of the night. He needed to walk to the wharf and find the hammock-vendors, as the locals called them. And if possible the hat-vendor. And he smiled and Nenúfar thought it was in anticipation of a romantic encounter. He realized that everything was so new, that even the same language used in a different way, made him happy.

Bas came towards them, "Eight pesos…well, you've paid, now what?" the pleasant man asked intrigued and in a playful mood.

"Ten pesos for you, Bas, because I want to be your friend and I want to ask you to take care of this wonderful young lady while I'm gone," he said handing him a bill.

"Thank you! Thank you don…" he said while he returned to his work. Nenúfar, the Whale, had found a good client and a generous one, at that.

Mandujano watched them leave. His client had left a bottle which was half full and that made him happy. Suddenly he noticed Nenúfar returning to retrieve it. He sighed. Well, he thought philosophically, some you win, some you lose. A business grows only if the owner tends to it. He was quite careful with his, because he had hopes of taking a long vacation. He wanted to see Tabasco well, travel in the river and maybe even get to the sea. Everyone spoke of Veracruz. Why couldn't he visit it?

Avelino Sánchez just sat waiting and was starting to get bored. He ordered a beer and rose to go chat with Mandujano.

That was the last thing Rigoberto saw when they were leaving. The noise and laughter floated in the night as a stench that did not belong to nature. Human bondage took place there because the men who arrived did not know any better and were ignorant of the language of Castille. But he did not want to think of that any more tonight. It was supposed to be his last night of freedom. Nenúfar was carrying the bottle and drinking from it from time to time.

They were near the river when they found the two hammock vendors who apparently were still hoping to make a couple of sales.

"Well, I need a hammock. Will you please choose it, Nenúfar?" Rigoberto asked her pleasantly.

She felt pleased at his request and proceeded to finger them all to compare textures and knots. It was difficult to see them, the moon was new and the light was scarce.

Rogelio lit a match to count the money for the vendors and they left in a happy mood.

"All you men are alike. All you have to see is money in your hands and you can't wait to get rid of it. Sometimes I see coins and bills on the streets. It seems impossible that these poor peasants get drunk and don't even know what they are doing! Look!" she said spotting a coin near her sandal. "See what I told you?" Nenúfar sounded angry and sad.

These were the nights in Tenosique, in *Heaven*, in the jungle. He wondered what it would be like up in the hill, in the *montería*.

They had reached the wharf and could barely see the water. They could only guess it was there by the croaking of the frogs.

"What hammock did you choose?" he asked.

"A blue silk one, my Love," she answered. "You deserve the best. It is not usual to take one of these up to the hills, but your category is high and you deserve the very best! And when you lie down and look at the stars, you can think of me!" she said sighing and taking him by the arm.

"Would you go with me if I asked you to?" he said suddenly.

Nenúfar choked on the brandy she was drinking and started coughing for a while.

"Are you serious?" she said finally. She could not believe his words.

"Yes, I mean it," he said firmly.

"Well, maybe you don't know what happens with the women in the *monterías*. I don't think you would like to have to wait for your turn while I was with the others. Would you? See, this it how it works. I would have to cook or help the cook during the day and during the night I would have to provide my favors to all the workers. And that is in case that the boss does not take a fancy to me because it is said that he likes his women. Anyway, we could not even say we are married, because you already are married if that ring speaks its tale and everyone knows me; I am 'the Whale', and secondly, I would not be accepted except on the conditions they set. And we are all aware of them."

They sat on the steps of the wharf. Nenúfar confided parts of her life to him. She came from Jonuta and she had had to leave town. The man she was living with, had abandoned her when he learned that she was pregnant. She had waited for her child's birth at her mother's house, and after much crying and cursing her luck, she had been forced to go to work. But she had been too young and did not know how to do anything. She tried to be honest and not steal from the peasants, but of course she had some money saved and one day she was going to go back to Jonuta to start an open restaurant in which to sell beer and crayfish in order to raise her daughter with the pride of honest work.

"Lesbia?" repeated Rigoberto, not willing to believe the name she had chosen for her child. "How old is she?" he asked.

"Three years old, same three that I have been working in *Heaven*," she said as if the consideration was for her benefit.

"Very interesting. Three years in *Heaven*…" he said because he was at a loss for anything else. He knew that the woman with him had had little choice in her lifestyle. He was amazed because he had never been faced with the situation in a direct manner. Women were cheap currency in the area and he felt their distress.

"And you? Don't tell me your wife cheated on you and you killed the man and that that is why you have to get lost. But that is not so serious. Half the men in the area have done precisely that and they are still working here in Tenosique. Nobody bothers them, you will see that…" she said vaguely hoping to have him change his mind about leaving.

"Worse than that. And don't ask me why, but I must go. First I need to ask you for a favor. Come, let's go to your place," he said taking her by the arm.

They arrived to a white brick building with three rooms. The roof was made out of woven palm reed that rested on chicozapote beams, which seemed to be an interesting and intelligent way of cross-ventilation. Tenosique was the extreme of the extreme heat.

Nenúfar opened a big lock and they entered into a patio that was lined with alcohol cans where different flowers and leaves were planted. Some were vines and they had started to cover the outer walls.

"The three of us like plants," she explained. We take turns watering and tending to them," she said casually as she opened one of the rooms.

"So I see," he replied, but his mind was elsewhere.

"Come to my room," she said penetrating into a room where she lit a candle standing on a bottleneck. He could see a bed and a big armoire with a broken mirror.

"The bed is clean. Would you like a drink? They change our sheets everyday, well, you can guess why. Here, have a drink," she said handing him the bottle.

"No, I don't want to continue drinking and I want you to stop . I need you sober so that you can remember what I am going to tell you," he said firmly.

"It cannot be a favor; I am going to love making love to you," she answered jokingly.

"Yes, but we are friends, remember?" he said looking into her eyes.

"My, my, my… It must be serious. What is wrong?" she said finally realizing that it was to be an important matter.

"I am going to repeat for the last time: I need a favor," he said again, staring into her eyes.

"Why so much mystery?" she asked suddenly alarmed.

"Because I am leaving tomorrow for the logging station, remember?" he said without taking his eyes off her.

"I have not forgotten. But just for the record, let us remember I told you not to go! But you've got guts, haven't you?" she said shaking her head sadly.

"Yes, I do have to go. I am going! I need you to remember that the contract is supposedly for one year, but maybe I will return sooner…much sooner…" he said waiting for her reaction.

"Are you already planning to escape? Is that it? Well, then you don't know that *montería!*" she was almost hysterical.

"Could be…could be…" he hesitated.

"No, you don't know what you are saying. Nobody leaves that hell-hole. They don't get out of there, alive or dead. At least nobody I know there. The *enganchador* hands the men over to someone else and he comes back to Tenosique to continue his work. They just send word as to how many workers they need and he looks for them. So, they need a new accountant for the store…hum, I wonder what happened to the last one. Maybe he stole something and that, that, they do not forgive. I have heard they are whipped to death or they die chopped up by the machete," she said shivering. "You say you are going to work in the *tienda de raya*? You don't even know what that is…you don't even know what you are wanted for! I am afraid…you will not return!" she sobbed hiding her face in the pillow.

Rigoberto sat at the edge of the bed and shook the woman. "Don't even dare say that! I *must* return! Here, I need you to keep this for me," he said handing her all his money. "It is the *enganche* money that Avelino Sánchez gave me. Next, if I do not come back in six months, it is yours. You can go set up your restaurant to sell beer. I ask you in exchange for that, that if one day I show up here you let me stay with you for a few days," he said saddened by the perspective of leaving Nenúfar in a situation like the one she was in.

"Yes, of course. But the money…well, if I don't keep it for you they will steal it from you or one of your fellow workers can kill you for that. Here, let me give you some cards to help you pass time…" she said getting up and looking again in the armoire for some Spanish cards. She handed him a pack of old cards.

"It is an old deck, but they complete. That way you can think of me…" she said trying to smile.

"All right. I will think of you. How could I forget you if you are my only friend?" he asked approaching her. He put his arm towards her and got close to her and kissed her on the forehead. He stroked her hair and said goodbye in the trembling shadows projected by the light of the candle.

"I can't believe it! I can't believe it! And why are you leaving?" she asked alarmed.

"Because we leave at five and I need to go find a hat. Then I need to eat something. It must be eleven. Yes, eleven. Goodbye, Nenúfar, and if you see Lesbia before I do, give her a kiss because one day I am going to Jonuta to drink beer in a bar called *Nenúfar* and you and I are going to laugh very much remembering this night and this ridiculous farewell. Please, one last thing. No one must guess that I am not your lover. Please, that is extremely important to me!" he said meaning it.

"I know; I know," she repeated.

She looked at him unbelieving and speechless. She was holding some bills in her hand and a ring with two initials, RR, and a date, which her failed lover was leaving with her. She would sit, sadly, alone, waiting for his return. She would stay there as he asked, sleep for a few hours and then go to bid him goodbye at the wharf, as if he were her man, which she hoped for in the future…And she had not even known his name! When she realized the fact, it was too late because the new accountant had disappeared into the night.

XVII

The sky had changed to an amazing blue, the color of dark sapphires and the stars shone like hard, cold diamonds. Everything seemed to be in order in the universe, like a miracle come true, or maybe a dream, he thought as he walked out of the hotel and into the night towards the wharf. He was lost in the reverie of contemplation, as if shut out of himself. He was attuned to the slightest sounds of nature. He could almost touch the sound of a leaf dropping or a tiny animal moving about in the damp freshness of dawn, the first respite he had felt in days. His eyes would marvel at the different pictures when the day was being born. These changed imperceptibly and with a speed that knew no time, as if all that nature's hand had to do was draw curtain after curtain in the sky until it reach a clarity of blue that was the translucent nacre of tropical daytime. Precise cuts were drawn by the black shadows of vegetation on the firmament, which one could almost touch. He was witnessing the bounty of nature as if to spite the agriculturally-impoverished soil of that latitude.

He barely noticed that he had reached the wharf's steps. There were two or three families already there. Tears were streaming down the impassible faces of the women who stood static, except for the occasional transferring of a sleeping infant in their bosom. The men that Avelino Sánchez had hired the night before looked defeated but tried to look strong. Only their square hands betrayed their true feelings. From time to time they would touch their hats or scratch their head. Their inner core had been broken.

Avelino Sánchez was also there. He was impatiently checking his watch and looked frustrated.

"Good morning, friend. How goes it? Can you appreciate what I have to put up with? Nobody has arrived…" he said turning his head towards the river.

"See that? Here is the kayak to take us to Santa Margarita and those bastards have not arrived!"

"Yes, people have a way of forgetting time," Rigoberto answered non-comittantly.

"I will take care of that right now. Why does it always have to be the same? My job is extremely difficult. Now I am going to have to bother my friend, Aladino Acopa. Well, too bad…" he said ready to set off to the chief of police's house.

"You take care of these bastards, sons of bitches. They might get the notion that they want to leave also… Then we have to track them down. They could even run away. Why do they bring those crying women? Boy, oh boy, do they like to complicate matters! They don't seem to have any guts!" he said angrily.

"All right. I'll wait for you here," he answered, trying to understand the scene. The women continued crying softly; the men looked sleepy and were certainly still drunk. Most of the men had decided to sit on the steps where two boatmen were also waiting. The kayak, which was carved out of a huge mahogany trunk, was gracefully floating on the tranquil river. The water which was closer to the steps was a dull olive green color but it gradually became a neat and shiny liquid mirror with the distance. One of the infants was crying quite loudly, and the mother proceeded to uncover her dark breast to feed him. It was a very natural act which shook him to the core; the child would grow up without a father, violently separated like bad weed from the precious one. The labors of poverty.

A few minutes later two policemen with rifles approached them. They were escorting four young men who were resisting. Acopa who had come with them was asking them to return the advanced money. They immediately remained quiet. Acopa was pretending not to look at Rigoberto, but he has shaking his head sternly.

Rigoberto pretended not to understand because he did not want Avelino Sánchez to notice the look.

Fortunately Avelino was busy counting the men. There was one missing but he decided to take off. "Well, please keep him for me in jail. I will return in two or three days. Sons of bitches!" he said addressing the chief of police, his friend.

He looked one last time, just in case… and spotting no one, announced to the boatmen that they would be leaving. The boatmen immediately jumped into the kayaks and picked up the oars. The bells of the church announced the hour of five and they were to profit from the freshness of day to travel the six leagues from *Barranco*, the wharf of Tenosique, up to Santa Margarita, the stately home of the Romano family in Tzendales.

The women could be seen standing, dumbfounded, as they watched the kayak take their men away. The children seemed foreign to the terrible drama that was being acted and feeling only the sense of confusion and grief their mothers were experiencing. Rigoberto could witness no more. The world had changed so violently for everyone in a few hours! He turned his eyes to the sky, as if to greet the star king, or *Kinich Ahau*, the procurer of life. Nenúfar would be sleeping a few more hours. The sonorous syllables of her name produced a bitter taste in his mouth.

"It is always the same with these damned broads," Avelino Sánchez was complaining.

"Well, their men will be back within a year. Time passes quickly," the young man said firmly.

"Maybe not, my friend, the jungle is a way of life. And those of us who know it, are sure of this. You will see for yourself. Sometimes one learns to like it and does not leave. For others, it is impossible to leave. The jungle is generous if you find its way. It is a world for men, *machos*, not for young girls. One must develop claws to handle it," he said lighting a small cigar. "I think don Fernando will like you. He needs someone he can trust for such a big station as his. He has a big responsibility, you know. Maybe you will come to love the rain forest, and you've got it made! A few years later you will leave being a rich man," he said looking him up and down doubtfully and shaking his head in disbelief.

The men sat down on the improvised benches of the kayak; the boatmen rowed with professional dexterity in the slow and quiet language of the motion. Everything was new. This silent language impressed him most, and then he found a name for it: submission to fate. It was a destiny that had chosen one, he included, to glide into the big virgin forests, into the tropical jungles full of the dangerous and the sublime.

The sun was hot; the freshness of the small hours had disappeared and soon it would be impossible to survive it: a vapor exuded by the entrails of the earth would envelop them while they were immersed in the warm water acquiring slight sun strokes. The men were clearly exhausted from the alcohol of the previous night and the lack of sleep; a few must be thinking of their families left behind. The indigenous societies had strong family traditions, vestiges of a milenary structure that continued up to them. Hispanization had not touched them and now it erupted into their world with the same brutality and devastation.

"Don Fernando is a strong man, but not always unjust. Let us say he doesn't have the best disposition, but he generally gets what he wants out of people. If you are loyal to him, unconditionally loyal, you will have no problems and when you have his total confidence, he might even send you down here once in a while. Life for you will be peaceful. Oh, I see! You even have a silk hammock! Well…" he shook his head dubiously.

"Nenúfar chose it. She is a pretty woman," Rigoberto said sincerely.

"Oh, yes…how many times I have heard those same words from men who are going into the jungle! Many times!" he said longingly.

"But I think it is true," he insisted. "I hope this hammock will do…" he said looking at Avelino.

"Well, yes my friend, it will! You will sleep like the angels themselves," he said with longing.

Rigoberto was also remembering the past. Not his, but the one of the Heredia family. Clara must have been enthralled by this beauty, because if it overwhelmed him and surprised him with its baroque leaves and strange animals and he had traveled quite a bit, whereas a young girl from a convent must have been extremely surprised to discover paradise.

He could almost touch her nearby. She had traveled this same river, seen the same water lilies that floated so gracefully in their delicate colors, esconced on the turgid, dark leaves, unbothered and serene in their watery substance. She had also seen the pink and orange rays of the early hours of the morning. He would follow her, step by step and see each scene with her new eyes.

"What are you thinking of my friend? Surely something with regarding to skirts," asked Avelino smiling maliciously.

"Why yes! I am thinking of a young, beautiful woman," he answered truthfully.

"I suppose you are here to forget her. Well, if there is no other way out, what to do? What do?" he said vaguely. "But let me tell you something. Women are a dime a dozen in the world. Don't be so upset by a single one. Don't tell me you found no relief in *Ballena*?" he asked laughing.

"Well, Nenúfar is something else…" he said hesitantly.

"Well, yes, we can agree on that. But it is better to be your own man than to stay at home caring for the squealing children or being bossed around by the old cows. Look, my wife is at home and she does not dare to even ask where I'm going or when I'll be back. One has to take this attitude to be really free and to act like a man. Now when one becomes old, well, one can stay home and let them take care of you. In exchange, they get to have you home all the time. That is the way it must be. Women are to produce children and take care of elderly husbands. But before that time arrives, one is free to act to one's own will and desire," he said spitting a thread of tobacco into the river.

"The jungle does not accept sadness. The jungle is struggle. You have much to learn my friend. We will talk a year from now and you will tell me if I was right or not. Forget your young woman; there are plenty of those here and with no complications," he said giving him the best advice he knew of.

"I wish I could! I really wish I could, but it is too soon. One day I will be able to laugh about this," he said with conviction. But before him he could see Clara's face with her water-colored eyes.

The trip continued in silence. Now and then the peasants looked at the sky. It was their way of telling time, a wise way that forest people would teach him too. They never uttered a sound.

Rigoberto thought it must have been around ten O'clock when they reached the walls of the deeply-incised river. They were extremely tall and intensely green and they rose proudly, guarding the shores and beaches of the river. The air was musty and warm, as if predicting the unbearable heat yet to come that day.

The two boatmen approached a sandy beach where a rustic wharf had been built. They disembarked, innocent as to the direction in which they were going and their final fate. They walked to a big house of tall ceilings surrounded by an infinite stretch of land.

Once there, they rested briefly. The cook had prepared a good breakfast for Avelino and he, in turn, invited him to share it with him. The miller gave the peasants a round ball of cooked and ground corn, wrapped in banana leaves, the meal he had heard so much about, the *posol*. They were to mix it with water using their hands. For that purpose they were provided with a bowl, which had been made from a dry pumpkin cut in half, a *jícara*. One of Mijares' helpers was watching them like a lynx, while the men approached the river to fetch the drinking water.

They sat on the kitchen which was in the back patio of the house where a thin and nervous woman had laid out a table with fried plantains, mashed refried beans and cheese and white freshly-made tortillas which she was still preparing on a tin. She proceeded to fry two eggs for each one of them, and to fill large jugs with coffee and milk. She then gave them a sauce that was terribly spicy prepared with tomatoes, onions, garlic and a special pepper called *chile de árbol.*

"Thank you Angelina. How have you been?" Avelino asked her.

The woman smiled temptingly, but did not answer and Avelino did not continue his inquiry. The two men continued talking about happenings in the jungle. Around them flies, butterflies and hummingbirds were roving freely.

"Look, don Rogelio, have you ever seen the army ants?" he said pointing to an endless line of black ants. They were indefatigable moving lines that stretched far and beyond their view.

Rigoberto had to remember that he had to answer to his secretary's name. He watched fascinated as the small creatures marched ahead, unstoppable.

They leisurely finished the meal and then Avelino called the guard in charge of the peasants. "Checo, I think you'd better start now or the heat will start bothering you. Say hello to don Fernando for me. Tell him one is missing but that tomorrow or the next day I will send another batch of workers, plus the missing one. Here is don Rogelio, who is an accountant. Made to measure, as unbelievable as it may seem. Don Fernando knows that he is not to ask too many questions. He will do, I believe, and he has been warned about being honest with don Fernando."

Avelino Sánchez was an implacable man without scruples and Rigoberto knew he was a product or had adapted to the law of the jungle, of brute force and merciless exploitation. In one word, he was a man without principles, and that fact made him a very dangerous one. Fortunately for them, he would be staying behind in Tenosique, and hopefully he would not see him again in a long time. Hopefully never.

Checo called everyone and he said goodbye to Aladino. With regard to himself, he understood that he was facing an entirely new way of life, one that could not be imagined even if endowed with a great imagination, one that could not be read, because he had never seen this described anywhere. And this is what Miss Heredia must have been awakend to, full of the adventurous spirit of her young years, youthful and light on her feet. Something told him that she was there, once again within the reach of his hand.

XVIII

The men had loaded a train of ten mules with sacks of jute containing grains and other supplies they would be needing during the trip. Most of the things however, were destined for the *tienda de raya*, a store which was a system Rigoberto had read about in his history books and later studied with his law professors. It was one of those institutions created by the Spanish conquerors where peasants could go shop and have anything available in the store charged to their personal accounts. Needless to say, the men never finished paying them off. These accounts also had the shameful characteristic of being inherited by the debtor's offsprings.

The trip would be long and difficult, especially for the men on foot and the animals. Two mules had been provided, one for the overseer and the other one for the new accountant. The party of twelve men walked alongside. They had taken with them two men, the *macheteros*, in charge of continuously clearing the way of bushes and plants so the party could continue. These were men used to swinging their machetes to and fro, as if it were an atavism of their second nature. These were hardened men, men who inspired fear because their passions were violent and so were their actions. Such was the caliber of the rain forest, of men who had mimetized with nature to such a degree that they had lost the notion of good and evil such as it was conceived in the world Rigoberto came from. Their environment was boundless: *chicle, rubber, chicozapote, wild avocado and papaya trees,* water canes and the birds, birds of paradise, small and big creatures and snakes and other deadly dangers, including man. Here also, lay treasures of medicinal plants sought after by scientists all over the world which the jungle and its keepers guarded zealously with an astonishing reverence. Terrible and legendary was that world which the favorite consultant of General Díaz had had begun assimilating in spite of the fact that he was suffering from sunstroke. The President was governing a nation of unknown dimensions, cultures and environments. A rich nation, which a century before had even been richer than its neighboring countries. It had the blessings of mines and seas and rivers; its forests were the few remaining "lungs" of the world. Rivers, who could forget them? Tabasco was water; it was also a state blessed with everything, including beauty and the unmolested serpent of death in its bowls. And he asked himself, while he halted for a brief moment to wipe his forehead with a bandana, if Clara had perceived it thus, or had she just simply traversed these lands with happy heart and clear new eyes? Had she even suspected where she was headed for? Or was she just accepting, protected by the youth of her age, of this beauty that was so total that it led to death?

Rigoberto López shivered for a short instant in spite of the sweat that was running through his body marking his underarms and his inner thighs and bonding him as one to his mount so that man and animal were undistinguishable. By now he could hardly remember his city dwellings and his city's perpetual buildings. National Cathedral was a blur and he could not focus on the exquisite and motely characteristic that lent it identity. He had, however, begun to have a recurrent and obsessive dream: his peaceful garden, as if from it his psique tried to draw survival strength. He had no way of knowing that this existence in no-man's land was just beginning. It was as if his timing and feelings were a still-life that he might never revitalize.

He would despair and concede, concede and despair. To what end? He had been hooked by the jungle; part of him had grown and another part had been irretrievable lost. For never in his life could he forget the beauty and the pain, nor the images of monstrous happenings. Nor could he forget the unsuspected sights such as the one they were just grasping.

They had reached *La Ilusión* where they stopped briefly and climbed to the small hill called *el Mirador* to admire the plane of Tabasco. They could see the famous *Cerro del Panadero*, green and stately, crowned by its jeweled clouds which were green rays of *Yax Kin*, the winter sun. And Rigoberto's mind went back to his textbooks where the Maya world had been an abstraction. And he studied the profiles of his fellow travelers and saw in them the high nose and slit eyes. Unsolicited and unsuspected, he was to love and begin to understand their world for they respected the stars and the sun was a diety, and they were in awe of the strength of a forest which could weaken the diety itself with its green winter rays, green smoke, that spiraled upward to taunt celestial gods.

Checo explained it to him. He loved the hills and the rivers; he knew of leaves that cured and of those that killed; he detected allergies and could cure them. Rigoberto listened as attentively as his physical discomfort would allow. Checo was strong, he was endowed with the inner core of jungle men. He knew what he ordered and was listened to. And Rigoberto was touched by the chopped syllables of the region's speakers and he learned from them new words and expressions. He was also confident that he could acquire some of their survival instincts and that he could learn to see and hear. He already felt that he had acquired the dignity of his humble mount, with which he had become one. This was great progress because he had never ridden without all the comforts and its trimmings. He was weakened by the city and its debilitating ways. He envied his companions their physical strength and their survival with only water from lakes and springs and food from innocent and unsuspecting creatures they knew how to hunt. He also marveled at their ability to survive on ground corn and water, because he recognized in himself the atrophy of the original man-hunter.

Sometimes they would rest or just halt to get water with which to prepare their paste of maize. One of the mules had been laden with *posol* and ground, dry peppers and salt for their trip through the *Negro* to the central headquarters of the Romano enterprise. Six more days, Checo was saying till they reached the main house. He liked the accountant because he was a mild-mannered man who did not seem to feel superior to them. Quite the contrary, he was surprised and expressed a desire to learn more from them. He had guided many men on this path and he had never quite seem anyone like him. He was innocently curious about him. He knew not to ask. Jungle people did not ask; they accepted. He loved his jungle; he was born in it and would probably die in it.

Checo was laughing wholeheartedly. "Don't tell me you're hot, boss. Heat, real heat in May, when one pays for one's sins and still has credit! Well, you'll see. It will be hell for you for a while. We are like the bulls, until they accept the yoke! You are lucky to be an accountant, because…" he said looking at him sadly, "no offense meant, you are a weakling!" He added without malice, "No muscle…no offense meant."

"I am a city man…or was," Rigoberto said humbly, as his secretary would have done.

"Agreed, agreed…" Checo conceded. "Not to worry, you will do fine," he said confidently.

"Snake!" came the alarming cry from one of the *macheteros* who had separated in two a black, long life.

"Four feet..adult *Nauyaca*!" cried the oldest of the *macheteros*.

The men immediately gathered around the animal who lay lifeless at their feet. The black head with yellow lines was triangular and protruding from the fauces was a threatening forked tongue.

"See, don Rogelio? We were miraculously saved! I arrive at don Fernando's with one less man and he would fire me, the very least, fire me. This is not possible, we nearly lost a man! If I had lost a mule, he would have had me skinned alive," said Checo patting his mule affectionately.

The *Nauyacas* were the most feared danger of all. They were undetectable because they possessed the high quality of mimetization. They would climb on tree branches to protect themselves from the sun. This would result in the invading hand being stung. The mountaineers would fall to their instant death. Nobody's fault. Serpents did not go looking for men to sting. Their territory had been invaded and they simply striked back.

Rigoberto realized how much he loved life when he was so moved by that small death. They should have left that harmonious world unmolested. Rigoberto would always love the weak, for he instantly empathized with them. He did not yet know it, but he would find hidden facets of his personality through that new world that absorbed and fascinated him. Suddenly the creature at his feet became terribly important and he wanted to touch it.

"Leave it alone, don Rogelio! You want the skin? We will give it to you so you can have the belt done. It is a belt you want, isn't it?" Checo had become conciliatory.

Rigoberto was disconcerted at the instantaneous way things had to be settled. They had to convert the enemy into an object as a sign of triumph. They might win many battles but in the end they would lose the war.

Before he had even finished drawing his conclusions about the rain forest, the vibrant animal had been converted into a long piece of empty skin. Now it was nothing in the scale of life!

They continued on their way until they reached the *Ilusión*, a mule station which was also used as a mail trail and that had been set up on the banks of the *Chocoljá* river. It was towards the evening and the temperature was beginning to descend. The sky had changed its colors and neither time nor calendar existed nor were they necessary. Life just flowed.

They gathered dead branches, they hung their hammocks on the long trunks of *chicozapote* under the palm woven ceilings which not long ago had been part of a *montería*. They collected water from the river and started a fire to make coffee in order to sit down to a dinner of dry, salty biscuits. The peasants were exhausted. As to him, he did not have the stamina to even try to get off his mule. His back had been broken into a thousand pieces; his legs were no longer his; life had become a prolonged discomfort that had nothing to do with him. Thirst and hunger had disappeared from the concept of the brain.

The men helped him dismount. Checo laughed with his good disposition. "Don't worry don Rogelio, you'll get used to it. Today, tomorrow and the day after, will be bad. It will be even worse later, but in the long run you will thank your mount for its great service to you in the hill," he said while keeping a supervising eye on the rounding up of the mules. Then they sat around the fire to eat their meager provisions. Nobody spoke. The breeze from the river helped lower the temperature somewhat; the flames danced their grotesque figures on the men's faces; those men that knew it not then, but were headed to be food for the monster. They listened attentively to Checo and were fearful of the two men with machetes and they never uttered a sound; they had retired to their interior.

Rigoberto did not want to think about the past. It seemed unreal. He then tried to concentrate on the mission and smiled thinking of his present situation and of how he had so unsuspectingly said goodbye to his wife early one morning not so long ago. And he wondered if he had done the right thing when ordering Acopa never to reveal his whereabouts to anybody, no matter who inquired and no matter how long his absence was. He had left him with his last wish, "I will return when I have obtained what I need, not one minute before nor after. I can be patient and hope you can too. It is the strictest of orders, Aladino. You simply lost track of me. You saw me but you never found out where I was headed for. If something is known, I hold you responsible, I assure you. Now, as long as my secret is safe with you, you will have all my support and we can be friends. I am a man who keeps his word. Will you keep yours?" he underlined as he left.

Aladino Acopa had tried dissuading him and explained the danger of his enterprise. "Quite the contrary," he said. "It comes as an order of the supreme power of this country."

Acopa had ended by believing him and the matter was over.

Checo was speaking with the two helpers: a small puma had appeared near Santa Margarita and don Fernando had had the skin prepared and had used it as a rug in the big house. Had they been scared! It was not often that a wild animal came so close to where people lived. This puma had, and it had paid with it with its life. Now it was merely an ornament. Rigoberto listened and learned stories unknown to him about dissected animals and legends, of *nahuales* and women. Now, more than ever, he realized the learning process was never completed.

They bathed that night in the river, in the soft light of the moon. Rigoberto still too shy to take off his clothes, had to sleep in a wet shirt and wet slacks. It must have been three O'clock when he woke up shivering. The fresh breeze penetrated to the very core of his bones, but it was possibly the most beautiful experience of his life. He had a tree for headboard and his roof was the infinite sky with strange formations, and he carefully studied Scropio that ruled over their skies and who silent and majestic, guarded their sleep. He could distinguish the Milky Way, Orion and many celestials which he had never seen. And he could see very clearly the day when in grade school his science teacher had taken them to the observatory in Tacubaya, and how surprised he had been when he found out stars could also be observed in daytime! And now he realized how limited the human mind was. Side by side, hand in hand, he had walked with a young girl whom he loved and who loved him. Now she was far away, and their separation was strange and unmerited. It was an adventure that would sadden him with the passing of time because he would lose faith in some types of human beings.

Other times he would think of his parents and his in-laws and he tried to imagine their reaction to his telegrams. Rosita knew very well that this absence was very much in spite of himself. And he spoke to her with all her heart. He told her to smile, that he would soon be back and that he loved her. He realized what a big treasure he had. And his mind traveled to General Heredia's house. They surely would continue their afternoons at the Virginia Fábregas theatre in the Puerta Falsa de San Andrés. Their daughter meant nothing more than a social blunder and offense. Maybe very soon they would forget her. He wondered what they had come up with to explain her disappearance at the foot of the altar. God knows! The general would go about with his peers, and he would continue to be

He fell asleep towards dawn with the obsessive power of a name. He had left the picture with Acopa, and the ring. How would invited to the Castle, to his friend's house, the president of their

Republic! How about Clara's mother? She was an unwilling ally of the men. She had not even been able to postpone the wedding. How would she feel to see Clara free? In truth, freedom had its downside. To walk six hours the first day, would not have been an easy task for Clara.

He fell asleep towards dawn with the obsessive power of a name. He had left the ring and her picture with Acopa. How would he find her now? Probably more beautiful because of the sun; more mature because she was free and happier, enjoying beauty. He seemed to have forgotten the human element.

XIX

Men, mules and machetes rested only to regain momentum for the following day's battle. Each new day brought its exclusive challenges, dangers and unique situations. Maybe they were repetitive in principle but the diversity of its elements demanded quite a different approach. This, Rigoberto felt, was the reason for people to have such a high degree of agility and instinct.

Their life in that long march became a routine. They would wake up around four O'clock each morning when the day was on the brink of dawn. The *macheteros* would instruct the natives to look for dry wood, start a fire and fetch water from the river to brew the morning coffee. They sat around the fire chewing dry, hard tortillas which they sometimes toasted near the fire or they would resort to eating dry biscuits from a tin. Then they would continue on an uninterrupted march and would stop again around noon to hopefully reach a source of water in order to mix the corn paste with their hand. One of the mules would carry the countless spheres of maize wrapped in the shiny banana leaves; the corn would become sour with time and this was even a better element of sustenance. To it they would add salt and dry, crushed peppers. In that manner they would avoid dehydration and deceive their yearning for food.

A better meal was procured at sundown when the day's assigned stretch had been completed. They could then rest, bathe in the river or lake if one was available, or lie down to study the sky from their hammocks. They were allowed to dream or sleep while others went to hunt and bring a prize to share, a *tepezcuincle*, the small wild dog from the mountains or an armadillo and if lucky enough, they would manage to capture a couple of wild ducks named *pijijes*. Sometimes they had even eaten iguanas, the cousins of lizards which had green, blue or red varnished coats and which were direct descendents of the dinosaurs. Other times they would hunt turkeys, central America's contribution to the world, or savage fowl or even wild hogs. They would kill, skin, clean and marinate the meat in sour orange juice and salt and then proceed to roast their prey. Sometimes they even spotted the wild avocado trees which gave them the black-skinned sweet fruit of little pulp and big seed. It was a day of rejoicement in which they found sapodilla, guavas, *guayas* and mangoes, fruit that was abundant but usually inaccessible. Other times they happily discovered *catate*, the younger kin of coffee with less flavor, but a treasure none the less, to help them start the day. The virgin forest provided everything. It was the primeval paradise from which they should have never left; nor should they have listened to the good will of the Spanish missionaries to go settle in newly-founded European-style towns and cities. They should have continued with their nomadic life, because in the jungle you could lose your life, but never your freedom. And another thing Rigoberto would discover was that the inhabitants had not lost their initial innocence; they did not have the concept of moral or religious limitations. They simply lived in harmony with their surroundings. This would be difficult to accept for a city person like himself. It was as foreign a concept to him, as his was to them. And yet, he noticed, they were more generous in accepting him: as if his need were a call to prayer heard from a distant church belfry.

He also came to learn the ways of silent, distant men who minded their own business when faced with unknown dangers from hostile worlds, the white man's, to be precise and which threatened their very existence. The best way was to observe and try to solve things with intelligence or inventiveness and to try to draw a lesson of each event in order to survive. This he would ponder in those hours of rest, in the tropical pink light of early evening when he could discover its nuances through the frame of wonderous leaves of unknown trees. He would lie in his hammock and study the changing moods of the sky and the flighty whims of the goddess moon, *Ix*

Chel, known to all as the fickle lady of the night. Time would prove that in spite of all his thoughts, no white man could really understand that world; one could barely scratch the surface. In the end he understood the answer to the riddle: to love without trying to understand; to 'become one with' without asking how or why. That simple rule of existing was the door to happiness. That freedom was nothing but pleasure with no major obstacles. The real world, or what he understood now to be real, had nothing to do with the buried, almost-forgotten instincts in the city man who had been alienated from his true nature.

It was with those thoughts that they traveled the second day crossing a river called *Cedro,* and paused when they reached *Chocoljá* river to eat and feed and water the mules. They were a bit relieved when they found plenty of *ramón,* a tree whose branches could be used as pasture. There must have been two hundred trees which made the place pleasantly cool. There he learned that from the seeds the trees yielded, one could manufacture an edible paste or that the seeds themselves could be roasted, ground and used in lieu of coffee.

They spent that night in a place called *Granizo,* maybe because someone had once seen hail there. Apparently the place was unusually populated by mosquitoes because Rigoberto could not find a patch of skin where they had not reached him. His whole body had small welts that looked like vaccines, and maybe they were, he theorized. Maybe they would inoculate him or maybe they meant contagion itself. He thought all sorts of things in that long night where he was so uncomfortable he could not sleep for an instant. He needed to learn to cope with it, although at times the pain made him feel faint. One of the *macheteros* approached him with a sour half orange which had been roasted in the fire. He handed it over to him instructing him how to rub it on his hands and feet. He found he could no longer walk; the massive aggression was too much. And he looked around to see the effect of his traveling companions and could not believe that they were totally immune.

"You have to get used to it," Checo sentenced wisely.

But he knew that it would never be so. Many months would pass in the same condition and it seemed like the mosquitoes would never stop their aggression.

"Your blood is sweet, your skin is white and new. Mosquitoes love that," said the older *machetero* smiling. "You'll become used to it," he added.

They left the site near the stream called *Granizo*, a tributary of the *Chocoljá* river, whose water was cool and with a chocolate color. Then they reached a place called *El Cedro*, where a field of tall cedars emerged like a whim of nature which extended infinitely at the river's bank. The river itself was endowed with a Nile green color. One thing could be said about nature here. It was apparently even, the same throughout, and yet those who were acquainted with its terrain could not mistake one place for another. They knew their land like the back of their hand. They knew the risks and possibilities and knew what went into play each time they decided to travel through it. And then Rigoberto wondered it that were not true of any circumstance; life was the other side of the coin of death. The eternal dichotomy. And yet these people felt at home. The forest was their habitat, their home, theirs and only theirs.

It was the fourth day when Rigoberto woke up in *Lacanjá* barely remembering how he had gotten there. He felt so different; he was in a terrible mood and terrified of the obsessive repetitive dream of his garden. He needed to analyze his new condition for he felt himself sliding towards this overwhelming nature and his mind was defending itself. It was the cool hour of the birth of a new day when the dew was plentiful and the rain forest seemed to have washed every leaf and blade of grass; it shone with an emerald's dazzling brightness.

He started to get up from his hammock when he noticed a patch of small plants he had never seen before. Minute white flowers in the shape of stars had taken their place in their center during the night. The earth moved his soul. The rain forest rewarded him for having conquered him. It offered him something very special for his eyes only. It was a message of love. He smiled loving it back, in spite of himself, for the innocence of an unmerited and magnificent gift. He had not wanted to be there in the first place and yet the conquest was in progress; he had capitulated under the bewitchment of total beauty.

They started out early that day to begin the eight leagues from *el Cedro* to San Pedro where a river with the same name was born. They had to try to get to a long strip of forest ornamented by a series of springs, waters that reflected the cloudless skies. Its beauty was so intimate, so natural and so soft that it took him by surprise, leaving him breathless. There they would spend the night.

He walked in reverent silence to the springs and drank from their sweet, cool and clear water and there he discovered his reflection in the quicksilver; and it was there that he knew that he and he alone, had been chosen to receive the grace of self-knowledge, of total insight. He was humbled for he realized that he was one of the creatures of the Magnificent Artist who had conceived the rivers and the oceans and the deserts. He loved His Perfection and was mostly thankful for the unmerited gift of the glimpse of total beauty. He thanked Clara Heredia for having guided him through her path, and fate for having sent her to this latitude and General Heredia for his limitations and for those who had thrust an innocent child into the vortex of life. His heart overflowed with joy: he communicated with his loved ones; he whispered words of love and affection to his wife; he gave instructions to his secretary and he finally greeted Nenúfar. Quite suddenly everything had changed; he could not recognize a bearded face with feverish eyes from which tears flowed unsolicited. He was terrified because it was the other image that he loved, the perfect soul, which had disappeared to give way to his material being.

"Don Rogelio," he heard a voice from the bottom of a pit. It was Checo who was quietly standing next to him, asking him to return to the earthly world. "Malaria. It is nothing; don't worry. You are hallucinating. Here, drink," he said handing him a bottle of a clandestine alcoholic brew. He felt fire run through his entrails and then cold, blue air, unwelcome snow-water which make him shiver. He was defenseless against it and swept away in cold convulsions. He lay exhausted and cold.

Checo was covering him and pouring more liquor into his mouth. It burned his esophagus and perforated his brain. Rigoberto was suffering from a delirium that must be a glimpse of hell. It was jungle fever, the price to pay for entrance to the Biggest Show. Before him he saw the sad outline of a child clad in translucent cotton, Clara Heredia with a headdress of golden rays. She was beckoning with her hand.

"Good God, don Rogelio! You had very high temperatures yesterday. Did you sleep well?" and Rigoberto realized he had returned to the conscious world and to a new day.

"I think so. I have a terrible headache," he could barely whisper.

"Of course you would! Now we have to go to the spring of *el Plateado* where the stream of *el Negro* begins, for a bath. There is nothing better. I have coffee ready for you to cure the hangover. When we reach the main house you will take quinine pills; don Fernando has some. Gosh! Bad luck! But it means nothing. We have all suffered this at one time or the other," he said shrugging and handing him a mug with coffee.

They reached the brook. All the men were there and almost ready to continue the trip.

"Day after tomorrow we reach the main house of San Román in *Tzendales* territory. You will feel better there. Maybe today you will feel weak, but you can't pay attention to that; come on," he said helping him to his mount.

The train of mules and men continued into familiar territory. Rigoberto was weakened and uncaring. The mule had to do all the work of travel.

Checo was always near him. The *macheteros* watched the men closely. There was not much need for cutting bushes and branches; it was the dry season. During the rainy season plants would spring from one day to the next, taking everyone by surprise. They had to travel for six hours, six long and anguishing hours of uncomfortable travel! Much as he wanted to think of the peasants on foot, he had little energy for anything else but his survival and that meant, to stay on his mount. He had to take care of his animal because he had to reach Clara. Clara was a distant echo with no response. He was too tired to understand the message. All he wanted was for night to come so he could lie in his hammock and sleep and maybe feel better. He did not want another hallucinatory episode because it might give his mission away and that would extremely dangerous. He could not risk his life because he could not risk Clara's.

Finally they reached *el Negro,* the river some called *el Plateado* because its colors changed from black to silver according to the time of day or the spirit of the onlooker. That was something that happened quite frequently. Many places did not even have names; travelers would baptize them as they were passing. He saw no more. He fell into a deep sleep. His hammock? Who had hung it up? Who had taken off his boots and hat?

After another blurry day of travel they reached the Main House of San Román, a two-story brick construction with aluminum roof. It was impressive to see a house in the middle of nowhere. Two of the workers came to receive them. Fernando Mijares lived on the top floor and the storehouse, the office and two rooms where workers slept were on the ground floor.

Mijares was one of the men. He walked between them inspecting the human merchandise and hesitated in front of Rigoberto who could barely stand and who was being helped by one of the *macheteros.*

"What about this one?" he asked, tapping Rigoberto's boot with the whip.

"It's the new accountant. His name is Rogelio," Checo answered nervously.

"What is wrong with him? Is he drunk? No, I guess he could be ill. Get him inside and tell the helper to give him a couple of quinine pills. I'll speak with Avelino; he needs to choose the men better," a gruff voice was saying.

That was the welcome he had received at the famous main house of San Román, and this was the feared man who stood before him. Rigoberto could think no more. He was sleeping deeply or unconscious. What was the difference when you could not register the happenings around you? He was freezing and sweating profusely at the same time. Someone was covering him as if he were a small child. It was a middle-aged woman with a look of concern. All he could feel was the dark cloud of terror that floated in the air.

XX

Rigoberto woke up in the early afternoon on what he supposed was the following day of their arrival. It must have been around four O'clock when the cook showed up with a bowl of chicken broth, which he was later to learn came from Fernando Mijares' table. Rigoberto felt the warm liquid as a comfort to his illness. He had no inkling as to the risk the woman was taking with that act of kindness.

"Don Fernando wants you to come down," she said calmly when he had finished. Her eyes betrayed enormous fear.

"Yes. Where am I?" he asked confused.

"In the room where the previous accountant slept. Better not ask too many questions of what you are about to see. It will be better that way; you will see for yourself. And please, oh, please do not mention what you have eaten. You had some *posol* with water," she said walking away.

The woman's demeanor seemed quite unusual. He was too sick to try to interpret it. He looked around. A squalid room with hooks for hammocks. His own hammock occupied the last two hooks. He tried to get up but the world started to swirl around him. He would have preferred to lie down again, but Fernando Mijares, the man in charge, had expressly asked him to go down. Nobody made Mijares wait, so he stumbled out of the room holding on to the walls.

He walked around the building to the back yard. There must have been some fifty men, two cooks and the miller in charge of preparing most of the daily sustenance. There was a strange silence and he was surprised to see that they had only been waiting for him.

"Come here, accountant, come see what happens to those in charge of the warehouse who steal or betray Mijares," the man with the moustache was saying. He was short, maybe five feet two and with a rounded figure.

"Twenty!" he said beginning to count with his whip on his own boot.

"One…two…" the man who was tied to a tree was feeling the force of the horse's whip on his bare back.

Mijares turned to look at the new accountant. "One of my brandy bottles disappeared from the store…" then he turned to oversee his task. He wanted to make sure that his orders were fully carried out.

Rigoberto turned towards a tree to throw up. He knew he was throwing up the broth, which the cook had so generously taken to him at great risk to herself. He knew, then and there, that he had found a friend. As to the scene he was witnessing, it seemed surreal. This was a greater nightmare than any feverish, sick mind could produce. That could not be taking place! No one moved; no one dared move. The men were paralyzed by the events taking place; the women were crying, hiding their face between their hands. Others simply refused to look, fixing their eyes on their worn, rough sandals and calloused feet.

The count had ended and Rigoberto knew clearly that there was no way the man could survive. The wounds on his back had opened as red flowers in bloom; weeping flowers from which flowed a reddish liquid. The unfortunate man had passed out. And Rigoberto found that he was to ill to fully digest the situation. He understood nothing because his mind would not believe the messages of the actions taking place.

"A bottle of brandy…" he whispered unwillingly.

"Many have died for less than that, Accountant," Mijares answered. "So, are you ill? Maybe you don't have the balls for this? I didn't think you would. So better you don't lose a single grain of corn, don't you think?" the man enjoyed his sadist mood.

"Yes, I understand," Rigoberto answered softly.

The lesson. Mijares was not only a teacher but a strategist. His first lesson had been taught when he was ill and weaker than the weakest, a blow below the belt. He had once and for all measured his opponent. Mijares was the boss with no one to answer to. He was free to deploy all his destructive brutality. He faced a killer, an executioner who thrived on others' pain. A tyrant, Mijares was, who needed no excuse to inflict his demons on others. He was a man to reckon with. He must act quickly. He had searched for Clara and Gerardo among those present. He would have recognized them instantly. Nothing. He had to act very carefully.

"Throw him into the river! Useless to dig a grave. We need people's time to fell trees!" the man in charge yelled in anger. Here was the man whose sole name made the jungle tremble with fear. He was infamous throughout the region. And he, being a city man, had never heard of him.

"A lesson for these animals!" he finally yelled and started to climb the stairs to the upper level where his rooms were. Rigoberto went back to his hammock while the rest of the men stayed on to watch a dying man end his worldly trials. It was like a frozen picture. They were paralyzed by the inability to change things. Mijares gave orders and there was nobody to contradict him. Right or wrong, they were carried out. And he understood that those miserable men could do nothing to change their fate once they had signed and received a downpayment in *Heaven*.

That night the obsessive dream of his garden visited him once again. It was a cruel sanctuary in the blessing of sleep. Next day he awoke feeling better. He washed up and soon Mijares called him to the warehouse. He looked him over carefully.

"Let's see, Magaña" he said as he took a sip from his coffee cup. He was sitting behind a wooden desk. "Let's get things clear from the start. It is not complicated. You will be in charge of supplies. If anything is found missing, I know how to collect. I think you saw that clearly yesterday. Here we have thick chocolate and clear accounts. Your past doesn't concern me, nor does your future. I need someone to have the store's accounts in order, to keep an inventory of clothes and food and that in case I need to leave, can take my place. That has never happened up to now, so don't be hopeful. I understand you need to get lost for a while. I don't care why, nor do I have time or desire to find out. But here, you walk a straight line or you leave…I don't mean leave from the *montería*, but from this world. So it is clear, isn't it?" he had had the last word without even looking at him. He then returned to his accounts without giving a second thought to Rigoberto who was standing firmly in front of the desk.

"What the hell are you doing there? Don't you have anything better to do? Get the hell out of here, but not too far. I might have to call you. Go to the kitchen," he ordered without raising his eyes.

Rigoberto walked to the kitchen where the cook gave him a bowl of black bean soup, recently-made tortillas and a mug with milk and coffee.

"You need to feed yourself well. You have lost a lot with the fevers, but you will recuperate. The other accountant had his breakfast here. The boss allowed him to. So if he sent you here, I can also give you something. I'm afraid that the rest of the day you will have *posol* like everyone else," the big woman said while she placed a huge tortilla on the fire. He watched her extend the next one with the palm of her hand. She would gyrate the white, ductile dough like an artist drawing windmills. Rigoberto had never seen tortillas elaborated in that manner.

"I have learned a lot these days," he said, unaware that he had spoken outloud.

The kitchen consisted of a woven palm roof, open on three sides. The flies and bugs came and went to their content attracted by the aromas emanating from the food being cooked. Rigoberto saw a flock of guacamayas cross the air like a wound inflicted on the sky. He could observe the birds feeding from the fruit of trees. Life was in order; it continued on its healthy way. The evil of man did not touch it.

"I like you, don Rogelio," the cook was saying while making a new tortilla. "But be careful. This is a very dangerous place, nobody escapes…" she said shaking her head.

Rigoberto turned to observe her. The good woman was wearing the usual attire of the women of the area. She had a piece of cloth wrapped around her to constitute a skirt. She was barefoot and streams of tears flowed down her rounded cheeks. From time to time she would wipe them with the back of her hand.

"The shop keeper, did you know him?" Rigoberto asked softly.

"Of course, I was his woman. I am the woman of the quadrille, and as you can see, when something happens to one of them, I cannot get over it. He always came for breakfast," she said turning the tortilla and adding more charcoal to her stove.

Rigoberto watched her with attention. He could not understand or imagine that this good woman aside from preparing food for everyone, still had among her duties to dispense sexual favors. His mind went back to Nenúfar and soon understood what the young woman had been trying to convey. He was now living the jungle and its men's fate.

"Don Fernando appears to have been drinking," he said trying to deflect her pain.

"It is always the same. He kills them and then spends the night drinking. Sometimes he goes on a two or three day binge. He is a very strange person. He doesn't ressemble anyone I have ever met. Yet one hears of such strange happenings…" she broke off looking towards the door that led to the house. It was imperative that no one hear them. Rigoberto understood that the woman needed to vent her anguish. She too, was trapped. Another thing, he hoped that she could shed some light on Clara's whereabouts. The big house would have been the logical place for a young lady like Miss Heredia. Where could she be? He did not dare risk asking anything. It was the first day of exchange of confidences and he had to dose his questions. He needed to see how the *monterías* were organized in order to understand the lumbering industry.

For the time being, he knew Mijares lived on the top floor where nobody was ever allowed. The cook took care of his meals, of this clothes or of calling him when something pressing came up. Everyone dreaded those times because generally it came with the punishment of whoever was responsible. Mijares' retaliation was nothing to be despised.

Rigoberto had worked for many years with shady characters, sometimes even with killers but he had never met such aberration, such an absurd specimen of a being, such a sick and evil man. He could not find the word that would best describe Mijares who was a formidable opponent. He had to be civil to him. He had a mission and that was something he could not forget. He would deal with him later, once he had left the *montería* taking Miss Heredia with him. He pondered if in trying to evade our fate we do not begin a race towards it. If Clara had thought her father was hard and demanding it was because she had never even dreamed a Fernando Mijares existed. And what in heaven's name had she come to do in this inferno? Maybe she had to, because the jungle was the only place one could see absolutes like beauty and evil, in one word, the bare soul of man.

"Don Rogelio, the boss wants you," said one of the helpers and they walked together to the big warehouse where one could see sacks of dry maize and beans where Mijares had the desk and was looking over the inventory while having his morning coffee.

"Here is everything. It seems to be in order, so I hand everything over to you and I have no room for tolerance. You will remain here until five O'clock. The cook will bring you some *posol* at noon," he concluded without looking at him. Rigoberto was beginning to understand. The man disliked people because he was afraid of them.

Mijares left without a further word and Rigoberto wondered where he was headed for. Would he continue to drink, as was his usual pattern? Would he go castigate and bother others? How could this man function as if nothing had happened yesterday? He had killed a man! It was then that he understood that the man was feared because he did not have what the rest of mankind had, a conscience.

XXI

Time passed slowly in Santa Margarita. Rigoberto understood that it was to be a lesson in patience and endurance. He felt jittery and ill at ease most of the time and he knew he must change that. The main reason was that Clara had vanished without a trace and then he was certain that Mijares wanted to be rid of him and could have him killed at any time. His life was worth that of any other unskilled laborer. To live or to die in these latitudes was a matter as simple as the toss of a coin. Then also, he had to change his demeanor towards Mijares. He disliked the man so intensely that he was afraid of betraying the peaceful subordinate behavior that he needed for his quest. His dislike had two reasons for being. The first was that he felt he was being swept into the sick degradation of Mijares' current and this clouded his judgment; the second was the realization that Clara was nowhere to be found and therefore, he was wasting precious time.

He must find a way out! He realized also that it was common knowledge that there was no possibility of leaving the infernal place, especially for him. He would either get lost forever or die in the dangers of the inscrutable jungle. He knew that even the men who had been born there and who were in possession of secrets of jaguar-hunting, of medicinal and edible plants and viper antidotes, feared the surrounding areas of the main house. Nobody seemed to remember anyone having escaped Mijares' hell alive.

However, being who he was, Rigoberto never gave up. He continued his systematic study of the surrounding geography, the customs, habits and routine of the logging procedures and the human responses, and mainly of the boss. Mijares lived in his own world, and in that manner resembled the creatures of the wild. He did not need of others to survive; even more, he did not want them; he needed isolation, calm and the chaos of the flow of whatever his mind produced. It seemed to be the only possibility of his personality: chaos and lumber. That seemed sufficient for the European lumber companies who carried away the treasures of that jungle: *canshan, bari, tinco, ceiba, guanacaste, guapaque, chicozapote, palo tinto,* cedar and mahogany, the latter being the most precious to the foreigners because of its delicate and even streaks. It was the purest, the most aromatic of all. The other woods, upon being polished, showed rich and ostentatious, intricate surfaces and colors that not always pleased a continent used to routine and smoothness. They would have felt the blue, pink, and intense brown hearts of other species as an aggression to their subdued taste. But the inhabitants of the area loved them and it was not unusual to go into a wooden home and perceive the pure aroma of recently-cut wood, for they used every piece of the surplus wood to live, build and cook their food. Their homes were mainly built this way and had been so for centuries. All they required for the roof was cut and dry palm leaves, which woven, would provide a type of freshness unequaled by any man-made material. Without them, May in the area would have been impossible to bear because he knew by his own experience, that people despaired due to the inability to cope with the hot dampness of the season. Many had preferred alcohol or even death. Passions became heightened and all kinds of evils surfaced, and alcohol was obtained even at the price of life, as he had witnessed in his first lesson. Even then, he could not understand how the workers accepted torture and execution as an everyday happening. Life was to be lived only by the survival of the fittest, the climber personality, the man who was able to turn his eyes away from Mijares' 'lessons'.

The *monteros* were mainly people from the region and during the idle afternoons, he asked himself unrelated questions. Did those men, descendants of the Mayan people know that their ancestors had been great doctors who possessed the secrets of tropical medicine and dentistry, astronomers who had a perfect calendar and who could predict eclipses, and architects who built pyramids for sacred funerary crypts with an exactness unparalleled by modern architecture and mathematicians that would astonish the world with their use of the zero? Time told him they did, even if it was only in an intuitive, collective unconscious manner. Theirs were the cities in ruins, the grandiose palaces which lay broken by history and time; the "houses of stone" where gods with different names lived, now partially hidden by the voracity of perennial vegetation, as the Spanish explorers wrote back in the eighteenth century, in awe, to their king; many of them had polychrome murals depicting the history of their military exploits and their victories. Theirs, too, were the exquisitely carved stellae buried in the growth of high *amate* trees and vegetation of all kinds: hidden bushes of huge leaves and flowers tiny and enormous, scented and unscented; the observatories where stars had been baptized and their movements minutely studied and recorded in delicately carved limestone tablets and handed down by oral tradition to a select few. Everything now lay buried in present-day state of affairs and in the forever memory of time. And Mijares hated them, the rich owners of an even richer heritage because neither he nor any of his, could ever equal the power and majesty of that portion of humanity. All that his incontrollable demons would be able to do, would be to unleash their fury on one of the innocent heirs of such wealth.

One afternoon when Rigoberto was reading pages from a travel book that had come from who knew where, and which he suspected had been written by the indefatigable traveler, baron Von Humboldt, Mijares walked in after his usual *siesta,* violently tore the pages from his hands and put a match to them saying he better watch the mice not eat the grains in the warehouse and instructed him to write the price of the loss in his own account.

Rigoberto did as he was told and read the astronomical sum he owed the main house. Then he went to inspect the jute sacks and found that the mice had almost finished eating the dry corn in one of them. He then wondered how long it would take him to get rid of the graceful, shiny 'miner' mice of black, hard eyes and then wanted to figure how to keep them away. Everything seemed so complicated because there were other calamities to worry about such as the ants, termites and all the unheard-of creatures of the rain forest that invaded them without mercy, but the locals knew how to fight them with methods handed down from ancestral times to their own and Rigoberto was not one of theirs.

A few men were called in to help move and inspect the sacks, to isolate the affected sack and to find and waste the small black lives. There was no other way. It was then he realized that he was failing the job he had been hired to do. He had failed, out of ignorance, to carefully check the warehouse every day otherwise the people might suffer shortage of badly-needed products. He had been too self-absorbed in his concerns and worries about a young girl and her fate and had forgotten the rest of his fellow men.

Surprisingly the men were eager to help 'the one who knew how to write' for they willingly contributed with their knowledge of the methods for keeping away the insects. They also taught him how to destroy their nests and how to follow their trails through tunnels and tunnels of underground construction. They had liked him and had never tried to steal anything from him. They had begun to accept him as one of their own, but never completely, because white was white. It was as plain and simple as that. They were puzzled as to why he had not awakened the sleeping demons in Mijares. They also knew that the accountant would have to pay for the lost grain.

He was surprised to see that their humanity could not be reduced, in spite of the serious threat it might mean on a certain instance. With time he understood that it was precisely this very kindness that Mijares could not tolerate because he considered it a weakness of racial inferiority. The Spaniard's own true and objective weaknesses were there for everyone to see and they were all reduced to one word: evil.

He tried with all his mind and heart to adapt and feel and see the world as one of the workers because he was in fact living as one of them. He wanted to know what made them vibrate, how their minds and hearts worked and with surprise he discovered time after time, that their main sensitivity was for the flowers and the small and big creatures, and their eroded temples from long ago and their gods, now with forgotten names and that they revered the rain and thunder and abundance; that they knew of an underworld and the submerged gods who inhabited it, of a death as palpable as life. He saw them in their daily greeting to the king star, the royal producer of golds and coppers, of reds and pinks and Rigoberto knew he had yet to see the enormous red sun when it shone in the total blackness of the night towards the west in the same way as he had experienced the green sun when he had arrived. He had acquired the sensitivity that the underground waves of rivers provided and their magnetism. He could now read the person in front of him as if in a transmission without interference. That quality was now his for life, because one could never lose it; just the opposite, one cultivated it to expand it in quality and quantity.

Rigoberto now was capable of loving the rain forest and his new life. He had become a sad man because the other world seemed to vanish from his memory. Even the face of his beloved Rosa was now eroded and blurred. He knew she had changed; he would no longer recognize the lines of her body and she was now a woman with other interests and another love, not unlike himself. They had been separated and the breach seemed insurmountable. He wanted her out of the way just now, because he was afraid of involving her in the demential life he was leading. And this made him wonder how one could love something in spite of the evil that dominated it and the answer was simple: one loved and knew not why.

This made him realize that he was falling deep into something extremely dangerous and that his hate for Mijares would harm him if he did not solve it. He knew him and now he had to stop him and it was imperative he find the way. For this, he had to find an escape route, get to Tenosique and seek justice.

On the other hand, the days were pleasant in spite of the growing degree of heat. They were in April, very close to May when the jungle provides beauty with new life, when the jungle bestows upon its favorite, spontaneous and unheard of colors. One could see the faintest of pinks in the *cocoítes*, and an unheard number of yellows and the purest of golds from the precious *guayacanes*, gold that outshone any of the competition without a trace of green. If one had the gift of seeing, which was different from the gift of sight, one could spy the parasites tolerated with good nature by the trees, the orchids that exhibited their exquisiteness only to the 'eye that could see.' Sometimes they would shamelessly hang down in acrobatic gestures betraying the dainty tones of whites, lilacs, yellows, pinks and browns. It was true that the jungle offered men the dangers of death; it also afforded them life and its abundant sustenance, like the *guapaque*, a sort of tamarind to flavor their drinking water and to soften their bodies because its seed was brown velvet. It gave them buried treasures like the *macal* and *Yucca gloriosa* which had edible roots which the trained eye could easily differentiate from other plants; wild coffee for their morning brew, and the pear-vegetable or *chayote* and wild oranges and limes. The *granadilla* fruit sweetened their water and their days. The rain forest gifted them with a free hand, a generous mother. And it was precisely this, which Mijares could neither understand nor accept. They were in possession riches he had been denied. In one simple word, he was an outcast. Nobody wanted him or needed him. Unable to do anything else, they barely tolerated him.

And what about himself? He had to scrutinize his own soul. He had to accept that the unfortunate Spaniard was probably the most interesting character he had ever met. Mijares was endowed with a high degree of intelligence and yet he was nothing. Rigoberto had dealt with criminals but he had never really stopped to dissect their souls, because he had been in a privileged position vis à vis them. He was extremely surprised to realize how much he owed to this cruel and vengeful being. He had never really had a boss before. He studied him minutely because he was interested in Clara Heredia's whereabouts and he knew the saying 'Keep your friends close and your enemies closer.' He needed to know the events of Clara's disappearance. He had foreboding suspicions If only he could find a clue! Both Clara and Gerardo seemed to have been swallowed up by the earth; and time and again he wondered if there was the remotest possibility of having been wrong.

He had reconstructed the chain of events, step by step, a million times and found no answer.

At that point Rigoberto had no way of knowing how close he was to learning a truth he had dreaded, all in the name of hope.

XXII

Rigoberto had gotten used to the peculiar smell of dust emanating from the corn and bean sacks. He had checked the accounts, which seemd to be in order. He had gone over the lists of the store of Santa Margarita of the San Román setup where some hundred and eighty nine workers appeared and whom he had never gotten to know because they were a migratory population that came and went to the *semaneos*, sites that sprung spontaneously according to the need of the overseers. These places were in essence similar to the 'walking cultivatable fields' for they moved to sites where they found better trees aged fifty or more, which they could fell. From his lists he knew what it meant to be a *boga*, or rower and that these had to own their own kayaks; and that the *gañanes* were guides; and the *hacheros* or hatchet men were in charge of felling trees; and that the *buyeros* or *boyeros* had responsibility of the bulls and their performance. He now knew that the *callejoneros* were alley-makers together with the *varaleros* who carried and laid down canes in order to form paths though which the bulls would transit in teams of twos and that of these yoked groups. The first one was to lead; the second one, the *cascos* would be the strongest in order to be able to carry the heavier load and then the third pair would be the *contracaso* in support of the second group.

From his lists he came to recognize a few of the workers but he had never witnessed any such operation of launching . He wanted to, in order to understand the setup and he wondered how to achieve that. He knew he was close to the end of his stay and that the jungle would always remain with him as branded flesh, a reminder of a past life somewhere in the immensity of the Lacandonia.

He had meticulously burnt into his memory the months spent at the main house, like one of the branded oxen, which turned him into a cog of the Romano setup. He had become an object with no personality, identity or importance, whose only mission in life was to see the correct workings of a warehouse, a store and the accounting books. It was only in the early evening when he came to have some contact with some of the workers. He remembered a few names and those he could identify were so because of their enormous bills. They were indebted for life and their children would inherit the debts. Once a worker had come to Mijares asking for money for a family emergency and Mijares told him it was impossible: he was facing the loss of a huge quantity of lumber which had been destroyed in the fury of the river. The worker had replied, "All right, write that debt in my account but give me the money I need now." They had no idea of how much sweat and toil their accounts represented. Some had no head for figures, nor did it matter, because it would have made no difference.

The layout of the main house was simple. On the ground floor was a huge room to one side, where the storage part was together with an office to serve as a store, then two rooms for a few workers to hang their hammocks from; the second floor was exclusively for Mijares' private rooms. Then there were twelve small dwellings on the grounds nearby. To the other side was the bull pen and to one side of that was the forge where repairs to the thick chains, hooks and shackles were carried out.

The Main House of San Román was the biggest of its kind in the region. In spite of that, they lived isolated from the world, in an artificial cosmos with its own rules and regulations and where justice was randomly exercised by its unmerciful tyrant. It could explain the reason why Rigoberto's search for Clara and Gerardo was fruitless. And the days were followed by nights and these by other days and moons followed crescents and new ones. Nothing happened. Maybe, just maybe, thought Rigoberto in despair, he had been mistaken and come to the wrong place. Precious time would have been lost and Clara would be gone God knows where. He no longer worried about leaving; he knew it was near, maybe a question of weeks.. Mijares, the lonely and distorted soul might trust him enough to send him to San Vicente or Pico de Oro or Tenosique itself.

He was hoping to see Aladino Acopa, but the man never showed up. Neither did another group of men. Then he studied the lists carefully and saw that they changed regularly, year by year, and that in his books there was not one single worker who had left with or without a debt.

Meanwhile, Mijares would walk back and forth, alone, lonely, searching in vain for something to assuage his wounded soul. Rigoberto never knew if he had family. It seemed he came from Asturias, a place whose name was never mentioned. He did not know if he had parents or siblings or friends. Nobody ever visited him, and he seemed never to have received personal letters. The mail would bring some bills, take money to San Juan Bautista where Pedro Romano, the sole owner of the enterprise lived and who controlled all shipments, payments, billing and documents of the lumber company. Little cash was ever sent to the main house. It was mostly all done on paper, work in exchange for ill-nourishment and debts. That, in few words, was the nature of the *monteros'* life. Rigoberto wondered if it were any different in other main houses. That too, he owed Mijares; he would make it his own personal crusade to fight the exploitation and depredation of the rain forest and the human beings employed in the industry.

Mijares was close to no one and Rigoberto realized that fear isolated him. He slept behind a locked door, a fact which was in itself unheard of in the area. He was not satisfied with a common lock but had a metal bar installed in his bedroom door. He rarely went out at night. Rigoberto had observed him for many days. Nothing. Mijares slept when he slept. Sometimes, though, he was too drunk to worry about his security and he would run through the fields and run after the bulls whose pen he had opened. Then he would go into the workers' room and rifle in hand, demand they get up to round them and get them back into the pen. Sometimes he amused himself by letting the chickens out of the coop, then he would run after them and catch one or two, ring their necks and

174

throw them on the kitchen table. The stench next morning was unbearable; the dead chickens were certainly not fit to be eaten. This, he claimed, was to help the cook who slept with him sometimes. Rigoberto knew the woman would have preferred to 'service' anyone else in the world than Mijares. She might have even obliged the miller, rumored to be gay. She was forced, instead, to stand on high alert for Mijares' whims and fancies. Her life too, was at stake. Rigoberto asked himself how Mijares had remained in such good health. Wouldn't it have been extremely easy to harm him? And how had he become immune to tropical illnesses, rancours and hate?

Where was Clara? Her whereabouts became an obsession during the slow days of duty in the storage room. It was only at night when he walked between the minimal houses and he could hear children's cries or matrimonial arguments that he allowed himself the luxury of nostalgia for his own family. This feeling suffocated him like a furious current. He managed to overcome the feeling by focusing on the small plants and animals, on the black monkeys that disappeared to God knows where when the sun descended but who come morning, woke him with terrible calling screams to show off their acrobatic stunts on the highest branches of the trees.

The surroundings of the main house were pleasant. There was a vegetable garden cared for with much labor by the miller. They managed to have a few vegetables of the region and spices. To one side of that they had several coconut palms, *pájaro* mango trees and a bush with wild raspberries. The cook kept all kinds of leaves, plants and flowers in the most varied castaway pots. Sometimes she would even place a few flowers on Mijares' table which only seemed to bother him. If the food she prepared was not to his liking, he would throw out the plate aiming at her head. Rigoberto had heard the commotion once and had seen a worried cook rapidly prepare something different for the drunken Mijares.

Marihuana leaves were brought to him openly. He would roll them up and smoke them in his hammock in the tropical nights. There the smell of burnt dry weed would mix with the tropical perfumes of flowers and blossoms that exuded their perfume for IxChel, the goddess of the night skies. And Rigoberto wondered if that faulty man was capable of appreciating some of the beauty that surrounded him; or if that beauty had somehow managed to move his soul or change it in some manner. He had to accept that it did not affect him in any way and that the sickness continued to invade areas which in the beginning had been normal. He rarely spoke to him, and when he did, it was only to inquire about supplies or figures in his books. The man in charge of bringing the mail was under strict orders to talk to no one and if Rigoberto had wanted to send a message to Acopa there would have been no way he could have done it. He could send a message to no one, not even Nenúfar, much less to the President of the Republic, Clara's godfather. In any case, what was there to say? That the man Díaz had trusted was unable to carry out what seemed a simple task? Another issue to consider was that he could not risk their interference in the very flimsy setup he had so carefully elaborated. Mostly his despair came from the fact that there was not the slightest trace of the girl.

Rigoberto knew something had to happen. His good luck had left him; or maybe had only temporarily forgotten him. Dorotea, the cook, liked him and always saved for him a small ration of the 'upstairs' food, a practice which he did not encourage because he knew the risks it entailed. But old Doro, as she was called by all, knew of Mijares' habits and had a fine ear with which she could distinguish Mijares' footsteps.

Nothing seemed to happen, in spite of his intent at making it happen. One morning he decided to broach the subject. Did the boss like women? What kind did he prefer? The cook looked up from her task at hand in surprise. She answered vaguely because she hesitated as to trusting him. Mijares liked all; whatever he coveted at the moment. "And if they don't accept…" the good woman stopped immediately. She had distinguished Mijares footsteps. It was the morning meal and Rigoberto had almost finished a bowl of bean soup which he complemented with the pepper called *pico e' pájaro* which birds relished and then disseminated the seeds in their droppings, and Doro's delicious tortillas. Rigoberto was finishing

the last drops of his black coffee and Mijares just looked in on
them and left as he had come, a silent ghost.

The accountant returned to his store and sat at the dusty desk,
which he began to clean. He concluded that Mijares knew everything
that went on, like a fine dog, and he knew that the man was afraid
of something in him. Was it his youth? His good spelling and
handwriting? Something was not clear and Mijares would find out!
At the same time he must not feel unduly worried. This was his
territory and Rigoberto was at his mercy. Nobody would come to
investigate or accuse. Was it possible to point him in another
direction? He knew that the men who were closer to him had orders
to report anything unsual. What could they have said? That he kept
to himself? That he trusted no one, spoke sparsely and was cook's
favorite although they were not on intimate terms? So? What else
could be said about him? Had he committed a crime or something
similar?

It was then when he realized that people of the jungle have a
special antenna with which they syntonize to depths unknown even
to the person himself. He was aware of what was whispered about
him: he was there because a woman had left him; that seemed to
satisfy Mijares temporarily. It was true, he had left a woman behind,
a woman who he loved dearly and this was the major tragedy in his
life.

Sometimes Mijares felt so ill at ease with him that he had
thought of sending him away, and this he told Doro in the nights
where alcohol blurred his memory. He feared him as much as his
own death obsessed him. Doro too, lived in fear, and Rigoberto
had seen black and blue spots on her arms and once, in a fit of
rage, the man had even made her spit a tooth. For the first time in
his life Rigoberto felt helpless. He would have made him disappear,
but first had to find Clara Heredia.

Finally, one afternoon, when Mijares had been drinking for
two days and two nights, the cook came to Rigoberto's room. She
was tearful and expressed her hatred and he asked her if there was
any possible way she could leave the area. She assured him there

wasn't. Mijares would send the men to track her down and kill her and he would demand proof of that.

Rigoberto knew that there was more to those words. Attentively he thought of them and then asked softly, "And what did the woman he just killed look like?" He did not really want the answer.

"She was young and very pretty; her hair had the color of honey," Doro replied sobbing. Rigoberto did not know if she cried for the girl or for herself.

"Why did he do it?" he asked shaking his head.

"She would not give in to his advances. It has happened before. This girl was not the first one. Other times he would just have them beaten until they gave in; most of them did. But never had the main house seen such a lovely young woman," she claimed still sobbing.

"Why didn't she give in?" he asked outwardly calm, but he felt the earth melting under his feet.

"I was the only one she told that she had run away from home and that she intended to marry the boy she was with. She told the boss they wanted to get married. He was never going to accept that, was he?" the woman said drying her face with her apron.

"How could they get married here?" he asked.

"The priest from San Cristóbal comes once a year to marry and baptize people. She was truly beautiful. She had big, green eyes and the hands as white and soft as the Virgin Mary's. She was very happy in the beginning," she said with regret.

Suddenly everything had fallen into place! He needed to know one thing more.

"What happened to the boy she was to marry? Was there anything he could have done?" he asked fearing the worse.

"Well, the boss doesn't like complications. He immediately sent him to San Vicente, there they killed him and she never knew. They were supposedly sending him to plant corn, but we all knew what was about to happen. That boy would have defended her with his life, he really cared for her," Doro said longingly.

"What was his name?" he asked, just to be asking.

"They were both from Puebla. She was called Maria, but of course that wasn't her real name! She was so young and pretty!

What can I expect? That man is worse than pork meat! And you, I have asked myself how you plan your escape. I know you are not here willingly because this is like being buried alive. I need to show you something. Come to the kitchen when it is dark."

The woman had hurried away and Rigoberto was left in the store trying to accept what he had just heard and which intuition had been telling him since he arrived in San Juan Bautista, when he had seen the long silver serpent, serene and smiling. Clara Heredia was dead, and he did not know how to give the news to her father and he did not know how he could get out to do so. Many months had passed and they might think he was dead. He had lost a lot of weight and his beard was long and he now had a big moustache. Only his eyes glared intensely.

He had to leave in the first opportunity. How? He was sitting there, thinking about his sole purpose until it was dark. Anyway, how could he leave the main house with no material proof that Clara Heredia had been there until a murderer had made her disappear? He needed some palpable evidence and he was certain he would find it now.

XXIII

Afternoon fell; the copper-pink ribbons disappeared behind the trees and the dwellings. Frogs began to croak near the spring that flowed smoothly not far from the houses. The young girls from the workers' homes were seen going in that direction with a bundle of clean clothes under their arm to take a bath. Rigoberto walked around, absent-mindedly, just for the pleasure of breathing the evening air, and free from Mijares who lay snoring in his rooms.

He enjoyed his walks in the freshness of his surroundings and he looked forward to the voices and cries of children that fragmented the air in a thousand pieces. He sat down to wait for the daily ritual of the peacock parade in the front yard of the house. They preferred the early evening to offer their luxurious robes, a green-blue-gold fan in silent display of temptation in the art of mating. Oh, for the male pride, whose beauty was far superior to that of the female! What they pretended to ignore was that females held real power. Sometimes they uttered endearing sounds, rough, scraping cawing.

Daylight was rapidly vanishing and Rigoberto insistently looked up to the second-floor windows. He knew Mijares would sleep at least one more day and its night, yet precautions had to be carefully taken.

His jaguar eyes, green and piercing, spotted the shadow of a figure near the Laurel tree, a small plant of firm green leaves and red flowers which produced a sour perfume. It was Doro, his friend. He studied his surroundings and slowly approached her. It was difficult to see her; her upper lip would have become more inflamed and the irreplaceable tooth that had been knocked out would make her look older beyond her years. He hoped that some day soon she could end up in Tenosique.

When he was close to the figure, he felt a hand in the darkness looking for his. A small rectangular piece of paper was placed on it. He grabbed it quickly and put it in his breast pocket.

"The boss ordered all her clothes burnt, but I managed to hide this. Maybe it is nothing, but it will protect you in your journey if you decide to leave one day." The shadow disappeared toward the kitchen to continue the preparation of next day's sustenance.

Everybody seemed to be sleeping, the people of the jungle were used to trimming the day in order to lengthen the night because in the early morning without even a faint light, they had to get up to begin their work. He too, walked quickly from the tree to the outhouse where stench increased with the evaporation of the heat. He took out some matches, damp, like all the others in that climate and he finally managed to light one. He was then able to study an image of the Holy Mother embracing her newborn, Lord Jesus. On the back he was shocked to read, "In remembrance of the First Communion of Miss Clara Heredia Amor y de la O." There was a date: ten years before.

The earth suddenly melted under his feet, and then he understood how the silence of the jungle, the music of the crickets, the dull-shrill cries of the cicadas and the intermittent light of the light bugs, everything was a complot to mark his descent into madness; and he heard the howl of wolves and the whip on the soft white skin, and the demented mind who drew mortal screams from a girl who had never harmed anyone; his useless search and don Porfirio waiting, his own pregnant wife needing him. The man had stolen more than life; his pathology had the ripple effect of touching many lives and destroying others.

He did not now how long he stayed outside, but the night became silver in the full moon, she too, pregnant with a male figure, when the lands shone with wonderful clarity, tempting him with a seduction he could no longer yield to, because his mind was already elsewhere. Escape. Now. But how? He had asked himself many times, he had traveled much only to return with empty hands. But he had to return with his life to help stop Mijares somehow. Nothing. He could not think. His blood had frozen in his veins, paralyzing him.

"Mission accomplished, my General," he whispered and walked with the slowness of defeat towards the main house. The upstairs windows were still dark. He went towards his hammock; the two other men were already asleep and he lay down to think. The first thing he must do was to pretend to forget and continue treating Mijares with the same courtesy and to seem to accept others' mistreatment with seeming indifference. He could not draw the minutest suspicion or he might never reach his destination alive.

He fell into a superficial sleep. The horrible scenes made him forget his true dream. Reality surpasses all our dreams, he said when the day began to light the sky and the cock sang the three O'clock alarm. Time to go to the mill to pick up the ground corn wrapped in green banana leaves. Time to continue someone else's nightmare which swept them all.

This was the dry season. 'I can escape,' was his last thought before arriving with Doro to seek a cup for his sleepless body. He then walked to the brook for the ablutions and prayer. Warm water, God, no respite from the heat! He washed in inferno water from a spontaneous and natural paradise. Somehow terms and concepts seemed inverted. No man's land and everyone's and he pondered contradictions as if his mind had run amok.

He now understood why so many people loved that latitude, why they were joyful and talkative, why they swore and played with words. Life was a big joke of unexpected, but surely tragic endings. Not even Mijares could understand the contradiction.

His escape seemed most urgent at the moment and he should think of nothing else. He needed good timing and perfect preparation for the escape. He had to wait for a night of new moon when there would be no light to betray his presence; it had to coincide with one of Mijares' alcoholic binges.

From now on his objective was precious, although there was no pleasure involved. He needed a routine that could see him through. After the early hours' plunge into the river he performed exercises which would help keep him in good physical condition for the demanding task ahead. He would then go to the kitchen to drink the morning coffee with Doro who would place the usual black bean soup in front of him, and the freshly-made tortillas. Then he would go to the store-warehouse where he would apply himself to books, numbers and orders and where he would write sum upon sum to add the bills to unheard amounts in unsuspecting workers' names.

The days followed one another in eternal, uninterrupted manner. The great heat was there, so were the bugs and minute mosquitoes called *pinolillo* endowed with a twisted needle like a corkscrew that penetrated the flesh in unsuspecting and unknown ways. The worse torture were the tics that produced an unbearable itch that only the learned knew could be covered with Campeche wax, which when applied hot, would seal off the oxygen, without which they could not subsist. The deer and cattle tick preferred the softer skin and their favorite place were the genitals.

He had learned the names of plants together with their characteristics, and of fruit, the edible and poisonous products, he drank teas and tasted foods, which nobody in his city had ever heard of. He had washed his eyes with the bloom of the *cocoíte* tree to be rid of spring conjunctivitis. He had seen a man blinded by the sap of the *chechén* tree and he himself had had to scrape his arm with sand because he had gotten too close to the tree; and from this he had suffered high temperatures for three consecutive days. He had seen people die infected by tuberculosis and wasted by the intermittent paludal fevers. One could say that the world had become the land of fate.

The old inhabitants trusted him with the secrets of the land that had contributed to the colors of the murals of Bonampak and its stellae, the big masks and medallions and he learned the names of different nuances of color like vermilion red, *rojo sinabrio*. He had seen the women dye their cotton cloth with orange *achiote* and *chicabante.* He saw Doro roast chicken with the flavor of *achiote* and wild *oreganón* and he learned to appreciate foods of the region like roasted plantain filled with pork rind powder. He was curious about the religious services but could not witness one because the itnerant priest of San Cristóbal had not yet arrived. He had heard the melancholic music of the woods in thin slabs which had given birth to the *marimba* and he learned of the *tikul* ancestral drums and cane flutes. He had helped the men process a tree bark by fermentation to produce a beverage called *Balché,* which the people of the region revered because it had been used for sacred rituals since the memory of time.

He had seen the men mimetize like the animals in order to climb the ramón tree with the help of spurs in order to cut the high branches and build fences and from the same tree choose the tender leaves to feed their animals. He learned to fish in the old way of throwing a vine called *brabasco* into the river where fish, sardines and crayfish ended by being trapped.

He had acquired many survival skills, but could he find a way out? Time continued to flow unstoppable, on its own, removed from them; time was its own time, neither master nor slave, and would complacently witness till the end of time, births and deaths, possibly his own. At present his only interest was to arrive in Tenosique. He was afraid Acopa might betray his presence there, even though he had express orders to forget him.

Some afternoons he played solitaire with the cards Nenúfar had given him; he saw her again and thought of her with affection and recognized her mastery over the concept of the men of the region. He had witnessed Doro and a young girl 'serving' the men and if an offspring were born, they recognized it in mass as 'son of the quadrille'. He had palpated that unknown world with his own skin and he knew its weaknesses and strengths and realized that women were kept in an unfavorable position. Only then could he understand how Nenúfar held the key to solving the dilemma. He smiled when he remembered that somewhere there was a child playing and living and breathing and that she carried the strange name of Lesbia and later he saw them both serving beer to the workers of the land. The child deserved a better fate and suddenly he felt uneasy and sad at the thought of a mother with her daughter and he was in a bad way for the rest of the afternoon.

He could not yet afford himself the luxury of thinking of Mexico City and its elegant, French-like and myopic life. Nor did he want to think of Rosita, his beloved wife who was painfully suffering this separation more than he was. She would have to give birth by herself, like a widow. And his heart ached. He did not want to think of her. Nor did he want to think of the joyful superficial women who went to the theatre to see and be seen, or who paraded through concert and dance halls and whose main worry was the color of the velvet to be used in their curtains and the china to be ordered for their homes. He did not want to think of General Heredia and his absurd life, nor did he wish to remember his secretary with mint breath, nor anyone for they had disappeared into the galaxies where they floated with the planets and were distant from him. He was in the world of the 'lord of knife and gallows' as Mijares was known throughout the region. He was the discordant element of Paradise. on earth; he was a sickness that could produce contagion to those who happened to cross his path.

XXIV

The months of dry, astonishing heat would pass slowly under the eye of a merciless sun, leaving sweat and illness as reminder of its yearly transit. Even the steaming nights were unbearable. Monkeys would roar their loud and frightful sounds. People would feel old passions and rancors stirred and alcohol and bad moods were the only answer to a freshness that seemed forever gone. Rigoberto, too, had suffered the intermittent fevers that the Anopheles transmitted and for the rest of his life the antibodies would remain with him. Malaria produced men who lay emaciated by fatigue and long-suffering abstinence and fevers. He had seen the men reduced to jaundiced creatures unable to perform the demanding labors of lumbering.

The spring months meant gentle warmth and the sweetness of flowers to the rest of the mortals; yet spring in that latitude meant the sheer madness of delirium, an exacerbation to the nervous system. Doro would press cold towels to his forehead during his illness. Who would be there for the others? Maybe the miserable presence of Death itself. Such was the dry season, asphyxiating, damp and full of electricity. Rigoberto could have never have possibily imagined that electric thunderstorms existed. It was another of the gifts of nature to assuage its flagelation. In the blackness of the night, one heard a thunder and then the most magnificent of lighting brought forth in pristine clarity, each blade of grass, and every being. The trees acquired a strange beauty, beauty of the night with the most potent of lights. Arrows of fire traversed the sky, showing the whole and then fragmenting it. *Hunahpú* and *Ixbalanqué*, the playful twins of the sky battled and the earth shook under their feet and it happened that one of their magic darts would once in a while defeat a giant, it would fall, now in mourning black, burnt wood, to the ground, executing in turn, blooms and saps with one swift blow. It was a visual marvel unequalled by any arts or crafts of human production.

It was also the season of great fires and many times one could see acres and acres of land go up in white smoke, jealous of the heights. The raze and burn of those called "walking fields" might mean the loss and degradation of the land. Rigoberto thought he liked the name but realized it hid an ecological tragedy. The poor, eroded fields were cultivated with maize and its yield was drastically reduced each year forcing the peasants to begin a new one on land close by. Ancient methods of agriculture were employed, a stick to make the hole in which to plant the seed in eroded soil. And so the fields progressed sometimes with great social complications, when indigenous farmers invaded the so-called private property. But did nomadic people understand or even imagine the artificial lines someone drew on paper? In their memory these were communal lands; they belonged to them, the planters and sowers of their forefathers' habitat.

Rigoberto, fascinated by the formidable nature, came to understand how a longer stay made people forget their initial origins and whatever knowledge they had previously acquired. They adapted to their new surroundings. He, too, had lost the blandness of his comfort, the memories of abundant food and drink, soft music, the touch of silks and the smells of bottled aromas and innocent pleasures like routine. His life would never be the same.

One day the great rains arrived. The beginning was deceitful. Only a few drops of warm liquid which seemed to taunt the scorched-dry mouths of Earth. And then he understood the godly states of rain and the exquisitely carved conchs of translucent flesh which symbolized the repetition of Infinity for the Mayan world: the vital circle. The inhabitants of the rain forest, uneasy and crazed, would pray, as prayed their whole universe of beings which had disappeared or lay in hiding, to Chaac, their god of Rain to stop his taunting and shower generosity upon Creation. And when he finally did, rain became a torrent, a serious matter for rivers that precipitated with a fury never imagined, a torrential violence sweeping everything it found on their way.

It was that precise moment, when the river crested, that the launching and floating of the timber had to take place, from the head of the *montería* or station, to the tributaries of the Usumacinta down to Ciudad del Carmen where heavy ships of ten or fifteen thousand tons would transport them to Hamburg, Liverpool and Le Havre. The sawmill had been forced to prepare squared timber of three thousand wood-feet 'big as the hope of the poor and high as towers' said the working hands while making ready for June. June was the most aggressive of months because all the heat of the earth became steam and men no longer could distinguish their sweat from that of the bulls' since they worked as one during the great launching.

All that time Mijares remained in the main house, animalized and inebriated, a capricious brute-tyrant whose inner jungle defeated the unborn man in him. And yet he had the exact knowledge to control the process. When Rigoberto had asked leave to accompany a quadrille, Mijares thought it was a good idea for the capable assistant to learn more of the process which would end for them in Tenosique. The rest was of no interest to him.

So the consultant of presidents set out one steaming morning to begin a three-day walk from the main house to a *tumbo* or 'throw' where piled wood lay in waiting for its launching. They would have to walk in the morning freshness fueled by *posol*; any other alternative would have been impractical. Only the young, strong mountaineers could labor in that manner; any other circumstances would have made it impossible. This made Rigoberto smile when he had a moment of relaxation in the late afternoon. He was grateful for more knowledge of his own limitations when he realized he knew nothing and that he was on the brink of wisdom. The jungle and its ways lent new demarcations to his personality and his shortcomings.

It was one red and insolent afternoon that he knew the time had come to use all his ingeniousness to free himself from Mijares and the main house and thus be able to escape. His mind went back to Acopa and he asked himself for the hundreth time if he had kept his word and silence. For the last weeks he had lived in dread that Aladino, in a display of zealousness, might show up in Tzendales and that the paranoid Mijares would feel forced to 'eliminate' him in an accident, as had happened with Gerado in San Vicente. His mind could no longer remember Tenosique, which had disappeared in the hellish steam of the first rains, nor did it matter. A type of lassitude and resignation had overtaken him. His mind told him something was discordant. He realized he might have been stung by the *Aedes Aegypti*, and was hostage to Dengue Fever or what was known in other latitudes as Dandy or Red Fever. He was a zombie lost in the jungle and he realized that he was onerous to the quadrille who had to deal with him every inch of the way. There was always someone at his side to take him to the river and the freshness of the water. The overseer carried aspirins that seemed like the only answer to the bone-breaker fever which made each nerve explode like firework needles in a million painful crystals. It made him walk haphazardly, in a "dengue manner" and he asked himself how many times in his childhood he had heard the expression without knowing the true meaning of the pain involved. At that point he once more began to fear for his mind.

Finally, on the fifth day they arrived to *Río Azul*, an affluent of the Usumacinta. They slept a few hours next to their precious wood which lay in waiting in huge piles in the "weekly," a name given to the improvised sub-station. Men and bulls strengthened by the *ramón* leaves would begin the launching process which had taken months of preparation. The group of ill-spoken and joyous men seemed more like soldiers than loggers ready for the big launch.

Rigoberto insisted on going with them, one morning when it was still night. But his legs refused to hold him well under the unceasing, warm and unforgiving rain. Walking seemed almost better than being in the river itself. Clothes had become sealed to the skin. They would walk through thick forests where one could see bald spots which had once rooted those admirable mahogany giants. They finally reached the river bank which lay two or three kilometers from the sub-station. The bulls would have to drag the wood through the mud which had turned slippery with the humus of the leaves and the stumble of the rocks. The pathfinders and machete welders went to work to form wide, rudimentary paths through which groups of thirty-two bulls could transit dragging logs of thirty or forty feet in length. Rigoberto was curious as to the manner in which the whole process was conducted and he sensed that under the hard work and good spirits lay a feeling of fatality and suspense. Those men were qualified to accept the higher rulings of fate and they just continued on its path. It was probably the only way.

They worked for a few days in the building of the "paths" and then they began to work on the hooks with big chains tied to the wood and which the animals would have to drag. The principle of the operation seemed easy and now he wanted to witness its practicality.

It was good to be away from the oppressive atmosphere of the main house, from Doro's kitchen and from the smell of dampness of the warehouse. He had left with the threat that anything missing during his absence would be charged to him. 'Write down what you wish, Mijares, the demons will repay with generosity,' he thought as he carried with him two bottles of hard liquor he had written down to his debit.

Tomorrow, before beginning the last stage, they would drink the first. The men needed some sort of recognition for their strength. He knew they appreciated his gesture. And in any case, he hoped the men would not tell Mijares about it because alcohol was strictly forbidden in all the setup.

Next morning the expedition started out: bull guides, bulls, and gurneys laden with the wood. They advanced slowly; the bulls' hooves slipped on the wet, round branches that formed the path. They advanced by millimeters, urged on by the most sacrilegious maledictions Rigoberto had ever heard, even though those men cared more for the black, shiny beasts, enormous and magnificient in their blackness, than for themselves. They were the engines of the whole operation. It was only the great strength of the muscles in their neck and the foam of their mouths that told of the effort involved. It was an earth-shattering event, not unlike to that of a birth of a new life.

Rigoberto took the whole scene in, resting upon the trunk of a *chakaj* or Slave, a tall tree whose magnificent and delicate skin was fragmented and the redness of blood sprang pointing to the blood of all slaveries. Here, in front of him were those beasts whose veins and tendons were about to break through the skin, and the men so occupied with their task that their own identity and conscience were erased on the chocolaty surface of the water that ran with no restraint and with enormous fury. It was now or never that the wood had to be sent down; but the bulls seemed unable to complete their task. The weight of the shipment, the slippery hooves and the round branches had vanquished. The bull handlers were desperate; the kayaks with its rowers and the 'throwers' in charge of pointing the wood in the right direction were desperate. The bull handlers continued to sound their whips in the air, edging the beasts on with names and surnames like 'Luzbel, son of a bitch' or 'Satan, great bastard' so that they would walk one more step; they in turn responded with their last breath, falling, broken and very dead under the whip, the water and the weight.

Rigoberto felt alarmed; he realized the futility of the failed effort. Affairs didn't look good. The men refused to stop even to drink the maize sustenance that the helpers had dissolved in muddy water from the river and which was rejected by passing the round, half-pumpkin container from hand to hand.

Hurt and with a few animals dead, the compact group of men and beasts finally threw the first lumber into the river. The boatmen were in the water with their kayaks, and the 'holders' were ready to guide those huge trunks though a safe journey, because otherwise they could get stuck in one of the beaches and that way it would take them a long time and they could arrive in useless and contaminating splinters to Frontera. The boats waited. They had been there for a long time and distributed their cargoes from Europe. They had brought low cost goods such as clay tile for the best houses, clothes, furniture, perfumes and niceties from France and the sailors loved those days of waiting, as they loved the local girls, thus leaving behind a living proof of their stay in the form of half-caste offsprings. They awaited the fruits of that great effort of conjunction that Rigoberto was trying to understand. He realized that these workers were the important men, those whose identity would remain unknown till the end of time, under the brand of a single name, San Román, and San Román was Mijares. The cruel despot whom nobody dared face if the task had not been completed. The trunks were supposed to arrive in Tenosique where they would be tied in groups of two hundred and sent down river in big rafts to ports where other handlers would be waiting for them.

It was an afternoon plagued by tragedy. The river had increased its strength so much that the handlers who waited in their kayaks to direct the wood fed to the water under the furious impact, had it snatched from their hands without a second thought. Ten men were lost that day, their remains swallowed up by the insatiable wave of roaring water. They died pulverized under the weight of their task without letting go of their precious treasure only to be diluted into the oceans. The magnitude of disaster the night in which the new moon of San Juan was born, led Rigoberto to open the second bottle and drink, because his crazed mind could not discern if he had witnessed a scene of blood and water or if it was the scene of the men of wood as described in the Mayan mythology, or if he had imagined it, like in a nightmare.

Months later he would continue to hear at night from his bed, the cries of the bull handlers, the whips that broke the air like lightening, the silent screams of the fallen and the mutilated and he could see the path dyed by the new and sticky blood which would vanish in an instant under the strength of the tropical downpours which were to last more than a week. The wood was waiting; the river grew hungrier for men who had to arrive from Tenosique to take the place of the dead. And everyone thought Mijares was behind schedule. San Juan Baustista grew desperate and soon they would see another group of mules arrive with recriminations from captains of the European ships.

What he saw that night Rigoberto did not know. He did not understand anything. Only later, when the impact had softened, could he bring himself to think of it. Meanwhile, he walked with three men to the main house to ask for reinforcements. Ribogerto left the second bottle for the men in spite of the prohibition, asking them not to betray his act.

It was in that manner that they left the macabre scene, little of which was left the following day. The mountaineers ate meat from the downed beasts; they salted some of it while others threw the remaining corpses and carcasses into the water to complete the sacred tribute of blood-letting to *Chaac*, the God of Rain

XXV

After the tragedy, one more in the history of logging in the Lacandonia, two trains of mules arrived in San Román. They had brought a new group of men, food and mail and had disappeared as suddenly as they had appeared. The days flowed under the copious rain, and at times the sun shone upon the renovated jungle. The dust was washed away and the limpness of the leaves had disappeared. New greens had been created, and with it life and hope.

Finally the rain stopped and the days were now more bearable and less wet. Rigoberto realized that they were well into August. He asked himself what was happening with his people in Mexico City, in another world which seemed less real each day, blurred and vague, so much so, that it seemed ready to vanish.

He was forced to wait until the torrential rains had completed the destruction, for the bodies of water to refresh into their clarity and for the appeasement of the roaring and furious serpent into a docile and even body. He needed to wait for a dying moon and for a kayak and for a cache of food.

Finally, when the climate seemed right Rigoberto took the first step towards the new enterprise.

That day he said goodbye in his mind to everyone. He procrastinated with the afternoon coffee in Doro's kitchen; he retrieved the First Communion card from its hiding place in a hollow part on one of the upper branches of a *guayacán* which had shed all its gold. Then he was ready to leave with the rebirth of the moon. He realized what was at stake and could almost touch his grave and felt close to his own dead as he looked in wonder at the banana trees pregnant with its strange purple flowers in the back yard.

Then and only then did he seize the message: new life was within his reach.

Conditions should be favorable. Fernando Mijares was exhausted from a two-day drinking binge. He hoped he would continue to drink. By now he had figured out that the man's main terror was the thought of death and his nightmare was life, things which induced him to drink himself unconscious. It was this constant cycle of life/death which was a challenge to his very existence. Rigoberto smiled the smile of a bitter thought. Mijares would probably be downed by a machete.

It must have been five in the afternoon. He had learned to read the hours written in the heavens, to recognize new and dying moons and so many other things. The frogs were ready to begin their orchestration on the opposite side of Tzendales. His warehouse was alone, the miller and the two women were busy grinding the corn for the *posol* paste and the tortillas for next day. The mountaineers were already lying in their hammocks trying to coax night in order to lengthen the new day by force.

He walked to the kitchen. Doro was just leaving. He handed her the cards and touched her rough working hand, all without a single word. Then he sat on a bench outside his store. He tried to concentrate on the hummingbirds, whose legs he'd spied and never seen, in the miracle of their suspension in the air and tried to memorize the lesson of those who lived for that instant of coupling with honey and dew. And he watched the parade of blues and golds and greens of the peacocks with the cascade of silver rattles knowing that such beauty came at the price of coarse cawing squawks. And when he finished, he looked around to make sure there was no one in sight.

He would continue the routine which he had initiated months back, so with a strong pat on his leg, as if to remind himself he had to travel, he stood up. Then he went to his room for a towel and his fishing cane. Today he was initiating the usual pattern of activities a few minutes earlier than usual. It had been his fishing expeditions, which had taught him how to master the river and its humors, and the possible routes it led to. He did not have to fear Mijares or the workers. Each was busy with his own affairs. Now his only enemy and his ally was nature. He had a good sense of orientation and the malice needed if he were to meet someone on his path.

The hours of apparent leisure in Chon's kayak in the previous months had helped him practice rowing skills and to acquire knowledge of the wind. He was now a graduate and could trust the risks he ran. Doro would not wait for the fish that night, but she would pretend to, so as not to arouse suspicions. The woman had a good feeling for him. He had helped her many times to clean the *pejelagarto*, that strange combination of fish/lizard that everyone coveted. She had taught him how to remove the entrails, to rinse and salt them and to protect them from other predators. Next morning she would charcoal broil them or if they were different species, she would marinate them in lemon and salt and fry them at high temperatures until they reached a crispy exterior. "This is truly fresh fish, Doro," he repeated each morning. His physical condition was good too, thanks mainly to the exercise routine he had followed when he was not exhausted by Malaria. He also realized that lately his body was doing better in responding to the fluctuating febriles.

He climbed into his kayak carrying with him a towel where he had inserted two cans of sardines and a package of water biscuits from Mérida. He touched Clara's card in his breast pocket and then he noticed two round spheres of *posol* amorously wrapped in the intense green banana leaves. Doro's hand. He smiled and set them next to his towel and then took off with silent oar until he reached the middle of the river, where he sat down to wait for night to fall. It was getting dark; he headed towards San Román into the Tzendales river and was aware of the need to navigate twelve leagues in order to arrive in Lacantún. He knew that if he rowed mid-river with enough care, he would arrive in four hours to San Vicente, where he would pretend to be headed to Pico de Oro. He navigated as swiftly as he could, guessing only the outlines of a landscape that was no longer visible.

Everything seemed to be going well; the river's stillness had helped him greatly. So when the first rays of light began to appear, he knew he had traveled the eight leagues which had separated him from the Salinas River and that he was in the Usumacinta. Luck had been with him because he had not crashed against stray wood that had run ground or which was floating undetectable in the darkness. The smooth current had aided the fugitive, and now he realized he was a fully-fledged river navigator. He smiled in spite of his exhaustion.

He needed some rest so he started looking for a brook, which was known as safe haven for the weary because it was protected by high, luxuriant trees. He surmised to have arrived to the town of *Tres Naciones* which had once been a *montería*. There he managed to tie the kayak to some bushes near the beach and lie down to an immediate sleep.

It must have been noon when he perceived a strange sound at his side. It was a small *cereque,* a delightful marsupial prowling around his towel. All of a sudden the small black animal had run from him. Rigoberto smiled, moved by his visitor. He opened one of the cans of sardines with a knife he had traded for his gold watch with one of the workers and of which he never let go and had a feast of dry biscuits and water from the river. He felt much better when he finished.

He decided to take ten minutes to gather his thoughts. Only ten. San Román must be in an upheaval; they would be looking for him in all possible places. Chon, bless his heart, would have gone to Mijares to say, 'That damned foreigner has disappeared with my kayak.' With any luck they might think his kayak had capsized during the night in a false move…maybe because he did not swim so well…he had surely drowned. It happened often, and nobody seemed to doubt unknown facts for long.

It was certain that Mijares would have his room searched. There they would find all his belongings, all his two shirts and a pair of discolored denim pants. Then he would send a worker whom he trusted to inspect all the dams and the river edge down to San Vicente. With luck they would find the capsized kayak because a body usually took at least forty-eight hours to show up. Mijares cared for no one. Just the opposite; he might be happy to be rid of a man who was better educated than himself. He had always mistrusted him. That was how his distorted mind would be rid of a witness to his crimes. The personality of a destructive mind was always shared with paranoia. He was well rid of him and he would have liked to find the overturned kayak to confirm his fears.

Rigoberto knew his ten minutes were up and that he had better get going. He needed to get to Agua Azul, and once there he could be sure they would pursue the matter no further. He tried to get up quickly and he realized that he felt so sore he could hardly move. He buried the empty can under some bushes and spread dry soil over the biscuit crumbs that the amazing sense of smell of the ants had already discovered. The indefatigable cycle of life would take care of those crumbs.

It took all his strength to push the kayak once more into the river and little by little his body adapted to movement again and he began to feel better. Day navigation was a very different affair. At least one could be more in control of possible dangers and their solutions. He had overcome his fatigue and he afforded himself the luxury of optimism in this first stage. He began to row and arrived in the early afternoon to a place where the cross-currents were very strong. He realized he had reached the deep incision called *El González*. He had to exercise utmost care lest he be swept away in the strong swirls of chaotic currents. He had been on the verge of falling several times, but he managed to control a most difficult balance and keep his kayak afloat. It was the longest league ever, until he could finally exit the danger zone. He would know he was safe when he could see the town of Filadelfia, private property of the Juan Buchanan Society.

It must have been four O'clock when he spotted a woman fetching water from the river. He got close to her and asked for the carpenter's house. He was looking for Primitivo Sánchez who had worked for some time in the shop of San Román. Mijares had wanted a new table and chairs for his house and Primitivo's stay had been that of two weeks. Rigoberto had befriended him, and in the evenings they would walk a stretch of the river or play cards. From him he learned that there was a safe way to get from Agua Azul to Tenosique. He had confided that there was a young woman called Nenúfar waiting for him in Tenosique. Primitivo respected a man's desire to be with his woman and made no comment. At the moment Primitivo's whereabouts was the only thing that mattered.

The door to the house was open, so he looked inside calling, "Good afternoon…good afternoon" and stepped in. A woman was preparing food. She claimed to be Maribel, the carpenter's wife who told him Primitivo had gone out to find wood for cooking, but that he should rest in the hammock. After drinking a glass of luke-warm lemonade, Rigoberto fell exhausted into the rocking of an undulating bed. He slipped into a profound sleep, with the certainty that he was in a safe place. Surely by now they had given up on him, and because there was no crime involved, they wouldn't bother to continue their search further down to Agua Azul.

The carpenter arrived with wood for his wife's cooking and he was surprised to see Rigoberto there. Upon hearing his story, he asked him to get up. They had to scuttle the kayak and try to send it down river about a mile from where it stood, because if someone were to spot it, it would endanger both of them.

As they walked to the river's edge, Rigoberto questioned him about the route to follow to get to Tenosique. The carpenter told him that there was no great danger, but that he was vulnerable because he was not from the area. However, he would help him in everything, point the way and provide enough food to get him to Tenosique.

They walked briskly until they reached the kayak and while the carpenter drilled its bottom, he instructed Rigoberto to find some stones to help sink it in the river. "Kayaks denounce their owners," he said firmly.

Once they had finished work, Primitivo proposed shaking his head happily, "Let us lie down a bit and plan your escape," and they lay down under the fresh shade of a tall tree.

"I know you travel to Tenosique once in a while and I can give you five hundred pesos if you let me go in your company. I have some money with Nenúfar," Rigoberto proposed casually..

"Yes, man, of course," he good man answered. "We will be in Tenosique four days from now. I had to go anyway to buy some screws and hooks to repair furniture and the only danger I can foresee is the Granizo station, because there we could meet a train of mules or people from Tzendales. But we will cope with that when we get there. I will let you know if anything comes up. Then we have to take a small detour to spend the night at Domingo Cruz' house. He's a friend," the carpenter said sensibly.

They got up and walked back. Primitivo must have been about forty and unlike the other people of the region; he was tall and had strange milky-blue eyes that were exclusive of the region. He was endowed with a helpful and happy disposition which would help him achieve his goal quickly.

"We will start out tomorrow morning and by noon we should be at Domingo Cruz' place, leaving behind the road to Tzendales and everything that smells of that pig don Fernando Mijares," he said passionately.

One thing Mijares could be sure of, was that with time he would become part of the black legend of the area. Rigoberto had been contemplating an idea which he had by now perfected about how to deal with the issue of bondage. He did not dare think much about it at the moment. His subconscious worked while his conscious focused on survival. He was safe and they would never suspect him of having friends along the way. No one had managed to escape from that particular logging station. Some had tried and had failed in the intent. They had become lost in the jungle and others had been found dead, perished in its dangers.

It was beginning to be dark when they returned to the house. Maribel was burning a mixture of sulfur, dry wild pepper and small fragments of the dry palm she had taken from the four corners of the roof. Next she took thecrying infant in her arms and rocked him in the smoke of the brazier; then she placed the peaceful child in the hammock and proceeded to do the same with the diapers. All during the process she prayed with a great faith, disregarding their presence. It was not magic; Rigoberto now witnessed the result and from then on he would not underestimate home-remedies.

"Is the tender one in a bad way?" the carpenter had asked his wife. The term 'tender one' was used thought the region when speaking of infants.

Maribel answered, "The foreigner has cast the evil eye. But he is fine now." She looked at Rigoberto with a smile on her lips.

She was a young woman in her early twenties with a joyful smile and smiling eyes. He saw in them the priceless peace that people of the city had lost. Progress in the white man's world came at a high cost.

Maribel had black beans she had fried with fresh peppers from the plants that grew near. Her tortillas were white as white can be. They placed before him some acid cheese from Ocosingo which was a luxury few of them had access to. Rigoberto enjoyed their hospitality and partook of their food and friendship. He knew he would sleep well that night and that he would be back in Mexico City within the week.

"Now, Mr. Accountant, sleep well because tomorrow we have to travel five leagues, two of which are the steep road of the *El Cojolita* hill. Me and my wife here, we will prepare everything and carry a good package that will feed us for two days, because by noon the day after we will arrive at Domingo Cruz's," he said setting about on his way.

Rigoberto lay on the hammock and stroked his beard. He asked himself what he might look like now. It was the first time in many months that he felt free and happy. Tomorrow he would feel even better because he would be closer to attaining his goal and to the beginning of Fernando Mijares' reversal of fortune.

The new day was being born. The sun was setting the day's mood. Pink sashes appeared from nowhere in the orient, predicting a clear, cloudless sky. They were to cross the Agua Azul river which was high, so they were forced to swim part of the way. They had to hurry for the climb of *El Cojolita* before it was too hot.

The stretch resulted like all the others in the area. They stopped around noon to eat cold tortillas and watered-down *posol*. Then continued on their way and slept that night in the shade of several *guapaque* trees. They could tell someone had recently been there. They lit the semi-burnt wood and roasted some jerky and tortillas.

The carpenter had improvised two mattresses of *guatapil* leaves and Rigoberto lay down to see the stars, maybe for the last time. "I have a confession to make, Primitivo, one sleeps better in the jungle than in the softest of beds of the city. You are lucky and luckier to be happy with that wife of yours…" he said softly, lest he disturb the sky.

"True, don Rogelio, true," the man answered smiling. We have problems up here, but I prefer it. My wife too. She is from an *ejido* and is used to a quiet life," the man said sighing contently.

The night was beginning and with it the orchestration, always new and original. The toads and animals, big and small, participated. He breathed the air that was beginning to cool down and realized it was still hot. He was no longer afraid of the creatures of the night and hopefully he would not suffer a night of fever.

"Your are right, don Rogelio. One is not afraid of anything here. Tigers attack when they are in heat or when they fear for their young. That is why I always carry my rifle. Their attack is a rare happening. Now, with the vipers, the same. Their attack is their defense. One must be careful when walking because they coil up on the logs. Otherwise they don't come near. It has happened, of course, that a man dies with bursted veins; but that is not so often. Stories tend to get bigger in the cities…Maybe you have heard them…" His voice trailed off and he began to snore.

It was not yet dawn when Rigoberto could detect the aroma of coffee. Primitivo had lit the fire to heat water from a nearby river. He was heating some tortillas that they would eat with crushed pepper. They drank the false coffee from a single container, ate their scanty meal and began their walk. The carpenter didn't seem to mind the rifle hooked to his shoulder. He was used to those long walks he was forced to make two or three times a year.

They walked fast in order to pass what might represent a dangerous place in the early morning. Two hours later they reached the crossing of Lacanjá where the road seemed wider because of more frequent traffic. This was the way in which roads were created and in which they acquired names.

"This is the road to *Tzendales*," Primitivo said, looking to one side of the river towards San Román and in the opposite direction to Santa Margarita.

"Two leagues from here to *El Granizo* and if someone is coming from *Tzendales*, they are sure to spend the night and should be here soon, so let's walk a little faster," he said, hastening his step.

They walked up to the station called *El Granizo*, surely it had hailed at some time? One could not imagine such a happening, but that was what it was called. About half a mile later, Primitivo turned left in a small trail that would lead them directly into Domingo's house. The trail was narrow and rarely trimmed, on purpose, because Domingo did not want unexpected visitors. They walked through rotting trunks and grown prickly bamboo canes for two leagues up to Domingo Cruz's house.

It seemed impossible that two leagues had worn them out, but they had to go slowly minding the snakes they knew to be there, for they coveted the freshness of the earth. It must have been noon when they found a clean pasture with about a dozen cows and he realized that nearby stood a regular-sized brook which was part of the Lacanjá River. To the other side there was a small group of palm-roof houses where chickens and wild turkeys walked freely. There were banana trees which held their precious bunches in different stages of maturation.

As they approached the house, some of the dogs started barking and the women came to the door. They welcomed Primitivo in a friendly manner and were introduced to Rigoberto, the shop keeper of Agua Azul, they claimed, on their way to purchase supplies.

Rigoberto already knew the story of this family. Domingo had arrived several years ago from Bachajón, where rumors had it he owed a life, nothing much out of the ordinary. A few months later his brother had tracked him down and had joined him. They lived in harmony, cultivating corn and beans and they even had a few plants of coffee and cacao. Their most lucrative business, however, was the manufacture of dark, rich molassess. They had planted sugar cane on two acres and had built a rudimentary sugar mill.

They sold their product in Agua Azul and Tenosique where they got a better price for it. Primitivo explained how he loaded some sacks in three mules and walked through the wild with only a machete in his hands until he got to Agua Azul and the stop of El Granizo and from then on, he continued on the Camino Real, which was a more defined road.

That evening would turn out to be memorable. Domingo's wife had killed a hen and cooked it in a stew with rice and spices of the region. It was the first hot meal in days. Then they talked till late into the night. Domingo and his brother Ausencio asked about news and stories from the logging stations to add to their repertoire, and transmit orally to their descendants. Then in exchange, they discussed the way they should go and where they should stop in the jungle.

The next day the travelers went on a three-day walk until they reached the valley of the Chocoljá, Chancalá and Chocoljaíto where there must have been some hundred brooks that reflected exuberant vegetation on their quiet surface. There they bathed and rested. Rigoberto pondered on things he had never even thought of: the principle of identity. Here were these brooks, all the same and yet so different, born all together and yet distinct and individual. There were no answers, he knew by now, only thoughts.

They proceeded to Chancalá for a technical scale, his companion said in good humor. The place belonged to a man named Tranquilino, who had arrived from Guatemala for mysterious reasons and who had decided to live there. He had married and begun a family. The helpful man had few things to sell to them. They bought a couple of packages of biscuits and *posol*. They bade their goodbyes quickly in spite of feeling very welcome, because they were eager to continue.

XXVI

It was the early evening when Rigoberto and the carpenter stopped in front of Nenúfar's place. There was no one. The women would be in *Heaven* starting the day's work; and because it was unwise to show up at the cabaret, they walked to a small restaurant in the downtown area and ordered a good meal. He knew he should sit facing the wall and fortunately nobody seemed to pay any attention to them. He had become one more the workers from the jungle, hungry, and with the signs of exhaustion. When they finished the well-seasoned hearty meal, he knew he would have to go find Acopa to get money to pay the carpenter what was due and to buy some things for the people who had been so good to them in the way. He knew it was risky to be seen in the streets and he was thankful for the night. Even then, he might be recognized by someone, like Avelino Sánchez, the man who hired. No one must know he had succeeded in escaping. He needed to disappear as quickly as he had arrived.

Once in the inn, he told the carpenter that he was going to find Nenúfar and that he would return shortly. The woman who ran the boarding house did not seem to recognize him. Too much time had passed and he hoped they would go unnoticed. He was thankful for the beard and the moustache which would help him move in relative safety through Tenosique.

He walked through the dark streets of Tenosique to the wharf where Acopa lived. He knocked on the door and found out he was not in. So he sat to wait for him, amazed at his wife's unsuspecting manner. She must have gone to bed after he had assured her that he could wait in the small patio where she had plenty of plants.

There was a hammock swinging empty, so he lay down to wait. He felt self-conscious of his appearance but he realized he could do nothing until he had gotten further away. He could not afford the luxury of arousing suspicions. His hat was so torn that it was surprising that it still held out. His shirt was spotted and torn and his slacks had been clean once, a long time ago. He could not figure out why Acopa's wife had trusted him. She was used to all kinds of people looking for her husband and she had accepted his presence without further thought.

It must have been around two in the morning when Aladino Acopa turned the key of his front door. He was obviously drunk. Then he realized someone was waiting and intrigued, he went towards the hammock. When Acopa realized it was Rigoberto, he suddenly became sober.

"Gosh! What a surprise! I am so happy! I didn't think you were alive! Don't worry. Nobody has looked for you. Only Avelino Sánchez asked around to see if someone knew what you were hiding from and why you needed to 'get lost' for a while. Nobody else," he said burping.

"What about Mexico?" he asked anxiously.

"Nothing. I have sent cables every week as you asked me to. By the way, the government owes me something…" he said burping again.

"I need a thousand pesos more immediately, because I am leaving as soon as it begins to get light. I have not been through here, I never arrived and you have never met me. As soon as I get to Mexico City I will see that what is owed to you is reimbursed immediately," he said firmly.

Nobody trusted anyone else in money matters. The man in front of him doubted for a moment and then remembered the President's letter.

"What about Mijares? How did you manage to get out? Did he send you on an errand?" he asked insistently.

"No, I escaped through the river. And now, don't ask me anything else. You don't know me and have never seen me. Remember I am in charge of something very serious and confidential," Rigoberto said, indicating that the conversation had ended. He did not wish to pursue it further.

Aladino Acopa headed for the station to get the money from the safe-deposit box. Rigoberto was to continue waiting in the house because they could not risk being seen together. About half an hour later he returned and handed him the money.

"Come back early in the morning so I can see if someone I trust can take you. Or better still, why don't you spend the rest of the night here?" he said simply.

"There is something I need to do and someone I need to see," he said nervously.

"Well, I suppose if you managed to escape from the logging station you will be all right roaming the streets of the city at night. However, I should inform you that Nenúfar was killed shortly after you left," Aladino Acopa said casually.

Rigoberto who was standing up next to Acopa was so shocked by the news that he slowly sat down again on the hammock. Acopa rushed into the house and returned with a glass of brandy.

"Another of the jealousy rivalries at *Heaven*. You know well enough that drunkards don't understand reason. She was a very attractive woman…" he said now, carefully watching his reaction.

"Was her family notified?" he asked nervously.

"What family? Who has a family here? We don't even know if Nenúfar was her real name… We don't even know what part of the state she came from. Her friends buried her in the local cemetery. The young woman had a few pesos saved up…" his look was intent on one of the plants. Now that he seemed to think Rigoberto had a personal interest in Nenúfar, he could not look him in the eye.

"How about the killer?" the young lawyer asked immediately.

"Escaped. He took to the mountains; they all do," he said shrugging helplessly. And then something happened: he looked into Rigoberto's eyes firmly, and said, "Forget her." Women like Nenúfar were not important; there were so many more. New account. Nights in *Heaven* would always be there, waiting their lethargic wait.

"I have to leave anyway. Someone is waiting for me. In a short while I will try to see if I can get a boat to San Juan Bautista and then to Veracruz. By then I can regain my identity. Maybe I can even take a shower somewhere, and go back to being a civilized person," he said lightly. "I would ask you, Acopa, to send the same two cables to Mexico with two words, 'Mission accomplished.' Don't sign them."

Acopa obliged, "I am going back to *Heaven* to ask the captain of the *Sánchez Mármol* when he is leaving. If it can't be tomorrow, you can stay here and you know that," he said shaking his hand in friendship. He was extremely happy to see the man had managed to return.

Rigoberto disappeared through the main entrance into the starry night. He went directly to the carpenter's room and woke him up. "Here, my friend. The money I had promised. I am also giving you a few extra pesos to buy some things for those kind people who helped us on the way. Now I have to leave, but maybe we will see each other again on these roads. I will never forget your hospitality, and please remember you never saw me!" he said patting his shoulder.

He walked beneath a beautiful sky, conscious of the aroma of the tropical flowers and freshness of the hour. He walked to the bank of the river where he could see the trees' outlines reflected on the even surface of the water and his mind recalled the green and fiery reds and he could guess the shapes of bushes and small animals and perceive the noises the tiny creatures made. His heart was happy. He had stored in it memories of beauty and kindness and he would have these for the rest of his life. Soon he heard the swish of feathers in the sky, near the treetops. It was finally dawn and with it came Nenúfar's memory and that of her unfortunate daughter who would grow up ignoring her mother's death and without even knowing who her father was. And there were many like her, born from chaos and possibilities, free seeds of unfortunate winds.

It was beginning to be light when he reached Acopa's house. He found him at the door, watching for him nervously. "You are in luck, my friend; the *Sánchez Mármol* is leaving at five. No one knows of our relationship, but I assure you, you will have no trouble finding passage in it," he said extremely satisfied he had found a good solution for the young man.

"All right Acopa. I am leaving because I don't want anyone to be able to identify me. I am very grateful for all your help and time and for having sent my telegrams," he said genuinely happy with the arrangements.

"I will be truthful with you. You have amazed me with your temerity. Nobody has ever been able to escape from the clutches of don Fernando. We hear horror stories about him. He is a real devil…they even speak of murder…" he said thoughtfully.

"They fall short, I assure you. I have lived through it. Well, now I have to leave. We will soon have too much light," he said receiving a package that the chief handed him.

"Your two rings, don Rigoberto. One was with Nenúfar and the other one belonged to Miss Heredia and I kept it here," he said carefully giving him both rings.

He walked slowly with the clean bundle of clothes Acopa had gotten from his nephew who was more or less his height. He walked to the wharf to wait. He sat for a while on the steps and replaced the ring on his hand. He felt he had recuperated his past and earned his future. A while later he saw people starting to board the ship. He walked up the plank, paid for a fare and sat among the workers. He needed to be one of them until they reached Veracruz. The truth was that he yearned for a proper bath and a good shave. He promised himself a good rest when he reached Vercruz but he still had a good wait.

As soon as they began to move he asked to borrow a pail and tied it to a rope. In that manner he could get water from the river. He would let the sand settle and then it would be as clear as it could get and he could take a bath of sorts. He changed into the clean, mended clothes Acopa had given him and went down to the stoves and handed the castaways to one of the men.

"I'm traveling and no one will be able to wash them for me. The young woman who could do it is dead," he said in answer to their surprise. It seemed enough; the men needed no further explanation and the clothes disappeared instantly.

He walked feeling refreshed and comfortable and mainly he felt relieved of leaving Tenosique behind as he watched the huge canyon that rose in its green majesty. And his mind went back to the brown, dry surfaces of land in the center of the country and he understood he would never forget that brave land that symbolized life; and he drank from the colors and from the trees and the water, as if wanting to swallow it whole, to take it with him, inside, safe, forever, a part of him, like an indelible metal plate or a perennial source of strength.

The people in the upper decks traveled in comfort and he thought of the process from a different angle, and he pondered on the difference money made. It was no longer important. He was one of those workers who had learned the secrets of getting fruit and wood from the womb of the Earth. And with them he loved their land and worshipped their brutalized gods. And with that in mind he said goodbye to sacred land, the rain forest where innocent creatures lived and died without knowing how or why. He said goodbye to the land where limits were blurred, where customs, air and land were different; where there was no help for the weak and no law to restrain the evil.

He took out Clara's stamp, a token of her first communion and he had a very difficult time trying to complete the puzzle with that last piece. He could not understand why she had to have paid such a high price for the freedom of her spirit and her thirst of life and knowledge to inspire her intellect. Everything has a cost, he told himself. Clara had paid hers. It was the price to pay for a woman ahead of her time; for her individuality and for having more spark than other pupils of her convent. It was the first opportunity that he had had to observe the card carefully. It was made in France and had been painted by hand. He studied the golden letters which were handwritten with impeccable style. That brought him back to the safe, monastic air of his childhood and of Rosa's house and he realized he could now afford himself the luxury of thinking about his family and allow himself to feel impatience. He needed to get home and see and hold his daughter, because his heart told him it was a girl. He still had to travel for several days, but at least now he had sent word to Rosita that he was safe and that he was on his way, which would represent a respite in her wait.

He studied the water, which for him had become a medium of the future. Golden rays colored the surface and he thought of Díaz in the castle and the Heredia family and of the jilted groom. He still found it difficult to think of the best way in which to present the facts. How could he tell them the girl had been murdered? Maybe he could think of a good excuse. She had died of malaria and tell the truth only to General Díaz. Someone had to stop Mijares. How? The place was inaccessible. He knew that upon arriving in San Juan Bautista he would again speak to the chief of police and begin his investigation into Mijares' trajectory. The roles had been reversed. Now it was he who was in persecution and Mijares better watch out!

It was the last time, he told himself, that he would see the Usumacinta, the river that led to the logging stations which provided the world with mahogany for their homes and furniture. Mesmerized he watched the silver serpent protected by the green. And his thoughts centered on that water which generated life and cleansed body and conscience. It was a magnificent reptile, he concluded satisfied.

XXVII

The capital city. The very thought suggested to the people from other provinces a magic world of lights come from Bohemia, of riches and opulence, of refinement where the music to be played was the Vienese waltz, where women dressed in heavy Sandong silks and brocades and men toasted with champagne and smoked pipes. True, that it was. Rigoberto had now seen his society from the second perspective, that of the working class. Mexico City was like a shining diamond, an eternal and transparent region that time would drastically change into a chaotic megalopolis. But now the air was fresh; the skies were clear and the purple-black mountains were visible in the surrounding area.

He walked to Vergara street, where a warm, loving home, a wife and a child awaited him. Of course he had wanted a daughter, but would love him as much were he to be a son. One had to respect nature's wisdom. Wasn't that the first lesson he had learned in Lacandonia?

His hand was shaking when he knocked. The gardener's familiar face showed through the shadows of the gate.

"Good evening. Is your mistress in?" he asked seriously amused.

"Yes. Who wants her?" the intrigued man answered.

Rigoberto remained silent. It was impossible not to be recognized in your own home. He smiled affectionately to the man who had been with them always.

"Boss! Mr. Rigoberto López! Come in! Come in!" the surprised man called in pleasant urgency. He had seen him as a child and talked to him about the garden, and then he had watched amused when he wore his first pair of full-length slacks, then he had seen him as a young man with a law degree.

The kindly man called out to the cook and in a great fluster he was welcomed home. The wrought-iron gates leading to the garden were opened immediately and he entered though the kitchen where he embraced the cook, then walked into the living room where the smell of wax and mahogany awaited him. His loving home. He climbed the stairs, two steps at a time and waited at the door of the master bedroom. From there he could see his wife's profile, breast-feeding their child. She was softly humming a lullaby while she cradled the baby.

He watched her and tears welled up in his eyes. He recognized the second of the Rain Forest's gifts; accepted sensitivity to the power of the cycle that perpetuated life. The room still had the warmth of the evening sun. The smell of infant's lotion permeated the space. He was there, thinking that this was perfection and thankful for his life. Suddenly his wife saw him and she gasped in delighted surprise: "Here, hold your daughter!"

And then he knew God had been complacent and granted him the gift. He took the child in his sun burnt arms full of superficial scars, the strengthened arms of a young man from the jungle.

"I don't know you anymore," his wife said shyly.

He lay the child down with extreme care on their brass bed and embraced his wife without uttering a single word.

"Your beard...I didn't expect that!" she said smiling.

"Maybe I left it on purpose, to show you that I am now a full-fledged *montero*, a man from the jungles of Chiapas. It is a very long story that I will tell you in detail," he whispered.

"Where is Miss Heredia?" she asked as if she had just remembered the reason for his absence.

He remained quiet. He did not want to sadden the perfect moment with what her absence meant.

"Tomorrow will be another day. Tonight is for my family and I don't want to tell you anything nor do I want to ask you anything. To see my two women is more than enough!" he said recuperating his joy.

"Thank God you are here. I do not like the fact that the baby has not been baptized," she said understanding that no good had come of his quest.

"Clara Rosa should not be without the state of Grace. We will baptize her as soon as possible. Now, let's talk about you…"

The hours passed slowly, and they had so much to communicate to each other and to love each other that all he could do was tell her that he was trying to carry out his mission, and asked her if Rogelio Magaña had visited her regularly. It had been so. The President himself had called on them twice and sent her flowers several times.

"Tomorrow," said Rigoberto, "tomorrow we will begin from the beginning but first I have to see the President."

Those were his last words and he fell asleep towards dawn. Far away, or did he dream it? he thought he heard a baby's cries. He smiled. He was home, once again in the warmth of his home and he was now a father, and a beloved husband. He felt very well, and his smile continued with his dream.

It must have been around nine O'clock when he woke up. He went into the bathroom and looked in the mirror to find the face of an eternal man. The beard did not look so bad, his face was tanned by the sun and somewhere he could distinguish eyes that had seen the forest, green, hard eyes like the jaguar-hunter's.

Once having showered and dressed, he went down to the dining room where his wife, his parents and his in-laws were sitting around the child. They hugged and kissed him, especially his mother and he announced Clara Rosa's immediate baptism.

"Where is Clara Heredia?" his father finally broached the subject.

"Dead," he answered definitely. "That is why I need to go see General Díaz immediately. I've had some breakfast and now I have to leave," he said getting up from his chair.

"Well, we have seen you safe and sound with our own eyes. We will stay to visit with our granddaughter and you will come to have supper with us when you find the time," his father said.

"We are leaving too," his mother-in-law said.

"Please don't go. Stay a while with Rosita and Clara Rosa. Have cook prepare some chocolate for you; she makes it quite well," he said disappearing.

Rogelio Magaña was deeply concentrated in his accounting books. Suddenly he sensed a presence at the door. He looked up and saw his boss.

"Sir!" he explained in surprise.

"Magaña, I see everything is more or less well here. I am going directly to National Palace to see if I can speak to General Díaz; then I suppose I will have to go find Heredia," he said as a greeting and goodbye.

"Yes, Sir," was all he heard.

He arrived at National Palace and climbed the stone stairway to the reception room from where he was immediately ushered to the General.

"My slow investigator and now with a beard," said General Díaz rising from his desk and inviting Rigoberto to sit across from him at their usual place. He looked at him. For the first time in his life Rigoberto experienced a loss of words.

"Far too much time has passed in your task. I hope it is justified," the imposing general uttered.

"Clara Heredia is dead. She was murdered in a *montería* in Chiapas," he said suddenly, unable to restrain the bad news.

"I knew you were in the area. We received your telegrams. Murdered? A child? What was she doing all the way down there? Did you say she is dead? She is my godchild, you know," he said sadly.

"It is a long story and fate seems to have had a hand in this. General Heredia was set on getting her married without her consent. No, still worse, against her will," he said to the general who seemed to have aged terribly during the last months.

Rigoberto proceeded to tell all he knew. He broached the working conditions of the southeastern state, the wood depredation and finally he concluded with his research regarding Clara.

"Tomorrow all the chiefs of police will be fired! How is it possible that a child escape from their hands?" the older man said impulsively.

"Extremely possible. She was not a professional; her actions were guided by her innocence and her thought was chaotic. She had one single goal in mind, to run and contradictorily, the police efficiency helped her go further each time to look for her truth. Finally she is her own person," and with that he ended his account.

"What am I going to tell her father? My friend?" the general said sadly shaking his head.

"That he should not have had a daughter like Clara. She was too much of a person for such a limited father! I understand her," Rigoberto said with the straightforwardness that was characteristic of his personality.

"Speaking of which, your daughter is very beautiful. I am glad you arrived because Rosita was very worried about the baptism. She has cried many times," said the general who was already thinking of Chiapas and its situation and trying to find a solution to the act of law called 'Empty Lands.'

The secretary came in bringing two cups of sweetened coffee which they drank in silence.

"Now...what would you do in my place?" the general asked studying his cup with care.

Rigoberto who had expected that precise question, had the answer ready. "I have thought long and hard about this. There is nothing that can be done. Death is so final. I think it would be better if I spoke with the family. Would you like me to do that?" and he handed over the small, religious card and Clara's graduation ring. "The card is the only proof of Clara's presence in the main house of Santa Margarita. The witnesses are too terrified to talk," Rigoberto continued.

They remained silent for a moment. Díaz looked at him and said: "Your mission has been impeccably carried out and I feel for you having to be away from your family. But you have rendered this nation a great service. We need to change many things in that area. The southeastern states are too far and inaccessible, as you have found out for yourself. They are almost inexistent for the central government. You have opened my eyes to these matters we have overlooked and to the reality of the injustice of the workers. I am thinking of calling for free elections. Even then, how can I revindicate this time of ignorance of those states? Well, one thing at a time. I wouldn't have given it a second thought if it had not been for your trip. Now, please go talk to General Heredia and explain the situation with as much tact as possible, which I realize is asking for an impossibility. Then you will take a long vacation with Rosita and when you come back we will be ready to tackle this. Now go; please try to talk to him alone. I don't think he will hold it against you," he said dismissing the young man thoughtfully.

Rigoberto started to cross the secretary's office when the colonel stopped him.

"Sir, would you please sign this?" he asked, handing him a pen.

"What is this?" he answered impatiently.

"A bonus and travel expenses for a year. Maybe I should send them to your office?" asked the young man.

"Please, I need to take care of something rather urgent at the moment," he said rushing down the corridor to the staircase.

He went out to the warm sun. He was in the main square thinking about the vacation the President proposed. He would like to visit Veracruz with Rosita and the baby. Was she too young to travel? He would ask the new mother. He wanted to go to Jonuta to meet a small child with the strange name of Lesbia. He was thinking about all this as he walked to general Heredia's house.

He knocked on the door with the brass lion head. The housekeeper opened the door. She was an elderly woman who wore her hair braided on top of her head and who was wearing cheap and excessive makeup, something unusual for her age. "The general is not home. He will be back soon. Mrs. Heredia is in the garden," she said in a high-pitched voice. He saw she was missing a few teeth and in spite of that she was a likeable person who must have been attractive when young.

"Fine. Please tell her I will wait for the General in the small room," he said going to the small room whose walls were covered with hand-painted blue tile. It was a sort of solarium with originally shaped stained glass windows. The sun penetrated through the colors giving a gaiety of surrealist quality. He looked through the window. Mrs. Heredia was speaking to the gardener who was bent over the roses. When the housekeeper appeared, they began to talk and Mrs. Heredia looked in the direction of the window. Maybe she had recognized him.

Two deaths would be felt in this house. The gardener, oblivious to the tragedy, continued with his task. He realized two children would be mourned in this house. His mind went back to Cholula and doña Remedios' hospitality. And he felt her pain. A mother's pain.

He could see Clara's mother approaching. She was still a beautiful woman and must have been even more so in her youth. He could hear the bustle of the kitchen where food was being prepared and he could detect the aroma of rice being cooked. Everyone ate rice; it meant home.

"Good morning. You were looking...? Mr. López! Where is my daughter? Why did you let your beard grow? Why are you alone?" Mrs. Heredia cried out, visibly alarmed.

"She could not come. Maybe..." he started to say but could not sustain the look into those blue eyes. Rigoberto did not find an answer because of Díaz' orders, but he could not lie to this woman. His mind went back to his wife and daughter.

"Malaria is frequent in certain regions..." He could not continue. He was misleading a woman who had trust and pain reflected in her eyes.

"She traveled to Chiapas, contracted Malaria and the intermittent fevers are very strong...She's dead," he said relieved to be able to deliver at least a partial truth.

The woman was speechless. She turned around, walked away from the rooms leaving a trail of freshly-cut roses behind her.

He walked from one end of the room to the other, looking out the window. The gardener was now trimming the hydrangeas. The

218

girls don't marry in a house that grows hydrangeas. Clara did not marry. Would never marry anyone. Never.

Half an hour must have elapsed when he heard a firm step and a low voice.

"In my library!" a voice ordered loudly to the housekeeper.

He waited for the woman to escort him to the library, entered and closed the door behind him.

"What does that beard mean, my friend?" the general asked angrily with a gesture of disgust.

"That I was in the jungle for almost a year carrying out a mission that General Díaz entrusted me with and that in order to report to him first and now to you, I have not had time to go to the barber shop," he answered without flinching.

"And what the hell were you supposed to be doing over there?" he asked walking from one side of the room to the other with his hands intertwined behind his back.

"General Díaz..." he began.

"My friend!" the man interrupted looking at him angrily from foot to toe.

"Yes, your friend. I had to go look for a young lady named Clara and I found what was left of her," he said handing him the religious card and the graduation ring.

"What does this mean?" he asked despectively.

"That she is dead and this is the proof. I hope that you are convinced because that is all I have. I had to follow her to Chiapas and go into the jungle to find these things," the young man said quite finally.

"What was Clara doing in the jungle?" he asked without believing his ears.

"She was running away from a dictatorial father who wanted to impose a marriage on her," Rigoberto answered plainly.

"How would you know?" he said slamming his fist on the big, intricately-carved desk which seemed handed down from previous generations.

"I have met a young man called Francisco Monteros and I have met you," he said without hesitation.

"Your opinion is worthless to me," the general said more calmly.

"I know; so was Clara's; that is why she preferred death, even though she did not know she would die. She was too sensitive for this world; the next one will be better for her," the young man said sadly.

"Get out of my house! I'm just sorry you are not in the military! I would have you shot!" he screamed furiously.

Rigoberto watched the man on the other side of the desk. His eyes seemed to be on fire and his perspiring face was red and distorted.

"Yes, indeed. I am the bearer of bad news. You are right, that was the fate that awaited them. And while we are here, let me tell you that I feel sorry for you, General. Clara was truly a beautiful free spirit. I know you thought you were protecting her, but your way was not the best. Maybe I am the last link of communication between Clara and you. She never did dare open her heart to you, or maybe she tried and you wouldn't listen," he said softly.

He did not wait to see how his last words had been accepted. He just turned around and walked out of the room and out into the garden. He spoke briefly to the gardener and asked him to transmit a message to Gerardo's mother and then, with a heavy heart, walked out of the oppressive atmosphere of the house. Once again he could evaluate what his happy life meant to him and he pushed away the sick, distorted figure of Mijares, who together with Heredia, were the culprits in Clara's death. And yet, he smiled bitterly, he would always be indebted to both of them!

Post Script

The mere name of Fernando Mijares or Tzendales, made the Lacandon jungle tremble. He existed, this cruel and merciless man, "Lord of knife and hangmen." He belonged to the Romano family and he was a partner and overseer in the logging station of Tzendales. This position allowed his sick mind to free his demons in the form of torture, mutilations, whips, shackles and even murders, which he rationalized to be part of his duties.

He was a man who insisted on exercising the "right of the lord" [*le droit du seigneur*]. This allowed him to spend the first night with any bride. Some of these tragic men like Polo Valenzuela had over two hundred illegitimate descendants, product of anarchic unions. It was the accepted behavior of the time and Mijares was no exception. Some of the young women would not submit to such treatment and would prefer death.

In the year of 1913 general Luis Felipe Domínguez, entered Tzendales, liberated workers; arraigned overseers and let his prey slip by. Mijares would return shortly thereafter to reinitiate operations. However, his luck could not last forever. In 1924 he was arrested on the murder charge of another Spaniard named Rivera, in an incident that had taken place in Tenosique. That same year Mijares died in the prison of San Juan Bautista, which is today Villahermosa and the capital of the state of Tabasco.

With regard to the ships and other characters that appear in the novel, they did in fact exist with the same names, and the descendants of some of them still live in the area. Others have moved or simply died. *Heaven* is still standing abandoned in Pueblo Nuevo, which has by now become part of Tenosique. The city continues with its history near the banks of the Usumacinta. Clara Heredia, Rigoberto López and their familes are the only literary creations.

The Rabasa Report

An investigator from the police station was sent by the governor of Chiapas to investigate a murder in Tinieblas [a logging station]. His report dated May 18, 1904 says that the *montería* was located and that "torture of all types is applied to free people." In another report dated the 21st of the same month, he adds that by orders of the overseer in charge of the logging station, they had murdered Daniel Caballero and that he had "found ten men with shackles on their feet and handcuffs and the women being tortured." He also assures that the quadrilles, which had been hired in Mexico and San Luis Potosí, had been hired to work in the estate of El Mirador in Oaxaca and had, therefore, been misled.

6-1-1906 *Archive des Affaires étrangères 2871 divers*
Brussels, Belgium